The Art Thieves

Guy Wilson was educated at Marlborough College and Gonville & Caius College, Cambridge. After a stint in the Royal Marine Commandos and a statutory attempt at being a schoolmaster, he determined to be a novelist. He and his wife Angela set off to Spain on a motorbike. This was the start of an adventurous and precarious existence: they spent three years in Spain, one in the USA, two in Algeria, three in Italy and one in Paris, supplementing an income from writing with starting and running English language schools. They then found themselves in charge of an international sixth-form college for girls, which they ran for twelve years.

Guy Wilson is the author of four previous novels and a volume of short stories. He and Angela now live in Hampshire.

By the same author:

Novels:

The Industrialists
A Touch of the Lemming
The Ardour of the Crowd
A Healthy Contempt

Short Stories:

The Three Vital Moments of Benjamin Ellashaye

The Art Thieves

Guy Wilson

First published in Great Britain in 1995
by Rampant Horse Limited
140 Whitehall Road Norwich Norfolk NR2 3EW

Set in 10 pt Times New Roman
Cover design: Chris Redman/Images

A CIP catalogue record for this book is available from the British Library

ISBN 1-898839-05-0

Printed and bound in Great Britain by Bookcraft (Bath) Ltd.

Part One

~ ~ ~ ~ ~ ~ ~ ~ ~ ~ ~

1

With half an ear, Reg Griffin listened to the Institute's clock. It chimed the four quarters, then after a portentous pause began to strike ten. What right had any clock to sound so goddam complacent?

His trainers resting half-way up the white-painted Victorian mantelpiece, he had been making an effort to listen to the undergraduate reading his essay. The fellow had some bee in his bonnet about sexual symbolism in El Greco's Death of the Count of Orgaz. It was to be understood that the bishop's crozier, penetrating the heavenly regions at the top of the picture, was highly suggestive and significant, as was the Count's spirit mounting through 'what is indisputably' an ethereal vagina to salvation.

It was a perfectly sound idea, Reg had been conceding, though not for the reason this ponce was giving. Religious painting and sculpture, especially in the Renaissance and Post-Renaissance period, was of course stuffed with sex, a kind of holy masturbation, safe sex in the age of the new pox...

So what? He got up suddenly, and padded to the window. While the rather nasal voice behind him paused in surprise before continuing, he watched a middle-aged don approaching across the square below. The man walked with a mincing, self-important step.

All his recent doubts were back. Wasn't that idiot down there what he would all too rapidly become if he stayed here at the Courtauld, a pathetic, effete academic, trapped into internecine intellectual warfare, attending committees, reading papers at international conferences, listening to endless undergraduate crap and believing it was all of world-shaping importance? Did he really want to spend the rest of his life raking over the stubbled acres of art-history from which all the goodies had been long since cropped, and for which he would be paid a pittance, when now, within his grasp, was a way out?

The undergraduate was limbering up for a purple finale. In a minute he would sit back with the smug look of someone delivered of a masterpiece. Pre-empting this, Reg went to the phone.

It was ten o'clock, but the voice was half-dazed. As it was too early for even Razzy Licknowski to be drunk, he was obviously still in bed. 'I'll do it,' Reg said crisply.

'Do it? Do what?'

'I'll meet you at midday. The same trough as last night.' He put the phone down. 'Right,' he said to the frustrated and now anxious genius. 'You've finished, have you? That's all then.'

'All?'

'All.'

'But – haven't you any comments?'

'None. Your essay is definitive. It leaves me speechless, probably permanently. Now if you don't mind?'

The ass blushed, and began to burble about the time. Didn't the tutorial finish at ten-thirty?

Reg opened the white-gloss door that gave on to the white-gloss corridor, and stood there until rid of this irrelevance in his life.

At midday Reg carried his pint to a corner seat. In deference to his old Etonian rules of throwaway nonchalance, Razzy would be late of course.

Reg had known from the moment Razzy made the laconic proposal here last night that it was the crossroads variety. North or south.

'This one has a goodish echo, Griff,' Razzy had said. 'There's more than is on the surface. Must be, or they'd have been on to the V. and A. or somewhere respectable, and there'd be a figure mentioned. The ethos seems to be: "Deliver and you'll be rewarded. Be silent and you'll live to enjoy the spoils."' Razzy's final words had added unusual flattery. 'And it's made for you, goddam it. It's as if the specification were written with you in mind. I wish I had your academic cargo aboard. I wouldn't be offering, I can tell you, if I had. You'll owe me big for this – I mean on top of the usual cut. I'm talking about favours, for life.'

Had his decision ever really been in doubt, Reg thought? Now it had been taken he was sure it hadn't. Its breathtaking finality stirred a deep nerve of pleasure. Who but the bored, the incompetent, or the destitute believed in luck? One *chose,* didn't one? And decision cleansed, inspired and, if you worked, got you what you wanted.

Needless to say, Reg's beer was half-gone before Razzy's unobtrusive entrance took place, *The Independent* tucked under his arm and folded at the crossword. Reg watched and admired the cool way Razzy dealt with the mob of competing males at the bar. You could not learn how to do that. There was no assertion, no pushing. Just, anonymously, in a matter of seconds, with no one objecting, he was somehow in front of them all and being handed his invariable Pernod and soda without a word being spoken by him or the barman. His quality of being totally unobtrusive would have made him a good spy, Reg thought, if he had not opted for his more remunerative profession.

Razzy settled himself comfortably at Reg's side, and trawled the bar lazily for ears that might be tuned. 'Now you know this isn't part-time any more,' he said, still trawling. There was an interesting note of resentment, Reg noticed. 'It's not like the Düsseldorf job, a week-end affair, a little on the side, for pin money. I've no details – I wouldn't have. But if you're taken on, I have the impression you'll be fully employed for a considerable length of time.'

'You said that last night.'

'You won't be able to take the fellowship, nor possibly any other afterwards.'

'I realise.'

'No more hunting and running at the same time.'

Repetition wasn't Razzy's style, and the agony column approach was tiresome. Reg asked for the nitty.

For some moments Razzy did not speak. He put the crossword on his knee, unhooked the silver pencil that was nestled in the V of his thick-knit, thought, and filled in one across, just the intersection letters. 'I've told you, there are no details,' he said, almost under his breath. 'First, it seems you have to get yourself a job. That, and that alone. A *sine qua non.*'

'You mean *a* job, not *the* job?'

'Precisely. And before that you have to get yourself an interview.'

'With the party concerned?'

'Not at all the party concerned as I read between rather brief lines. Step one is just to land the job. If you don't get it, that's the end. You get yourself the job if you can – against, I gather, other candidates, and without making a formal application, for which it's now too late. Then one supposes, if you're successful, there may or may not be developments. I have no doubt my imprint is big enough in the circles we're talking about, but they'll be bound to check on you themselves. If they don't like your vibes, you'll hear no more. If they do, they'll no doubt contact you in their own way in their own time.'

An answer to another clue was hatching. 'By the way,' he added when it had gone in, 'I have hinted about Düsseldorf. It should have an encouraging effect if I'm not mistaken. You'll need a heavy credential.'

When he thought about it afterwards, Reg was conditionally encouraged, too. The second-cousin-three-times-removed aspect was worrying. Razzy supplied the name finally, and a photograph, of the guy he had to contrive to meet. Somehow the unexceptional face was not totally unfamiliar, though he was sure it was not one of any consequence. And there was a London address. But no more to speak of, except an injunction to get a move on. The man was 'available' in three days' time, and it had, it seemed, to be 'a chance encounter.'

What if he got this unknown job, lost the Courtauld in the process, and then failed to qualify for the goodies, whatever they were, at a later stage?

But Razzy's sour tone, not to mention the lecturing, was not like him. Reg decided that Razzy was jealous. That had to be a good augury. *'Ya se arma el gordo,'* as the blind Spanish lottery-sellers say.

It had better be a fat one arming itself. He was burning a fleet of boats. And, to further mix the metaphor, he had not been playing with a straight bat all these years to hit singles. Düsseldorf had been to convince Razzy, not for 'pin money'.

2

Robert Caine said goodbye to the last applicant and closed the heavy mahogany door of the luxury flat. Like the Italian lot he had seen in Rome, they had been worthy but dull. Was it Fine Arts departments or the profession, he wondered, that attracted such uninspiring people these days?

He turned away to face an empty flat and an empty evening. Mortimer Ready's 'little *pied-à-terre*' – Mortimer's phrase – did not revive his spirits. Some *pied*, some *terre*, he thought with grim humour. In Ashley Gardens, among the dwellings of the rich and the titled, it was big enough to house a Victorian family. Rather ample, you would have thought, for a small-size expatriate Englishman and his tiny oriental wife who would have fitted, both of them, into one of the commodious tallboy drawers. It would have been more tolerable had there been any evidence of taste. There was none. Filled with a miscellany of valuable furniture, there was no idea of co-ordination. Victoriana cohabited with the age of elegance, baroque with chinoiserie, brass with copper, like an excuse-me dance in Noah's Ark. It could be a very upmarket antique shop.

He wished now he had excused himself from Mortimer's insistence, almost certainly inspired by the thought that it would reduce his expenses, and stayed in a hotel at his own cost. Occupying one of the five bedrooms reminded him too much of how in pawn he had allowed himself to become to this petty dictator of the art world. He felt the need to escape the place.

He gave the last applicant, a young woman, a minute or two to disappear. Then, taking up his raincoat in the hall, for a storm was forecast, he walked down the carpeted stairs into the still crisply bright April sunlight. He stood for a moment in the paved piazetta in front of Westminster Cathedral. He tried to imagine himself as he had been when he left Cambridge twenty years ago with his double first and Ph.D., with Mortimer's amazing offer of a new directorship in his pocket and recently wed to Kate. Surely then there had been excitement, expectation, as sharply defined as this light? How was it he had allowed such priceless commodities to slide into the comfortable everydayness in which he was now jellied?

An extravagant idea came to him. Why didn't he go out on the town? He was alone in a capital city which provided every conceivable pleasure. A classy night-club, an attractive young girl? Who would know?

He had hardly finished the thought before he rejected it. He didn't even know the name of a night-club, and even if by some effort of will he got himself to such a place, what next? He saw himself at a solitary table, the not-so-attractive girl making her professional approach, his conditioned liberal instincts dousing automatically, like activated fire-sprinklers, any feeble semblance of lust. On Victoria Street he bought an evening paper. He went into a shadowless café lit with yellow neon to read it and drink a cup of tea.

He glanced at a so-called 'sensation' on the front page which was meaningless to him, and found the cinema list. Scanning the unknown titles and actors' names and the exaggerated phrases attached to each advertisement, his eye fixed on 'Le Bonheur' at the Baker Street Classic. He had seen it years before and remembered – yes, with a definite tingle – how it had affected him. Would, could, his feelings be the same now? It would at worst be an interesting experiment. There was only an hour until the next showing. He took the tube.

The careless joy of the young man, who thought he could suffer no consequences from loving two women at the same time, one of whom was his wife and the mother of his child, the visual beauty and poetry of the film, once again lightly tore apart the sexual morality his genes had programmed him to. For who could say the young man was 'wrong', and leave it at that? The only difference was that where those years ago the lack of guilt had excited, challenged and uplifted him, now, equally moved, he felt not only saddened by the human tragedy that destroyed the radiant happiness of both the marriage and the affair, but also faintly, in some undefined and paradoxical way, jealous. At least the characters had lived.

However, there were still shameful and mawkish tears on his cheeks as he shuffled up the aisle at the end trying to be anonymous. In the grip of his emotion he forgot his raincoat stuffed under the seat.

'You left this.' A young man, a shade taller than himself, in jeans, an open-neck shirt and an odd grey hairy garment that most resembled a waistcoat, was grinning at him infectiously.

He felt foolish. The type didn't appear to have been moved by the film at all. He looked humorous, with an interesting air of restlessness. Robert thanked him for the raincoat, and they shuffled together in silence through the doors and up the stairs.

The forecast had hit the spot all right. During the film, thunder had rumbled intermittently. It was now pelting in the darkness outside. The chap had no mac. In the crowded foyer Robert was wondering if he could offer to share a taxi perhaps, when the man suddenly turned to him.

'You live in Italy, don't you?'

It startled him. 'How on earth do you know that?'

'Italian name on the raincoat – the cut of your clothes. And now I guess I recognise you. You're Dr Robert Caine, aren't you, of Etruscan fame? Director of the Villa Aemelia.'

Robert blushed, though whether from pleasure or confusion he was not sure. He could hardly claim to be that well-known outside the narrow precincts of scholarship, and certainly not in England.

'That's very perspicacious of you,' he muttered.

He was going to ask if the man's name was Holmes – it was after all Baker Street. But he was too slow.

'Home on leave?' the man asked.

'No, I've been interviewing as a matter of fact – a curatorship vacancy. We had a bit of a tragedy. That is to say, we've now to assume it was a tragedy.'

An interest seemed to kindle. 'What happened?'

'Well, one of our curators disappeared. He went off one weekend to walk in the Abruzzi, as he sometimes did, and we haven't seen him since. This was two months ago, and as the police have found nothing, we must assume that he either fell into a ravine or did himself in. He was a depressive, I'm afraid...'

The young man's interest, if such it was, died, or rather, switched. Impatient again, he was looking up dubiously at the weather. The lightning seemed to be over, but the heavy rain looked set in. Cars and taxis were sluicing up Baker Street. The cinema crowd jostled about them, donning raincoats, putting up umbrellas. Of course, Robert thought, a chap like him would hardly be interested in a deceased museum curator in another country.

'I say, you're going to get a bit wet, aren't you, with no coat?'

There was a shrug. Robert hesitated. But he thought of Mortimer's flat again, and the words were out of his mouth.

'Why don't we have a drink? There's a pub just round the corner, if I remember.'

The fellow said he was hungry, and asked if Robert had eaten. There was a restaurant almost next door. Robert found himself offering dinner.

For a moment he wondered if he should have acted on impulse like this. What on earth would they talk about?

But if he had doubts, his companion did not apparently. As they sat down, he immediately seized the leather-covered menu from the red and black check tablecloth and began to run his eyes down the two pages like a scrolling computer. In a matter of seconds he passed the menu over, having made his choice. He began to search impatiently for a waiter. One was passing and would have ignored them. He leaned backwards on his chair and seized his arm.

'A carafe of white wine please, on your way back. You agree?' Retaining the waiter's arm, he gave a token glance at Robert for confirmation. 'OK. And we'll order as soon as you're free.'

Direct, to say the least of it. Had his offer of paying for the dinner sunk in, Robert thought? But he immediately dismissed the scruple as one of those silly social correctitudes to which Kate had conditioned him. Instead, he felt an absurd rush of youthfulness.

The wine arrived promptly, dumped off a full tray the waiter was carrying to another table.

'You haven't told me your name,' Robert said, pouring.

'Reg.'

'Reg ...'

'Griffin.'

'What did you think of the film?'

Amazing pale blue eyes fixed him firmly, like those of a Burmese cat. 'OK. But the guy was a bit naive, didn't you think?'

'Imagining he could run two women simultaneously, you mean?'

'He didn't exactly take precautions to keep them apart.'

'No, but…'

Wasn't that the point, that he didn't? 'Le bonheur' – the assumption that anything pleasurable and happy is right, that life is so easy and uncomplicated? Should he plunge further in? He thought not. He made his escape.

'Well, I suppose nowadays all three of them would have hopped into the same bed, produced two families and lived happily ever after.'

'I like them one at a time myself,' Reg remarked without humour.

The implications of this remark spread like shot from a gun. But there was no chance to pursue any aspect of it. The waiter came into their catchment area again. Reg raised his eyebrows, and the palm of one hand. The waiter came and turned back a leaf of his notebook. Reg immediately ordered an expensive steak with three vegetables, Robert, after some dithering, a Dover sole with none.

This bothered Robert. 'Look, I'm sorry about the wine. It should be red for your steak, shouldn't it?'

Again, the shrug. 'I ordered it. I prefer white plonk actually. Don't they say there's less they can tip into it?'

Conversation was in rushes like this. Robert let hares out of the trap. Reg coshed them. Was it nervousness or indifference?

The waiter brought the food and deployed it. Between them they had already made inroads into the rather mean carafe. 'Would you bring another of these, please?' Robert said to the waiter, tapping the depleted vessel. Perhaps the wine would help to ease things.

As they began eating, he enquired what Reg did for a living. A more adhesive interest showed. 'Same racket as yours as a matter of fact.'

'You mean you work in a museum?'

'The culture business anyway. I'm a don, or almost one. Fine Arts. My corner's sculpture. The later Renaissance.'

Robert stared. Was such a coincidence possible?

'But how extraordinary.'

'What's extraordinary?'

'My ex-curator's field – Carlo Pelucci's – was that period. Not sculpture specifically, he was more of an expert on furniture. But he covered sculpture in the museum, too. You may know his name?'

'It's familiar, yes.'

There was a silence. A first segment of steak went into the rubbery, rather sensual lips and an investigatory chew began, his head on one side, fork rather unpardonably in the air. Robert felt a further ignition of amusement. Reg was droll, likeable. He laughed. 'Well, I think you'd better apply for the job.'

'You mean you haven't found the person you're looking for yet?'

'Nobody I've seen makes up my mind for me. Carlo's shoes are difficult to fill.'

'Do you want to measure my feet?'

'Are you serious?'

'Yes.'

'You mean you have no job at present?'

Reg swallowed. Apparently the meat met his standards. He took his time replying. 'The Courtauld want me back. I'm teaching there part-time at the moment. But I'm not sure I want university life. I've thought of museum work, and Italy certainly attracts me. I spent some time there not long ago, and speak the language. It's a good place to be, wouldn't you say?'

'Well, yes.'

Robert had to rein back his excitement. He would never have suspected the man of being an academic. He had placed him in television somehow. On the technical side probably, all action, quick with the witty riposte, but without much thought. It might well turn out that his credentials would not withstand scrutiny, but there was something about him that was intriguing, not least, now he thought about it, the cool way he had accepted the coincidence, as if – yes – as if he expected life to be surprising. How refreshing that was. Reg could not be in greater contrast to the earnest people he had interviewed.

'Why didn't you apply for the job? You must have seen it advertised. There aren't that number going.'

'I didn't see it. I've been busy teaching.'

Robert convinced himself before they parted company that evening that Reg Griffin was no run of the mill art-historian. Age twenty-seven, first class bachelor degree, a good doctorate, wanted by the Courtauld, a couple of books published already, one on Bernini (hence the interest in Italy, and Rome in particular), one on some Malaysian stuff he had recently got interested in. And he was clearly no desiccated academic. Given the necessarily commercial aspect of a major private museum, and with Mortimer's materialistic breath daily down their necks, that could not be a disadvantage.

Griffin repeated that he wanted to be considered for the job. The next morning Robert set about the checks on the telephone. He got through to the right man at the Courtauld, who said Reg Griffin was outstanding.

'A voluptuary of Decameronian dimensions when he was an undergraduate here, and by all accounts nothing much has since changed in that direction. A bit of an oddball. It's always been understood there's some kind of tragic family background, though this has never been clear, and he's as conceited as a peacock. But he is immensely energetic. Socially, he's pleasingly unplaceable. And about his ability there's no question. It's top class.'

The professor confirmed Reg's publications, also that the Institute had offered him a fellowship and would be sorry to lose him.

Robert had Reg come to Mortimer's flat in the afternoon. He grilled him a lot more severely than he had the night before. He was impressed by his mind, and even more by the humorously nonchalant way in which he seemed to regard his own talents. Wasn't this just what the museum needed, what he was looking for?

Towards the end of the interview indeed, he began to grow apprehensive that Reg might lose interest in the post when he heard how miserly the salary was. But this did not seem to worry him.

Afterwards, he thought it mildly odd that Reg had shown such little curiosity about the job from his own point of view. 'I think I know the kind of thing to expect,' he had interrupted, when he was trying, unbidden, to inform him. But on reflection Robert liked that, too. Griffin had obviously, for his own reasons, quickly decided he wanted the job. It was pleasing to find such decisiveness, and such an apparently unmercenary and professional attitude.

Robert would normally have taken time to reflect on all the candidates, and there were still two more due to be seen tomorrow. But in a sudden heat of certainty, he decided he could put off the remaining two and offered Reg the job there in Mortimer's culturally schizophrenic dining-room. It was accepted at once.

Later, he wondered how Mortimer would react to his choice. Almost certainly badly. He would not be able to classify Griffin in the way he usually liked to vilify academics, and it was hardly likely he would appreciate Griffin's laid-back attitude, which he would interpret as, *a priori,* insolence.

This added to Robert's satisfaction. He had the same feeling of outrageous triumph a spur of the moment, expensive purchase can give.

3

Reg was puzzled by aspects of his triumph. Given the luck of Caine's not having found anyone before their meeting, it had been easy enough. A bit of hanging about outside that dismal Catholic pile and the café, a tube journey at rush hour, with admittedly the danger of a slip-up, then the cinch of the cinema and the meal. But why the super secrecy? They could have given him more than the name and address. They could have told him it was the Aemelia, couldn't they, told him it was Rome? Could it be a practical joke? Razzy's idea of fun and games – to lose him the Courtauld and get him walled up in a minor museum like one of its exhibits? The idea bore his stamp. Razzy had never liked universities, probably because he did not go to one.

Since Düsseldorf, he had afforded a mortgage on a terraced house in Clapham. On his new doormat a couple of days later was a hand-delivered, executive class air-ticket, single, London to Kuala Lumpur, Qantas, for the next day. This improved matters. He believed in the development. Mean bastard that he was, Razzy would not have gone to *this* expense for a laugh.

There was a baldness. No note accompanied the ticket. There was also an amputated element about the lack of the return leg, or, more accurately, an unspoken conditional clause. If he did not deliver in some way... But the arrangements so far had a certain style about them. That had to be encouraging, he decided.

Was this the big one then, churning in the lottery urn, Reg thought several times as the plane journeyed over the blinding white lands of Araby, then the brown ones of the Indian subcontinent? The next twenty-four hours were probably going to reveal.

It was after midnight when they landed. The equatorial heat and humidity snatched at him with clammy fingers as he emerged from the aircraft. You could hardly see the control tower, let alone the sky, for moisture-laden haze, and the place stank of a cellar-like mildew. He only hoped the accommodation would suit the class of air ticket, with five stars and air-conditioning. He felt raked with lag. It was like being luggage in advance. His body would follow on a later plane, due in about a week.

Not a sign of red carpets in immigration. He queued for twenty minutes and got an unwelcome stamp in his passport. He had an instinctive dislike of leaving his scent. But in the customs hall an ugly little sod with a fuzzy head like a coconut, wearing khaki shorts and a pineapple-motif shirt barged him aside and took over his trolley.

'Follow me, plees.'

Apparently, customs were fixed. The officials didn't even raise their eyes as they made for the exit. Outside, a little away from the flare of neon light, a Jaguar waited – the four-wheeled variety, he wouldn't have been so surprised if it had had four legs and a snarl. In the front seat was a figure.

The man with khaki shorts was the driver, it seemed. He opened the back door for him, then set about stowing the suitcase in the boot. Reg got in. The head in front of him did not turn or speak. Reg also kept his mouth shut. The onus of greeting was surely on the host nation, and weren't the Malaysians renowned for hospitality?

He knew a fair amount of Bahasa Malay, but there was a short exchange he didn't catch between the driver and the chaperon. They set off. Soon they were gliding through jungle vegetation towards the reddish loom that was the city. Was it ominous? Reg decided to think he was simply in the presence of servile reticence.

At the modern skyscraper hotel, it was the same. The chaperon came in, but did not utter a word to him. He spoke briefly and unintelligibly with the male night receptionist. A registration pad was swivelled and a pen handed with lowered eyes. When he had finished signing, the man was on his way out, passing the incoming porter entering with his suitcase. The porter was handed his key and the two of them made their way to the lifts. In the lift he thought of questioning the porter, but the blank face raised dutifully to the floor indicator did not suggest inside knowledge. At least he was in a bona fide four star hotel.

The usual post-jet routine set in. For four or five hours he listened to the hissing breath of the air-conditioning. His body and mind felt wound up like clockwork. They would take their own time to unwind, and there was nothing he could do but wait. Just as it was beginning to get light something seemed to relax. He slept.

He woke after midday, feeling drained. He got up to have a shower, and only when he returned from the bathroom saw the note that had been pushed under the door, together with the *Straits Times*. His name, *'Mr Reginald Griffin'*, was hand-written on the envelope. Inside was a stiff, thick card with bevelled, gilded edging. *'His Royal Highness the Tunku Raschid will see you at his residence at 6 p.m. this evening. Please make yourself ready in the lobby at 5.30 p.m. A car will be sent for you.'* There was no signature.

By five-thirty, lunch, a swim in the hotel pool, and the thought of a live Tunku pending, had gone a long way to restoring Reg to something nearer normality. When he went down, the driver – a different one – rose from one of the armchairs as if he didn't really belong to it and led him out to the car, this time a Mercedes.

Apparently the Tunku's day staff were a bit more extrovert than the night shift. The man seemed to have a perpetual grin. He thought it a joke that Reg preferred to sit in the front seat, announced his name was Selim, and was quite prepared to chatter. Reg learnt that Tunku Raschid was the brother of one of the Sultans, of the State of Panjung, that the house they were approaching was only one of a dozen he owned in various parts of the world, that the family owned huge areas of rubber and palm-oil jungle as well as mines, that the Tunku had four wives, the 'latest' being a young Hawaiian girl. The 'last one', a beautiful English woman, had been pensioned off somewhere in Europe.

Reg rather expected a palace, or perhaps part of *the* palace. In fact it was a sizeable but not vast two-storey modern building built round three sides of a swimming pool in an ordinary street in the more fashionable, residential part of the town. The only sign of security was that the villa, the pool, and a small garden were surrounded by a ten foot wall surmounted by spikes which looked like the front row of pikemen at Agincourt, and an aged guardian who sat in a hut beside the one modest, wrought-iron gate that breached it. The gate was for pedestrians only. Cars were apparently garaged elsewhere. Selim indicated that Reg should get out. He did so. He entered through the gate that was electrically operated by the guardian, and another man appeared from an outhouse. Apparently the latter was the butler. He bowed courteously from the waist and in Jeeves-perfect English asked Reg to follow. He led the way to a table and a group of chairs set in the shade of the house beside the pool, and asked if he could bring Reg anything to eat or drink.

Waiting for fruit juice to arrive, Reg looked about him. The house was motionless, and silent except for the single, rather insolent call of a tropical bird which should have been in a zoo, sitting out of sight in one of the short bushy trees. He then became aware that there was someone beyond the trees, running. Heavy footsteps pounded ponderously. An upright figure appeared in a blue track suit, running with his hands clenched in front of his chest and with knees exaggeratedly raised, like a soldier running at the double on parade. He turned at the wall and retraced his footsteps. He was running up and down in this absurd way, it seemed, in the fifty-yard space between the walls, letting out his breath in artificial expulsions between pursed lips.

In a moment a beautiful girl came out of the house in a pink cheong-sam. She was holding a large bath towel. She stood dutifully at a distance from the runner. The 'latest'? The butler returned, and confirmed that the male figure was the Tunku. The Tunku took 'a constitutional' every day at this time, he explained, 'as regular as clockwork'. Nothing had ever been permitted to interrupt it, he added impressively.

'And the girl?' Reg asked.

There was a pause of whose timing Jeeves would certainly have approved.

'The Princess Irene has just joined us,' said the butler faintly.

Reg began to enjoy himself. The iced mango juice had a flavour that went with the bird of paradise in the bush. There were no doubts left in his mind. This was no joke, and Razzy had been right, the client was big. You could smell it. Information about the state of Panjung was arriving in his mind. Sipping, he watched the ceremony of the bath towel. Her hero having finished his exertions, the girl bestowed a token wiping of his face and neck, standing on tiptoe. What delighted Reg was the way they completely ignored him. They both went into the house without as much as an acknowledgement. This was the East all right. Not a bourgeois manner in sight.

It was half an hour and a whisky and soda later before the Tunku reappeared. He emerged suddenly into the deep shadow of the arched loggia that kept the downstairs windows from the full glare of the sun. Showered and spruced – had other therapy also been bestowed? – he had an equestrian look about him. He wore a spotless white shirt with a multicoloured neck-cloth, black strongly tapered trousers and black leather shoes with silver buckles and raised heels. One almost expected to see spurs. It was a good bet he was a product of an English public school and a good regiment, though – not quite the image – he had a plodding, rather laboured walk, as if he had some deformity, which had not been apparent when he was running. That would surely have precluded the army.

'Good evening, Mr Griffin. You will forgive me for keeping you waiting. Abdel has seen to your wants, I see.' He barely raised his voice. 'Abdel?'

The Tunku did not need to speak. Abdel had appeared a few discreet seconds behind his master. Raised eyebrows, and a manicured, ringed hand stretched forward, on which a large, surely priceless Burmese ruby was prominent, suggested the same again for Reg. Reg declined. The Tunku's eyes did the rest of the ordering. Abdel withdrew to execute wishes apparently as standard as the evening jog.

Reg had a batch of small talk ready. But though there was a long silence, which it was tempting to think needed filling with western conversational expertise, Reg withheld it. The Tunku's attention seemed riveted by something in the pool. From his seat he peered forward, both hands on the arms of the chair, frowning heavily. In a moment he leaned back in the chair and they sat in silence again.

Abdel reappeared with what looked like a glass of sparkling water. There were two pills beside it on the small, English, silver tray. The Tunku did not look at Abdel, and spoke in English.

'Abdel, the pool is filthy. Will you kindly attend to it at once.'

Startled and puzzled in equal proportions, Abdel gazed at the pristine expanse of blue. He and Reg spotted the offending item simultaneously – a white feather gently rocking against the overflow rim at the deep end. Reg and the Tunku watched while Abdel oversaw another male servant with what resembled a butterfly net, and a red plastic bucket.

'I have an incompetent and idle bunch of people at present,' the Tunku explained, as he took the glass and threw the first pill vigorously to the back of his mouth.

Reg felt a further silence was necessary to absorb the aberration and perhaps bestow sympathy. If this could be transmitted by a nod and blank features, he was not averse to doing so. Again, he waited.

The manner then changed abruptly. So radical was the shift of expression, Reg could not think in this moment how he could have imagined the man deformed. Suddenly the face was all action. The black eyes blazed, the high cheek bones suggested a fearsome medieval warrior.

'You took a first and a doctorate at the Courtauld Institute, where you have been working recently as an auxiliary tutor. Your speciality is High and Post Renaissance sculpture. But I gather you know something of Malaysian art, which was a subsidiary subject in your first degree course, and that you have had some employment at Christie's, both on the public relations side and as a valuer for important auctions.

'I have in Panjung quite a collection, mostly of Malaysian artefacts. For various reasons I want it realistically valued. Naturally, I require total discretion. If your knowledge is what I think it is, and your valuations are convincing, you will be well paid. Any books you need can be supplied. I would like you to travel early tomorrow morning. Do you accept the assignment?'

Reg would have much preferred to fix the remuneration and be assured of a return air-ticket. He did not think he would get an answer if he asked about this. As the religious say, there are some matters that require faith.

4

Sunshine, striking the rising wing, distracted Robert Caine's concentration again. Almost imperceptibly they were altering course. For longer than one would have imagined, the pilot held the turn before lowering the wing gently on to the new bearing.

Reg Griffin's appointment had certainly had one immediately good result. He was on his way back to Rome a day earlier than he had planned. But though he was trying to read a long article on a new Hittite discovery in the *Italian Archaeology Society Journal,* he found it hard to keep his mind focused.

Just then the intercom pong-ed and the line was live. There was a long stagey pause while the engines droned on dutifully.

'This is your captain, Captain Waterman, speaking . . .'

The languid, all-is-well voice began, as if its owner were basking in a deck-chair on a Caribbean cruise, idly contemplating the quirks of the rest of humanity.

Robert looked down quickly through the small porthole to the uniform layer of cloud below. The voice added to the disquiet he felt and, practised in stalking himself as he was, he immediately suspected why. He imagined the captain in shirtsleeves, relaxing up there on the flight deck. Several days a week he did this, endlessly traversing placid ponds of water or cloud. Every time, at this point in the journey, in that self-satisfied tone he gave his passengers their height and airspeed, and pointed out Mont Blanc on the port side.

It was the demon, he knew, that had got at him in London, up to his tricks again, for did not his own life similarly voyage, with a parallel predictability?

He quickly tried a catechism he had used before as an antidote. He could not be said, surely, to have done so badly in life? Without total immodesty, he could claim, could he not, to have created one of the few viable private museums of Europe? In the field of scholarship he had made his contribution, was continuing to make it. His name was known, even if only to a handful of specialists of a similar bent.

As regards personality too, where ultimate judgements had to be made, need he be so despondent? Some people saw him, he was sure, as an amiable plodder, an academic distanced from reality, pushed around by Mortimer Ready, and married to a woman who thought she deserved better. But did his compliance spring from weakness? He could claim it didn't. Weren't understanding and forbearance worth something? He felt he exercised both.

It was no use. At a deeper level he did not believe himself. He had not done so for a long time. The animation his London appointment had temporarily aroused in him was already fading. What difference would a new young man on his staff make?

They were kept waiting in the aircraft after landing at Fiumicino, just off the runway. No other aircraft seemed to be landing or taking off. After ten minutes, the captain came on the intercom again, rather less languidly, and apologised for 'a temporary administrative hold-up'. But when police cars started flashing about the tarmac in front of the reception building, a male American passenger in a tartan cap got more than curious.

'Say, darlin', you ain't goin' to tell me this is an admin snarl-up. It's a goddam bomb scare,' he said loudly to one of the beleaguered air-hostesses doing her best to reassure.

It was a bomb scare, in the terminal building. In the end the captain had to come on the blower again and tell them so. At once pandemonium broke out. Most of the Italian passengers, the majority, started talking at once, shouting and gesticulating.

Robert was amused. He loved Italy and the Italians, and his affection included an appreciation of the Italian excitability which burnt on a pilot flame and could flare up like this at any moment. For was not this the reverse side of their intense interest in life, their insistence on the moment, their immense capacity for emotion? He sat back in his seat, enjoying the drama around him as he idly watched through the porthole a yellow Agipgaz vehicle turning under the wing.

The bomb was apparently a hoax, but it was an hour before the place was cleared and they were allowed to enter the building.

Robert's more genial mood persisted. Broad, easy, knowledgeable, careless, disorganised, fitfully and spontaneously affectionate, Italy, his foster parent, took him back. The crowded airport was its usual mixture of private animation and official inefficiency. As they walked down the long corridor, the overhead television screens had a fit of the blinks. In Customs, in such preferable contrast to more officious behaviour in other airports, sullen officials with slouched, shallow-rimmed caps loitered and could scarcely raise the energy to place their yellow scribbles on the suitcases, as if to put in its place the whole idea of the tiresome controls they were forced to operate. And on all sides private intercourse raged. A small dog belonging to a woman had a coughing fit. She was surrounded by solicitous strangers offering advice. He was home, he thought amiably. 'Oh, for a beakerful of the south.' He was not the first Briton to need Italy to convince him he was alive.

He emerged with his one modest suitcase into the balmy spring evening which smelt of the nearby sea, and sought out his car in the huge open air park, a very old resprayed and indestructible Citroen D.S. with rather gaudy cerise upholstery he had bought second-hand years ago. It started almost at once, and he waited in pleasant anticipation for the hydraulic suspension to elevate him. He had thoughts of a cool gin and tonic on the balcony. It was just possible Kate had organised a little more than tin opening, their usual custom on Sunday evenings. And perhaps his absence would rekindle a little the surely still glowing embers of their relationship?

The Citroen lapped the grassy waste of the Pontine Marshes with lofty, unhurried speed, and he was soon negotiating the scruffy environs of the Eternal City. The serpentine route wound its way through a web of suburban streets, spun by an active and insular proletariat bent upon its own purposes and unmindful of the traveller trying to reach the centre of the city. He drove down endless avenues of battered plane trees with the torn election posters of umpteen political parties, unmade litter-strewn pavements where unattractive brown dogs foraged under café tables, ugly concrete blocks which were a maze of telephone wires and washing hung out of the windows. Only when past the

Porta Ostiense and inside the great Aurelian walls did the ancient world and therefore some dignity take over.

Robert's mood lifted further as he passed the long oval of the Circo Massimo, the ruined palaces of the Emperors on the Palatine that overlooked it, the massive Arch of Constantine, and finally, rounding the Coliseum, the Forum on his left. The classical symmetry, even in silent ruin, reprimanded like a respected elder the chaos of the Italian city that seethed and bickered about it. The study of ancient Rome could never be quite his love as it was Kate's. He liked a lot more between the lines than Rome seemed to offer, and he could never quite rid his mind of the notion that the Romans had pinched so many of their central ideas from his Etruscans without acknowledgement. But he understood Kate's absorption in the subject. It suited the lust for that Augustan definition and exactitude she had inherited from her determined, self-made, scientific father. And whatever his personal regrets, Rome, glorious, crumbling, decadent Rome, which had long departed from these classical certainties, was his city, an uplifting, daily pleasure.

Through the walls again, he broke free of the stranglehold of traffic as he entered the Borghese Gardens. The Villa Aemelia was in an ideal position for a museum, isolated, surrounded by pines, left alone in a fume of resin to brood upon its treasures from the past. Though he suspected that Kate, in her moods of social pretension, took private exception to the concept of living over the shop and often apologised for it to the well-connected friends she cultivated, when the public had disappeared in the evenings she had been known to say it was a lovely place to live. They inhabited the flat on the top floor, which had a superb terrace. How many rich Roman families had this almost rural peace?

As he drove on to the tufa-paved area in front of the palazzo, he slowed for a moment to reconnect himself with the familiar sight. The Renaissance facade was particularly beautiful in the glow of sunset, when its ochre-painted rendering – together with terracotta, one of the two standard colours of old Rome – turned to a lavish gold. The three storeys of well-proportioned windows, handsomely grilled on the lower floors, rose majestically to the high wooden eaves jutting almost horizontally, like someone shielding their eyes contentedly from the sun. In the centre, at ground level, was the welcoming spread of half a dozen shallow steps leading to the front entrance.

The house was almost square and was built round a central court. The Caines' flat was on the third floor at the rear. The approach to it was by a gravelled road that rounded the building on one side, and then through an archway that tunnelled through the ground floor on the far side and led into the inner court.

The archway was defended against unauthorised vehicles by a chain, slung between two stone bollards. As he drove round the building, Robert hooted lightly to warn Kate he was back. To his surprise the bulky, athletic figure of Pietro Buongusto, the concierge, sauntered from the door of his flat in the middle of the archway, followed by the inevitable Faro. Pietro was seldom separated from his mongrel.

'Non si preoccupe, lo faccio io.'

Usually surly and ever-conscious that he might be being put upon, Pietro would never normally have considered undoing the chain as part of his duty. But he did so. Puzzled but grateful, Robert thanked him through the lowered window, and drove into the court.

There confronting him was the explanation. Mortimer Ready's Rolls was parked next to Pietro's absurdly huge and ancient Mercedes. Pietro was standing guard. Robert's spirits took a nosedive. He kept his manner calm, however.

'Mr Ready is upstairs?' he asked, in Italian.

Pietro had followed him into the courtyard. The podgy, self-centred, boyish features betrayed, as they usually did, his predominant emotion. Obsessed with notions of 'bella figura', Pietro sycophantically admired Mortimer, largely, as far as Robert could judge, because of the Rolls. Robert's own standing, in view of the old Citroen, was correspondingly low.

Pietro used the most insolent weapon in his repertoire – English. 'Mee-ster Ray-ar-dee telephone your wife,' he pronounced with relish. 'Your wife telephone me. He is here since one hour. I not go out. I make certain I expect for him.' He raised his crafty brown eyes insolently to the third floor. 'Meester Ray-ar-dee very angry, I think. He expect for you upstairs.'

Robert took his suitcase out, locked the car, and left Pietro standing there. The man had been difficult ever since last summer when he had demanded a loan, undoubtedly to finance an affair he was carrying on with an English girl on holiday in Rome. Robert had refused, and Pietro had gone to Mortimer who swallowed the lies and gave him the money.

Access to their flat was through the museum's rear door in the corner of the court. He gave their private bell the usual tinkle, opened the door with the electronic gadget he issued only to himself, Kate, and to one or two of the senior staff, and disconnected the alarm system while he went up to the third floor, where he would reconnect it. He mounted in the ancient lift, which was also used for shifting heavy museum objects to the upper floors. As he rose, he tried to get his pulse in line with the stately movement. The last thing he was going to do tonight was to be angry if Mortimer was indeed on the rampage.

They were out on the terrace with empty glasses. Kate, groomed and immaculate as usual in a white silk blouse, stylish green scarf and matching skirt, raised her hand to the level of her shoulder. He held it ritually for a second until she disengaged it.

'Why the hell are you so late?'

Mortimer's small, blue-suited, gingery figure was enthroned in the large basket chair, which was one of those with a wide, fanned back like a Tudor ruff. He looked lost in it, like the smaller Ronnie doing that old solo act of his.

'Someone playing bomb scares at Fiumicino. They kept us in the aircraft.'

'Well, I've been sitting here an hour waiting for you.'

What was implied – that he should have opened an emergency door and jumped, just *in case* Mortimer happened to be waiting for him at home? Kate, he noted, was already informed of whatever it was, and was as usual outwardly in cahoots with Mortimer. She refused to meet his eyes.

Mortimer realised his last remark had not been exactly gallant towards Kate. 'It's only fortunate,' he mumbled as a postscript, 'that I've had Kate to keep me company.'

The remark convinced Robert it was nothing catastrophic. If it had been that urgent, Mortimer would not have played about like this but gone straight to the point. He relaxed, and though mindful of his new thoughts, put an old routine into action. The first thing was to get the fuses out.

'Good,' he said. 'Well, whatever the dread news is, I want a drink first if you don't mind. Can I fill you up, either of you?'

Kate shook her head. Mortimer continued to look cross, but didn't answer. Robert went inside.

He took his time pouring the whisky. They had demolished the soda, so he went to the kitchen to get another. He was aware of them sitting out there, waiting for him in silence. It seemed they had already run out of things to say to each other. He had never understood why Kate was so polite to Mortimer, even when speaking about him when he was not there. She had even less in common with the man than he did, and really despised him. Was it part of her unspoken punishment of himself? Probably. He was responsible in her eyes for landing them in the predicament of their relationship to Mortimer, so she was making the best of a bad job. Was that what she wished to imply?

'That Bruneschi woman's got to go,' Mortimer said, as soon as he returned. 'I wish to God *she* had disappeared and not Pelucci.'

Robert had rather expected Kate would melt away at this point, now she had handed on the baton. She usually did when museum talk developed. She sat her ground.

'Gabriella? How has she transgressed?'

'To begin with she's quite obviously administratively incompetent. I cannot think why you leave her in charge. And apart from the fact that she's a bungler, what you once chose to call her "frilly pinkness at the edges" is getting starker red every time I see her.'

Robert sipped. 'What happened?'

'Does it matter precisely what happened? It's a general situation I'm talking about. This isn't a university, Robert, it's a commercial enterprise. Let her rabbit on about social injustice where it does no harm. A university would be the ideal place for her – if she could get into one, which I doubt.'

'Gabriella hardly "rabbits" – but what has she been up to?'

Mortimer flushed. '"Up to." That's a typical phrase of yours, isn't it? As if the whole thing's a childish game. Well, I'll tell you

33

what Signora Bruneschi's been up to. I happen to be meeting the Minister tomorrow in case you've forgotten. It's your darned highbrow exhibition, which is going to lose me a packet of money again, that I'm seeing him about, isn't it? Where would you be with it if I hadn't used my influence in high quarters? I need the precise list of exhibits. If the Minister's going to pressure the Spaniards, he will need to know what an important exhibition it is and what a gap the Escorial Crucifixion will leave if it isn't there. When I phoned her yesterday morning, Bruneschi says airily "she'll see what she can do". An hour, two, goes by and not a squeak. I phone again. She's been "caught up", she informs me. The lights had fused on the ground floor, or some triviality. When I pointed out the urgency of my request, she told me, "other people can have emergencies too," or some such phrase. I tore a strip off her and told her to get the list immediately or there would be consequences for her. I still haven't got that list.'

'You mean she didn't get back to you?'

'Your secretary got back to me this afternoon to say the list must be in the safe and that you went away with the keys.'

'That's true.'

'I'm not going to be treated like this by your curators, Robert. You have the right to hire and fire, but I expect a certain minimum of civility. She must go. As it turns out, she couldn't have got the list. But that's no longer the point. The point is, she isn't the kind of person we want round here. With her ideology and attitude, and those of that red husband of hers, there's a security risk, quite apart from other considerations.'

Robert was on the point of defending Gabriella on the last count. If security had anything to do with it, which it didn't, Gabriella was hotter on it than he was, quite apart from being the straightest, most honest person he knew. It was also absurd to say she was red in the way Mortimer was suggesting. He stopped himself. Instead, he got up.

'I'll get you the list of exhibits and their donors,' he said. 'I'm sorry, I had no idea you were seeing Palomero so soon. You didn't actually say, you know.'

When he returned from the office on the floor below, Mortimer was standing and Kate was handing him his brief-case. He snatched the sheet from Robert's hand.

'At last. I really don't expect to have to come into Rome for a piece of paper from you. Get rid of that woman, any way you can, or there will have to be consequences.'

Robert was going to accompany him down to his car. But at the lift he was dismissed.

'I don't need nursemaiding, thank you. Pietro will let me out – one of your smarter and more loyal employees, incidentally, a damn sight smarter than some of your so-called intellectuals. Next time, perhaps you can leave keys with Kate when you go away.'

Robert went back into the flat and alerted Pietro on their communicating phone, as if he needed to be. When he heard the door boom downstairs, on a reflex action he reconnected the alarm system.

Kate was in the kitchen, putting the glasses into the dishwasher. He tried to revive his earlier feelings.

'Well, a somewhat dramatic homecoming,' he said lightly.

'Indeed.'

'Why didn't he send someone in for the paper? He didn't have to come himself. He could have phoned and I could have sent it out to him this evening for that matter.'

'He was clearly angry on the matter of principle.'

'What matter of principle?'

'Gabriella Bruneschi's behaviour.'

Robert turned away.

'Then I have the feeling I haven't heard quite all of the story. From what I have heard, I can't discern any principles at large.'

'You certainly *haven't* heard all the story.'

'You mean Gabbi really shot her mouth off?'

Kate was being unusually domestic. Fastidiously, at arm's length, item by item, she began to rearrange two or three days' crockery in the machine.

'Among other things I gather she called Mortimer a fascist.'

'Oh no.'

'Mortimer is right, you know. She doesn't control her tongue.'

He sat down at the table. 'No. But neither of course does Mortimer.'

'Mortimer happens to own the place.'

'Yes, and thinks he owns us as well.'

'Well, in a way, I suppose he does, doesn't he? You, and the staff anyway, apropos the museum. Anyway, his influence is useful, isn't it, with Cellini? He is good at cultivating people in high places. I would have thought you'd all see that Paris, or Madrid in this case, is worth a mass.'

Robert again applied the brakes. What she said had some truth, though her tone had a personal edge which went beyond the situation. In spite of the implications of what she had said, paradoxically he had a spasm of that old affection for her. For what the Italians so graciously call 'sulla quarantina' – she was actually forty-four, four years older than he was – she was still pretty athletic and youthful. She was still, surely, beneath the irrelevant layers time had built, the girl he had fallen in love with on the Cambridge backs? They were regarded in those days as the ideal pair, she the daughter of a distinguished and eminent scientist and in her own right one of the best undergraduates in the Archaeology Faculty, he with his own bunch of laurels.

'All right, I agree,' he said, with humour. 'The Escorial Crucifixion is worth a mass.' He paused. 'And it's nice to be home.'

'Nice to have you back,' she said perfunctorily.

She was shaking soap powder into the plastic compartment, amateurishly, at arm's length, as if it were not her job. It amused him to watch her. Did he not really appreciate her refusal to be domestic, which was part of her immense integrity as an archaeologist?

He hoped the subject had gone away, but it had not.

'What *are* you going to do about Gabriella Bruneschi?' she said in a few moments.

'Oh, it'll blow over.'

'I rather doubt it this time. You didn't see Mortimer when he came in.'

'Mortimer's fury evaporates as fast as it bursts out.'

'Do you think Bruneschi's competent?'

'Of course she is. She's by far the ablest person here.'

'Then it's a pity she hasn't got more tact. Can't you ease her out somehow? If she's as bright as you say she is, she should be able to find another post easily enough.'

He turned to her, astounded. 'But Kate, quite apart from common justice, I don't think Gabbi wants to move. Her husband's a Roman.'

'You mean you're going to take her side over this business?'

'I didn't say that.'

'Well, what are you saying?'

'I'm saying we'll see, and that I'm hungry.' He looked around the room for evidence of food.

She had done nothing about a meal. She apologised. She had been going to, she said, but Mortimer had 'shifted the agenda'. He suggested they went out somewhere, to Trastevere perhaps. They hadn't been there for years. She said she really didn't feel like it if he didn't mind. She had a hard day ahead of her, out at Viterbo.

They had a tin of asparagus soup, and a tin of salmon, with a salad he made. At least, he thought, the subject of Gabriella and Mortimer had been buried. During the meal Kate chatted comprehensively about the new villa dig she had been invited to examine. The villa had belonged to a rich commercial family and some interesting graffiti had been unearthed which could be useful for her new book on first-century inscriptions.

As an afterthought, she asked him about his visit to London. He had looked forward to telling her at some length about the candidates, about his chance meeting with Reg Griffin and his feelings about him. In the moment he found he had no relish for the story, related it baldly, and made his method of choice sound even more casual than it had been.

'A bit risky taking on someone like that, isn't it?' was her tangential comment.

'He has as good academic credentials as the others. Better in fact.'

'Well, let's hope he isn't another Bruneschi,' she added more crisply, 'and that his politics are a little more sophisticated.'

The evening died. They went to bed as on any other day. He might not have been away, he thought gloomily. He knew that he had not really expected it to be otherwise.

5

Back in his hotel, Reg Griffin was having second thoughts. The outlines of a routine job of tediously recognisable proportions were taking shape. Not a word yet about Rome, and what *could* a job in a Roman museum have to do with the valuation of an art collection? Razzy's 'instincts' were not infallible. Perhaps it was a hoax after all, if not Razzy's, someone else's – or a cock-up, two different operations with crossed lines. Perhaps he should get figures straight with the Tunku before the next move, possibly an advance. He could be landed with peanuts, with a hotel bill and the return fare to pay, not to mention with the mess of having signed a contract for a job in Italy he didn't want.

But money was a bit difficult now, even if he could get the Tunku's phone number. Incidentally, the whole bunch of them seemed to have a very ex-directory approach to life altogether. He had not even been given a visiting card.

A car was to be at the hotel at six a.m. Reg was glad it was Selim and the Mercedes. At least there could be conversation. He took the front seat again.

He was also glad of the air-conditioning. Going outside the hotel door was like stepping into an extra-hot sauna. He had calculated about a six hour journey. The place was on the Pacific coast, about three hundred miles from the capital. Selim said it would take nearer seven hours. He had forgotten a couple of mountain passes they had to negotiate. He got the feeling Selim had been briefed to keep his mouth shut. His attempt to get him talking about the Tunku met with giggles and a brush-off. All he got was confirmation that none of them liked 'the latest', chiefly because she wasn't the discarded Princess Elena – who had apparently been much loved. Selim wanted to talk about American films.

They left Selangor State and sped through jungle relieved only occasionally by sparse villages of houses on stilts. They entered the state of Panjung. After an hour of travelling across a fertile plain forty miles wide, Selim remarked with a snigger that it all belonged to the Tunku.

Reg presumed the Tunku lived in the Royal Palace of Panjung – perhaps a wing? – and, whatever banality was in store for him, he looked forward to seeing it. This Sultan had one of the few surviving wooden buildings, seventeenth century as he remembered. Unlike some of their colleagues, the Sultan's predecessors had maintained cordial and placatory relations with the European interlopers – Portuguese, the Dutch and finally the British – and profited accordingly. He could imagine the spread of beautiful and priceless objects that awaited him. It would be a museum of Malaysian art as well as whatever else they had stashed away over the centuries from other parts of the Orient. Perhaps, even if the whole thing turned out to be a flop, there would be this footnotal compensation.

As they entered the park, his pulses began to beat a bit faster. Suddenly, through some trees he saw the palace. He recognised at once the tiered roof of copper and zinc shingles, the gilded spires, and the beautiful carved pillars on which the building stood. But at the last moment Selim took a road that peeled off from the main drive.

Selim saw his disappointment. 'Tunku's house shore-side,' he said. 'More big than palace. You see, more big, very more nice.'

Selim's loyalty to his master's taste was hardly compensation. The Tunku's residence, which was some four miles from the Royal Palace, was a great deal larger. The palace was still not large by royal standards, and the fretsaw effect of its woodwork made it look smaller than it was. But this house was hideous – a curry of styles borrowed from Europe. The steep green gables curved upwards in oriental style, but the grilles on the windows were Spanish, each had a rounded canopy of striped orange like a Parisian restaurant, and the main structure was of a small, very dark brick reminiscent of Amsterdam.

In front of the pink glass porch another car was parked – the Jaguar that had met him at the airport. He had noted the registration number, an automatic reflex. Selim's face fell.

'Ah, Haji Kassim is come.'

'The type who met me at the airport?'

Selim nodded. He seemed agitated. He parked and, leaving the engine running to keep the air-conditioning going, motioned to

Reg to stay where he was. He got out, did not approach the front door, but disappeared round the side of the house.

He returned in five minutes. 'We go to hotel,' he said, briskly. 'Return later.'

Reg could gain no further information, except that he was to stay at a luxury hotel right on the beach.

'Very nice luncheon,' Selim said as the place came into view. 'If wanted, very pretty afternoon girls.'

Reg was beginning to form a high opinion of Selim's sensitive nature.

He had expected Selim to pick him up at five. But when he went down to the lobby, it was Kassim who was talking in low tones to one of the managers at the desk. Reg had not really taken in Kassim's face the other night. He realised how disagreeable it was, small eyes peering from between a protruding brow and unnaturally bulging cheeks. One cheek had two not quite parallel scars. The lack of symmetry – the other cheek was not adorned – suggested violence rather than ritual.

Seeing him approach in a mirror, but making no acknowledgement of it, Kassim turned towards the door and with an ugly jerk of his head indicated he was to be followed. Reaching the car, he opened the back door and, leaving it open, went round to the driving seat.

This was becoming absurd. Reg slammed the back door and sat in the front passenger seat. 'You're Haji Kassim?'

The head of jet black hair, neatly parted in the centre like a schoolboy spruced up for Sunday school, made no movement. 'Tunku Raschid wishes you to do the inventory now,' he said distastefully, in syllable-perfect, educated English. 'He will come this evening.'

'You mean he expects me to complete the entire thing tonight? It's out of the question. If it's any kind of a collection it'll take me several days, and I'll certainly need the books the Tunku said would be available.'

'Those are the instructions.'

Further expostulation was justified. Reg kept it to himself.

The house had been shut up, it seemed, in anticipation of a prolonged absence. They entered by a side door that led into a

40

basement area where apparently the servants lived when the Tunku was in residence. At present Kassim and himself seemed to be the only people in the building. Kassim unlocked and locked doors as they went up to the ground floor. All the furniture in the hall and the front rooms was covered with white sheets. There was a dank, mildewy smell. Either there was no air-conditioning, or it was not turned on.

They entered the main salon. Kassim began rather aggressively to whip the sheets from the furniture as if he were undressing and about to rape the entire harem in a fit of sadistic rage. He left them where they fell on the rich Chinese carpet.

'You will start in this room,' he said finally. He produced a large pad and a biro from the drawer of an inlaid rosewood table and threw them on the polished surface. 'List all the valuable objects, their date of origin, a brief description, and your valuation. When you have completed this room, ring that bell.'

He indicated a velvet tassel. He tried to put the lights on at the door, but nothing happened. He left the room, locking the door behind him.

A dense silence descended. The windows also, Reg noted, were all locked – not that they needed to be with the grilles behind them. God, the place was like a morgue, and how was he going to see in this gloom? It would be dark soon. Then, as if answering his question, the lights came on and a huge ceiling fan, like three large banana leaves, began to turn. He was grateful for the fan. The heat was suffocating.

He saw the room was stuffed with minor treasures. It was ridiculous working without reference books. He would have to make this plain again to the Tunku when he came. But there did not look to be anything of immense difficulty here. He would make a start, and work at his normal speed. There was not much else he could do.

He began on the contents of two glass cases, which looked to contain the most interesting items. One held a collection of Malay musical instruments. There was a selection of coconut drums of differing antiquity, a five-gong chanang, some spike fiddles and decorated Malay oboes. The other case was a mixture of weapons – kris, and a fine group of keramabit, tiger-claw daggers with magnificent ivory handles – and various objects of metal. There was a gold, jewelled tobacco box, a beautiful silver Malaccan pedestal tray with a lotus motif, silver bracelets, and a brass betel box, probably Thai.

He was so carried away with the task, it was some time before an essential fact occurred to him. This was all very well. There were interesting things here, and this was only the first room. But why call in an expert? The total value was perhaps ten grand sterling so far. That was not a vast sum for a man like Raschid. Why did he want a valuation anyway? He did not give the impression of being on the verge of bankruptcy. Insurance no doubt, but none the less...

Losing interest for a moment, his attention strayed to a door behind a drape he had not noticed before. Was there anything more valuable in the room beyond it? The door would be locked of course, but he tried it. To his surprise, it opened. He switched on the light.

Was he meant to be in here? The dust sheets were in position. It seemed to be Raschid's study. Books bound in a uniform red leather lined one wall to the ceiling. He lifted the corner of the sheet covering the largest piece of furniture and revealed a huge mahogany desk with a circular-back chair drawn to it. A fine ornamental moon-kite hung on one wall, and in a corner, also with no dust sheet, as if on guard, stood a fully-armed warrior, probably medieval from the shape of the helmet.

Nothing so very marvellous in here either, he thought. Then he noticed that on two of the walls two sizeable objects must have hung, of the same dimensions, probably pictures from the rectangular shape. There were remnants of cobwebs where the top edges of the frames would have been. They appeared to have been removed recently. The salon did not otherwise suggest slovenly housekeeping.

Reg could not entirely explain to himself the next action he took. He kept a small extendable measure in his pocket, always useful in cataloguing. Standing on a chair, he took exact measurements to the millimetre of the unfaded patches and made a note of them.

At this moment, alarming in the silence, there was the sound of an approaching helicopter flying very low. There was a crescendo of din as it hovered over the house. He switched the lights off, reshut the door, and hurried back into the salon. Darkness had fallen now, but lights had been switched on in the garden. The helicopter was coming down on the lawn.

The blades slowed and stopped, the door opened and the Tunku appeared. Kassim was approaching from the house. The two of them came in together, making apparently for the same side door Kassim and he had used. There were footsteps in the hall, the key grated and Raschid appeared.

'Hard at work?' he said absently. He walked straight to the windows and began pulling down blinds and drawing the curtains. Kassim trotted in behind him and assisted.

'I've made a start, yes, but I shall need the books I mentioned,' Reg began.

The Tunku was not listening. The blind-pulling continued. The Tunku turned towards him. 'You have begun your inventory, I see, Mr Griffin. May I glance at what you have done?'

He took the pad from Reg's hands. Already reading, he sat on one of the sofas. He flicked a finger sideways in Kassim's direction. 'Drinks, Kassim,' he commanded.

This time Raschid defied his religion with a whisky and soda. Reg asked for the same, taking some pleasure from the position to which Scarface had been demoted. While Raschid sipped and read, Kassim lurked unemployed by the sideboard. What was he, some kind of secretary? He was subservient enough to the Tunku, but several cuts above a domestic servant one would have thought. He certainly wasted no energy on being polite to visitors.

After some minutes, Raschid threw down the pad on the table.

'That'll be all, Kassim.'

Raschid waited until the door closed. 'I see you do know what you're talking about, without the aid of reference books,' he began. 'It also seems you're thorough, and get on with whatever is in hand without asking irrelevant questions. I rather imagine, I don't quite know why, that you don't like small talk. Is this so?' He did not wait for an answer. 'If you come to know me better you may come to the conclusion I share your view.' He paused. 'I think I may also hazard the guess that you realise certain objectives in life cannot always be reached entirely within the confines of scholarship and academic life…'

Reg let his eyebrows make any necessary comment on this. A sort of Gaullist 'je-vous-ai-entendu' line was what he aimed for.

'I did not of course invite you to Malaysia without making some enquiries.' The Tunku looked aside rather distastefully. 'Let me relate to you some of my findings. You recently took an apparent Fabergé brooch to Düsseldorf for its owner, allegedly with a view to selling to a German industrialist. You had the brooch in the flat you rented. You claimed that while you were out on the town the flat was burgled and the brooch taken. The police interrogated you, didn't they, for a considerable period? There were some difficult features to your story. But you kept your nerve, and got away with it. The insurance was collected – a great deal more than the brooch was worth in view of the private doubt the owner had as to its authenticity – and you collected your share of it.' The oriental mouth twitched. 'I gather you very prudently invested your spoils in property... I don't know quite why, Mr Griffin, but I've formed the distinct impression from all this that you have rather a single-minded attitude to money, unusual in an academic, and a most reprehensibly flexible attitude to legal procedures.'

Raschid looked at him. It seemed to indicate that some response was expected. Reg kept his face impassive, and crossed one leg over the other. 'I've an idea I haven't been summoned here to value your possessions?' he said, by way of a preliminary.

'On the contrary, even the small amount that you've done this evening is most informative. When I had your particulars described to me I saw at once how useful your subsidiary knowledge of our art would be. Not only did it give me a good reason to ask you to come here, your inventory tells me the first thing I need to know. You are not an academic amateur. One thing life has taught me is never to depend on other people's estimates, even when the testimonial is from a revered authority. You are not an academic amateur, and you have a commercial sense. That is a combination, as I say, rarely to be encountered.'

The Tunku rose and went to one of the windows. He opened the safety lock with a key concealed behind a shutter, then pushed up the lower pane. A welcome breeze entered. A pity Kassim had not thought of that, Reg thought. They could just hear the wash of the ocean on the beach about five hundred yards away. Nearer, a night creature bayed intermittently.

The Tunku returned to his seat, crossed his arms on his chest, and regarded Reg flatly. 'But yes, the instructions you received in London – which you carried out with dexterity and with such triumphant success – *will* be suggesting to you that matters beyond valuation of my collection are involved. I congratulate you, Griffin. I must confess to you I didn't think you would manage what you have. Our adversary is, I gather, a man of careful habits, and I can only say the way you handled him was quite masterly.'

'Adversary?'

'You rightly pounce on the word. No, it isn't really the right one to use, is it? Robert Caine should not be looked upon as an adversary. Certainly not from an *operative* point of view. Rather, he should be seen as our unconscious accomplice. I think this starts us off very much on the right track – assuming, of course that you are willing to undertake the further mission that lies ahead?'

'I can hardly do that without knowing what it is, can I?'

'Ah, but that, I am afraid, is what you will largely have to do. The job depends, you see, on a number of contingencies. Your first task you have magnificently achieved. But that is only a beginning. What I am saying to you, Mr Griffin, is that our association, certainly in the earlier stages, will have to have its basis in a mutual trust and regard rather than in specifics. You know, among many other things I admire about you English are your proverbs. You are such splendid retailers of morality. "One thing at a time." "Patience is a virtue." "Don't run until you can walk." There's a choice for practically any situation, isn't there?

'I've now made up my mind about you. It's a question at this moment of your own inclination. I have to warn you, there is risk, and danger – considerable danger, physical and otherwise.'

It was the crossroads again. Reg had no hesitation.

'I'll do it,' he said.

'Good. I rather fancied you would.'

The black gaze was lowered to the carpet.

'Finally then, we have money to discuss. I thought, if you accept the mission, for your visit here, which is now terminated, a thousand pounds would be appropriate, plus expenses and the air fares of course. On your arrival in Rome, which I realise involves your turning down a fellowship, ten thousand would be available. Then at a rather later date, very naturally, we might be into a different scale of remuneration.'

The Tunku was looking bored again.

Part Two
~ ~ ~ ~ ~ ~ ~ ~ ~ ~ ~

6

The day after his return to Rome, Robert promised himself the luxury of a few hours writing up his paper on Etruscan dentistry. The finds at Spina and Caere had thrown up so much, including this fascinating new aspect of their genius that could prove to be a lot more than a footnote.

He imagined there would first be some work in the office. Gabbi would have dealt with everything with her usual efficiency and decisiveness, but his secretary, Franca, quite possibly would have kept some things back from her, out of spite more than necessity. Franca, devoted to him and the museum, was not attractive. Gabbi was.

Nonetheless, he thought a couple of hours should do it. Kate had departed for Viterbo at dawn in the Citroen. Duty done, he could wallow, perhaps for most of the day, inviolate in the silence of an empty flat.

Rising at eight he made himself breakfast and ate it on the terrace, while leafing through the notes he had made and beginning to think how he would shape the essay. Already the morning sun was warm.

Just before nine he saw Franca's Cinquecento appear round the building below and disappear into the courtyard. Soon after, he went down to do his duty in the untidy high-ceilinged office on the second floor which always, even in summer, smelt faintly of damp plaster. Franca's slight bespectacled figure was lying in wait for him. He knew at once from the determined look on her face that he had anticipated correctly.

He first gave her the present, a bottle of toilet water snatched at Heathrow at the last moment. She took the parcel with her usual embarrassed sniff of pleasure, opened it, and thanked him. He knew she valued the gifts he always brought her when he had been away. He had heard that she boasted about them to the curators. But this was a mere stay to the avalanche. She held up the label to her short-sighted eyes, gave a quick smile, put the bottle in a drawer of her desk, and in a matter of seconds was in full spate.

She recited first her version of Gabriella's brush with Mortimer Ready, slanted strongly needless to say against Gabriella, and followed it with a list of other disasters. Latent as always was the implication that he should not have gone away. Franca's tempestuous loyalty could certainly be tiresome.

Involuntarily, his whole morning was consumed in a frenzy of largely unsuccessful administration. The thunderstorm that had fused the lights and caused Gabbi to be rude to Mortimer had also discovered a hole in the roof, through which a storeroom had been flooded. Reputable builders proved overworked, or the Rome telephone system made sure others were unapproachable. Robert then spent twenty minutes in the telephonic labyrinths of the Ministero dei Beni Culturali trying to contact the official who had visited while he was away without appointment, and declared that several objects 'of clear national importance', and therefore within their authority, were displayed with 'a prominence inconsistent with their cultural significance'. Franca scornfully quoted the words verbatim. And for half an hour one of the full time curators, Giuseppe Gasparotti, whom Franca had only just headed off from sending him a cable in London at museum expense, paced his room in a dapper blue suit and white shoes complaining of 'the plainly prejudiced attitude towards armour in this museum', which allowed 'such meagre resources as were available' to be 'lavished' upon pictures (another slap at Gabriella) to the detriment of his own speciality. Gasparotti 'could not think' that this disparity was the result of 'a prejudice based in any way upon seniority, or' – he paused significantly – 'still less upon personality,' but at times it was difficult for him not to think so.

Giuseppe's feathers were easy enough to smooth by dint of a little flattery and a very small concession to the armoury budget, but these Latin sideshows plundered one's time and energy. At one o'clock Giuseppe was still there. As a Parthian shot before going off for her lunch, Franca triumphantly brought him a stack of letters to sign.

He reread and signed the letters, and went upstairs to the flat. As he threw a bag of instant gnocchi into a saucepan of boiling water, he heard the distant boom below, which denoted that Pietro had shut the front door for the afternoon

Suddenly there was peace, the peace he had anticipated and,

surely, looked forward to? The roar of Rome was pleasantly removed, here in the centre of the Borghese, and he could feel the familiar, benevolent silence rising through the building. A warm breath of April breeze, faintly scented with pine resin, came through his open window and impishly winnowed some papers on the kitchen working top. As if a switch had been thrown, the cicadas started their siesta shift. *Wasn't* this what he had waited for?

To his dismay, he found he did not feel elation, only the dull ache which, in this moment he had to recognise, had been with him since last night. It quickened now into something nearer desolation.

The reason? Was he really going to continue kidding himself? He had known throughout the morning what it was, hadn't he?

All through Franca's loyal strictures, Giuseppe's posturing, he had been aware that, because she was off work today after her week-end duty, he would not see Gabbi until the following morning. Her vitality, her total integrity, her alternating moods of sweet gravity and delightful, explosive gaiety, her beauty and entirely feminine presence, which had come in recent months to be his daily solace, were being spent on that worthless, utopianist husband of hers, who couldn't even get himself a job and lived off her labours.

A crazy idea surged up. Why didn't he walk round to her flat on the other side of Termini? He could make the Mortimer situation the excuse. For a few reckless, frenzied moments he contemplated going. Giancarlo, by some luck, might not be there, and she would be alone and surprised, delighted, to see him. Hilariously, no doubt, despite his initial resolution to be otherwise, they would discuss Mortimer's latest absurdity. In five minutes he would be restored to sanity.

But his romantic vision, even as it danced ahead of him like a happy, innocent child, was already underlain by the knowledge of its impossibility. How could he go to Gabbi's flat and not be mis-understood? In a couple of minutes he could destroy everything they had together. It was spring madness.

He ate the food, went to his study, sat himself at the desk and with an effort began to work.

The idea came to him untripped, when he was no longer thinking about Gabbi. The new showcase of course. It had arrived while he was in London. He seized the phone before he could think himself out of it. Gabbi's vibrant, deep voice answered. Her 'Pronto', he thought, was dull, unexpectant. Was her day off so lacking in animation for her? He was encouraged.

'Gabbi, it's me.'

He thought she lit up. 'Robert, how nice. You're back safely. I did phone Franca this morning to make sure you were back and that I needn't come in. A good trip?'

'Fine.'

She paused. 'We had some fireworks. You heard no doubt?'

'Yes.'

'I'm sorry. It was just that on Saturday...'

'You don't have to apologise. It's not what I'm phoning about.'

'No?'

He heard her relief, then sensed renewed anxiety in the quality of her silence that followed. If not Mortimer, what else? Was she wondering that? Could she have no inkling of his feeling, of what was driving him? He composed his voice to matter-of-factness and dropped his intonation an octave.

'It's just I've had a mad notion. I was going to work this afternoon. Real work, I mean. My new paper on dentistry. But the morning was the usual bedlam, and I find I can't bring myself to it. It must be the relief of getting back here after London. I'm not feeling in the least studious.'

'And?'

'Well, you know the showcase arrived? I thought instead I'd start assembling the stuff, try to work out how we arrange it. I was just wondering if by any chance you felt like giving me a hand.'

'You mean today?'

'It's unforgivable of me, I know, on your day off. I expect...'

'I could a bit later. I've got my neighbours' children with me for another hour or so. You know I run a crêche here?'

He did know very well about the crêche. Gabbi organised this relief whenever she could for the mothers in her block of flats. Joy overwhelmed him. Was it possible she was saying yes? In his euphoria, he almost spoilt it.

'Are you sure Giancarlo can spare you?' he asked.

'Giancarlo's at a meeting,' she said.

Her voice was dull again, and carried justifiable reprimand. They never discussed Giancarlo, but such was the intuition that operated between them, Robert was sure she knew his sentiments in that direction. She had spotted at once that his question was hypocritical.

Robert had held a long debate with himself about the new showcase in the Etruscan room. There was always jealousy if any department was allocated money. If it was his own, he could expect the resentment to be doubled.

It was hardly a princely sum, not much more than the cost of the case and the extra insurance, for the objects had been donated to the museum in gratitude for the advisory work he had done (much of it in his holiday time) on the two remarkable sites in the north. But that would not still the tongues if they were inclined to wag. More important, he had to decide if he was putting his own interest above that of the museum in another way. Could it be said that a whole case devoted to the artefacts of Etruscan medicine and dentistry – in a collection that sought as its macro-aim to give a balanced view of each phase of Italy's history – was relevant?

He had persuaded himself that a major point was being stated. The contrast between the Babylonian achievement in the field and the advances the Etruscans had made, was surely a graphic and specific way of setting the Etruscans in history and thus of introducing the visitor to this section of the museum? And it would certainly be discourteous to the donors if the gift were not displayed.

Gabbi, who was excellent on design, had helped him with the blueprint of the (admittedly expensive) showcase. This involved photographs of the digging sites, which were to be a backcloth to the display, and the clever, curved shelving on four different levels which allowed the maximum number of objects to be displayed without crowding. He had done the smaller captions for each item from the inventory they had sent him, also the larger placards that gave the general information, and had had them printed before he went away. Everything was now ready. There was just the pleasant job of setting the objects in place.

As soon as he put the phone down to Gabbi he went to the main storeroom in a converted attic, where the two large packing cases containing the pieces had been locked. One at a time he took them down to the Etruscan Room on the ground floor, using one of the hand trolleys and the large service lift at the back of the building. Then, having returned to the flat to get pliers and a hammer, he started the work of unpacking. His idea was to have everything ready when Gabbi arrived.

He always loved being in the Etruscan room. As he stripped the showcase of the protective wooden frame in which it had been delivered, he felt around him the friendly company of half-sitting tomb figures, so strangely twisted at the waist and with their enigmatic, fawnish smiles, the casefuls of terracotta and greened bronze objects. He had his usual fantasy that when no one was about the brooding spirits came alive. The idea that ghosts appeared in certain defined areas was after all as old as mankind. Why should they not do so in the homely atmosphere of a museum devoted to their memory?

The case had been beautifully made in mahogany, in keeping with the other furniture of the room, and as far as he could see exactly to their specifications. The sliding glass doors opened smoothly, and had been fitted with the concealed, electronic locks they had ordered. Gabbi's blown-up photographs had been tastefully cut and mounted on the vertical surfaces between the glass shelving.

Having manoeuvred the case to the position in which it was to stand, he began to take the pieces from one of the boxes and unwrap them from their straw. He had also brought down a dust sheet from the storeroom. Spreading this on the parquet floor he put the objects on it.

Absorbed, he forgot the time, and was alarmed to hear a car pulling up by the front entrance. He flew to the window. It was Gabbi. He sped to the small room under the staircase to disconnect the alarm system. By the time he regained the hall, she had let herself in. As always, his spirit stilled at just the sight of her. At work, Gabbi was always neat and professionally tidy. Her relaxed jeans and white sports shirt gave him almost a feeling of privilege, that he was being included in her private life.

'Oh, you've begun,' she said, going ahead of him into the room.

'Just the unpacking.'

They stood together by the case.

'They've done it well, haven't they? Our blow-ups look tremendous.' She turned to him radiantly. 'Don't you think?'

'Your blow-ups.'

She laid her long hand on his upper arm. 'Rubbish, Robert. It was your idea. All I did was choose which ones and cut them about.'

They turned to the unpacked exhibits. They were like children, he thought, kneeling together on the sheet and admiring the hoard. Yes, with the innocence and frankness of children. Wasn't that just it? With Gabbi there were none of the irrelevant accumulations of normal adult relationships. In each other's presence they were at once centred, immersed in, what was clear, immediate, and important to them.

Robert had already begun to sort the goodies into categories as he unpacked them. She saw at once what he was about.

'You've almost made the main layout choices already, haven't you?' she said. 'Dental-stroke-medical is one obvious distinction? Then it's a question of either further functional subdivisions or simple chronological ones?' She paused, continuing to read the augury spread before them. 'But you're leaning to the temporal divide, aren't you?' She was regarding four heaps of dental instruments some of which, though clearly having the same function, were differently shaped. 'Your grand theme of the *progress* they made – on from the Babylonians? Is that what you're thinking?'

Robert could have engulfed her in what would have been, in impulse only, a purely platonic embrace. He almost did until an instant later he realised how quickly this would have become, for his part, something quite other.

'Top of the class,' he said, aware this sounded trite. 'I was beginning to think, yes, before you arrived, that though chronology can be dogged, in this case it's justified. It is after all

55

the justification for including all this in the collection. What we need is a set of Babylonian teeth, and one or two of their dental artefacts, to get us going at the left end of the case. I must look around.'

'With that fine Etruscan set as the finale?'

She was regarding this magnificent object, once part of the ruminatory equipment of an aged male Etruscan of a very late period, which showed clearly the sophisticated dental therapy carried out. How quickly things were resolved between them, Robert thought. No fuss, no argument into which personality or politics was loaded, as was nearly always the case with the other curators. If he and Gabbi disagreed, which was not infrequently, it was always substantive. Eventually one of them acknowledged that the other was better informed on the subject.

'A whopping idea,' he said.

They went to work automatically. They had a brief discussion about the shelving, what went where. He then continued to unpack and sort, while Gabbi began to make a preliminary positioning of the objects.

Robert did not realise how the work had postponed a remaining dilemma. As they laboured, he had thought that this was all he wanted. Simply, that Gabbi's presence, their easy everyday professional connection, should be renewed. It was not until he looked at his watch, and saw that in a few minutes Carmina Manfreddi would be arriving to open up and take charge of the entrance hall, that he realised how things had changed for him in the last hours. He looked at Gabbi's back, turned to him, her copious brown hair falling forwards as she bent to her task, her slender waist, the curve of her hips, and knew that he loved her, that he had done for months, and that this was the one involuntary, indisputable certainty of his existence.

He felt breathless. Would he ask her up to the empty flat for a cup of tea? He imagined a scene up there. His – no, not a declaration. Between him and Gabbi there would surely be no need of such an overture? If it happened, they would both have to know. It would be instantaneous combustion, or it would not happen.

She finished positioning the last object and closed the glass door. 'There. What do you think?'

He came to her side. 'It looks about right first time.'

'You think? We can leave it, take it by surprise tomorrow. We'll have to cover it tonight, won't we? There won't be time to put all the tags in position.'

He realised they had spoken of nothing but the case since her arrival. Of Mortimer's paddy, his London trip, not a word. Perhaps, after all, the tea upstairs?

But she looked at her watch. 'God, I must go,' she said in her almost flawless English. 'Giancarlo will be back, screaming for food.'

Giancarlo would be back, with it her duty to him, and why should he assume she performed that duty with anything less than joy? The surge of emotion he had felt curved and spent itself like a broken wave.

7

Reg woke and felt the bed shake. It took him a moment to realise he was back in Rome and that he had company. He sat up and observed the girl, who was already up. She was sitting on her side of the bed pulling on her tights. She wore white gloves for the operation and was otherwise naked.

'You're up bright and early. I thought you had the day off.'

'I have.'

'Just bright and early?'

He put one hand behind his head, comfortably. She had the things on now and was wriggling them straight. He observed anew her breasts, which were in the fair to middling category he preferred and milk white below the tan. They swung slightly with her movements. He also liked the Australian accent, warm and caustic by turns. This morning, it seemed, they were into a caustic phase.

'And what will you do when you're dressed?'

'I'm going.'

'Going where? I thought you wanted us to spend the day together?'

There was no answer to this. She got up, clawing behind her back at the attaching mechanism of a white brassière. Why didn't someone invent something easier for them? It was like a pilot climbing into harness.

'Well, I'm sorry if we're not. I was looking forward to it.'

'The part you looked forward to is finished, isn't it?'

Now this was plain unfair. She had enjoyed it as much as he had, as on the other occasions, and who had made the first sighting and approach last night? None the less, he was prepared to concede. Perhaps she had eaten something.

'Have I transgressed in some way, Lucy?'

'No.'

'Then why am I in the doghouse? I didn't seem to be last night.'

She sat on the bed again, faced him, and dropped the aggressive manner. 'It's no good, Reg – this nibbling between meals. Not for me. I swore when I saw you a month ago it would be the last time.'

'But when you saw me in the hotel last night you changed your mind, right?'

'Yes. I'm not blaming you. You know you always turn me on. The fact is, as you well know, I'm *too* fond of you. But you're so…'

'I'm so?'

'Well, you don't want a proper relationship. For you it *is* titbits here and there. You've got a vital part missing.'

'Not getting the main course from me, you mean, Luce? I thought you always were. I thought we had fun together.'

'We do. We do have fun. Sometimes there's no one I'd rather be with. But underneath you're always sort of distant. Being with you is like seeing someone you know in another train travelling on another track. And the fact is, Reg, I'm twenty-six. I've got to think of my future.'

He did not care for the trend of this conversation. Simplicities seemed in danger. But he seized with some relief on this last statement. It was perfectly clear what this was about. When women like Lucy talked about their futures they meant only one thing. He left a short silence in respect for this reality.

'What you mean, Luce,' he said then, with sympathy, 'is that you've met someone you want to keep.'

She looked sulky. 'Perhaps I have.'

'In England?'

'No, Kuala Lumpur. I met him there on a stop-over about three months ago. He wants to marry me. I think I'm going to.'

Reg sweated about this for a moment. Not about her intentions, but the place. Christ, he had forgotten she sometimes did the Rome-Melbourne run. He could have bumped into her. She could have been on his flight out or back.

'OK, Lucy. That's a very nice decision.'

'You do understand. You know it's nothing to do with – what we were talking about. If you were a different sort of man…'

'What I understand is that you don't want away fixtures any more. That is fair enough, entendido, entendu and capito.'

She proved difficult. Now she had got her intentions off her chest she expressed an inordinate desire to spend the day together

59

after all. Wasn't it always the same? They wanted it both ways. It was OK while they were breaking it off. They enjoyed that. But when you cheerfully agreed, they wanted to hold a memorial service for the deceased relationship. There was a lot of stuff about how she would write to him. Would he write to her sometimes? And how there was no reason they shouldn't meet and spend a platonic evening together from time to time on her stop-overs in Rome, as his attitude was 'so mature', and 'if he was free'. He liked that last phrase.

In the end he didn't spend the day with her. After a long spiel from her about the virtues of her husband-to-be, on the whole, he said, he thought it was better they made a clean break of it.

When she had gone, he had an unexpected trap-door feeling as if ground that had been there was not any more. This made him peeved. He liked Lucy. It had really seized him seeing her again, especially while swimming in the uncharted waters of the Tunku's purposes. He could even imagine circumstances, circumstances that might not now be so far round the corner, in which things could be put on a more permanent basis. But not with her going in for this sort of amateur character analysis.

'Distant.' Of course he was distant. Everyone is distant. People inhabit separate bodies. You cannot crawl into someone's armpit and nest there, as she was suggesting.

He forced himself to return to essentials. The plain fact was he had allowed himself a highly unprofessional lapse. Flying Qantas he could not easily have avoided, since he had been issued with his ticket. But when the Tunku's minion had phoned and said he had to be in the Excelsior lobby last night at six p.m., it just had not occurred to him it was the hotel used by Qantas crews. Lucy had been far from his mind. The brief conversation with the type was over when she breezed up. She could not have heard anything, but she saw them together on the sofa, saw that they had been talking, and she had had a ringside view of the man. His face was not a variety that bred confidence, nor was it easily forgotten. The brutish bald head looked like a boulder balanced between his shoulder-blades, and his eyes were like the black centres of two Remembrance Day poppies.

'Who the heck was that beauty you were talking to in the hotel lobby?' she had said later in the evening.

One thing was sure. If he ever went to Kuala again, he would not be flying Qantas.

It took him a time to get his cool back. But this he finally managed. Apart from the small aberration of Lucy Tremayne, things were going well, he told himself. Boulder-Head had not exactly been explicit, neither had he delivered a cent of the promised cash, which he had rather set his heart on receiving. But in a croaking voice the senior Godfather would have envied, within a few days of his arrival Boulder-Head had, like the Angel Gabriel, delivered the next clue in the treasure-hunt, a time and an address. There could not have been anything on paper of course, and nothing explicit on the telephone. Again, the style was convincing.

There was another plus point. If he did nothing stupid or precipitate, he suspected the urbane and easy-going Caine was going to graze nicely at his feet. Caine seemed pleased at the chance appointment he had made. Things were surely going forward as evenly as could be expected?

He gave himself to more positive speculation. Would it be the Tunku himself he was about to see again? He hoped it would be. He was beginning to feel an affinity with the man he would not have thought possible that equatorial evening – was it only three weeks ago? – beside his swimming-pool. He had no doubt now he was into the big time. Razzy had come up with some homework, and sent a coded message to his flat address. The dimensions of the missing items on the wall of the Tunku's study were precisely those of the twin Frans Hals lifted from the Rijksmuseum in Amsterdam two years ago in mysterious circumstances. The coincidence was too great for another explanation to be credible. As he remembered, the police had no idea how the Hals had been stolen. No clues, immaculate. Just, one morning, they were not there. All the hallmarks of a master craftsman at work.

He was puzzled nonetheless. The Villa Aemelia had many objects of great interest, a few of some value, including a couple of Titians, but nothing that would be in the Tunku's league one would have thought. Even the Titians were not of immense value.

The delectable Gabriella Bruneschi, incidentally an area to be examined, was unsure of the authenticity of one of them. The other was not all Titian's own work.

Well, tomorrow would presumably throw some light on the mystery. Dismissing the subject from the day's agenda, he gave himself to a re-examination of the newly rented attic flat in the Campo Fiori in which he had lived during his work on Bernini. He was lucky to get it back, even with the crippling sum of key money he had had to put down to have the temporary incumbent thrown out. There were the same horrors he had never got round to changing, like the crumbling mirror whose imperfections made you think you had blackheads, and a more than usually obnoxious crucifix (raised knees, lolling head, bleeding wound, the lot). What a dismal religion Christianity was, he thought, compared with, say, the Hindus, who stuck jolly pricks and tits on to anything they could lay their hands on. The plumbing, too, left much to be desired. The wash-basin and bath exit pipes seemed to be in direct sympathy with a main sewage conduit.

But the flat pleased him. It had a superb roof-top terrace, crammed with terracotta brimming with flowers and with a view that included the shallow inverted saucer of the Pantheon dome. Inside, crowded with once-distinguished baroque furniture and lampshades artistically decayed, it had a faded charm. Dim, brassy lustres made one feel one was inside a Rembrandt interior. And to crown his aesthetic pleasure, as he was re-admiring the place, Attila, his ex-nomadic roof-top tom, which had no doubt noted his reappearence with speedy sagacity, dropped in with a thud from the open skylight. He gave it the head of the fish he would be frying for his lunch. He watched it, half-crouched and violently masticating on the kitchen floor.

The next day he found the Galleria Ottavio on his street map. It was not so far from the flat, in a narrow side-street just off the Piazza Navona. The appointment was for ten to one. He made sure he got there in good time. He spent a moment or two observing the place from the other side of the pavementless road.

The street was not Rome's most elegant, but the dark green paint and matching awning of the shop, the gold lettering, denoted class. In the window was a single large flower painting in a gilded frame mounted on a miniature black-painted easel. He watched two well-dressed women enter.

He gave the women half a minute, and followed them in. It was a long, narrow room, carpeted in a paler green, stretching back the depth of the building, the walls on either side stuffed with the sort of expensive-looking rubbish you would expect in a place like this. Half-way down one side, stairs mounted with an ornate white balustrade to an upper floor and, presumably, more exhibits. The women were attended at the far end. There were two other well-dressed men, one seated at a desk, and a younger one in attendance near him. The older one said something inaudible.

Reg pretended to view a pretty, modern representation of an opera taking place in the Baths of Caracalla – Aida by the look, there were a couple of live elephants on stage (the artist had omitted the red shit buckets they kept handy for an emergency). Out of the corner of his eye he saw the young man go to the door, lock it, pull down the blind, and turn the sign to 'chiuso'.

Nothing happened. Should he announce himself? He had an instinct that he should not. At the far end of the gallery the women continued to talk. In a minute or two they left. The man attending them let them out of the door and relocked it behind them. Of course. The coast had to be clear.

The young man approached, paused momentarily beside him, then turned and continued. It seemed to be an invitation to follow. He did. As they passed the desk the other man did not speak or raise his eyes. For Italians, they were unusually expert at silence.

They went through a door into a poorly-decorated passage and down some stairs. At the bottom was a toilet, and a small dingy room with a table covered by a green baize cloth. Apparently minor picture repairs were carried out down here. There was an open cabinet full of small tools, and several frames stacked beside it.

'Aspette,' said the youth. The unadorned subjunctive was bared, in a similarly un-Italian way, to the necessary. The door shut, and the footsteps retreated upstairs.

Reg waited ten minutes. Then he heard voices briefly at the top of the stairs. Someone was coming down. He listened for the slight impediment of that leg, and found himself short of breath and standing up.

The door opened. Revealed... the unillustrious and very unwelcome and black-suited personage of Haji Kassim. For some reason he felt his skin tighten across the top of his scalp. He sat down again quickly to counteract the sensation.

'Good afternoon, Mr Griffin.'

There was an ironic, slight dropping of the head, which revealed the familiar jet black hair and the central parting. Not unexpectedly, there was no trace of a smile, only a disgusting stink of oriental aftershave.

Reg made corrections to his instinctive response. No doubt Kassim fancied himself as the Malaysian equivalent of a Grand Vizier, bureaucratically ordering heads off for the Sultan. But he was nothing of the sort, he told himself. He was a time-serving creep who had had his sense of humour removed at birth, and to be treated as such.

Kassim was carrying a smart black leather brief-case with brass corners and locks, one finger over the edge. He put the case on the table, well on his own side of it.

'I think you will prefer it if we go straight to the business, yes?' he said as, after inspecting the chair for dust, he committed his small buttocks to it, eased his crutch, pinched his trousers at both knees, and clasped his fingers in front of his face like a priest about to pray. His dismal features then assumed an even more disagreeable expression.

'I am first to communicate to you the Tunku's satisfaction with your services so far. He wishes me to congratulate you again on your handling of the matter in the Baker Street restaurant, which was, in His Highness's word, "immaculate".'

He paused, seeming to need to restore himself. One could not imagine Kassim found congratulation of anyone much to his taste.

'I am also to inform you that he considers your approach to the person we are talking about, here in Rome, to be along the right lines. A cordial relationship is much to be desired. Only upon this can any meaningful structure result. We have of course noted the progress you have made.'

Reg swallowed quickly. He was realising, a lot too slowly, what this was about. Kassim had been ordered to offer these palliatives no doubt, and was doing so, but he was making full use of them.

Behind the suavity, he now saw, was the ugly conclusion he was meant to draw.

He rapidly drew it, and made the mistake of going public with his finding. 'Are you telling me I've been under close surveillance here?'

Kassim's contempt also went public. His mouth twitched, he made a small movement, and fully recovered his poise.

'You will find, Mr Griffin, if you continue in Tunku Raschid's employment any length of time, that he is a very meticulous man. There is nothing he leaves to chance. You are very much a newcomer. Naturally, yes, precautions are taken. Would you expect otherwise?' He paused. 'Shall we now proceed with more concrete matters?'

Who would be the sleuth in Rome? Someone in the museum, one of the guardians, Pietro perhaps? Reg was astounded that he had noticed nothing. He had been looking. But he kept these further thoughts to himself. He had already handed Kassim a couple of tricks too many. He arched his back, folded his arms, and sat back in his chair.

'Proceed away.'

The brief-case was being opened, two little explosions which Kassim took care to make simultaneous like a child setting off a small firework. It was filled with Italian bank notes. Kassim swivelled it like a commercial traveller demonstrating his wares.

'I am next to give you this. It is exactly fifty million lire – that is, rather more than twenty thousand pounds. This represents payment of ten thousand pounds for services rendered to date as promised, and a further ten on account. If you wish to count it, please do so.'

Reg stared, and again felt the ghostly presence on the upper part of his head and neck. Money did not appear like this in such quantity without strings, especially when it was double the sum offered. It seemed Kassim read his mind.

'I see you do not wish to count the money? Very well. I will come to the main point. You are now entering an entirely new phase of your work. The Tunku is being generous. He is displaying a degree of trust which I have to say is – unusual. I hope it will not prove misplaced. I should like to point out to you that from this moment there is no question of withdrawal on your part. Acceptance of this advance is a total commitment to the greatly more difficult services you will now be asked to carry out. You will be from now on in possession of privileged information. Do you give this undertaking?'

'My actions so far indicate I do.'

'I hardly think so. All you have done so far is to get yourself a job. You have not taken the smallest risk and are in no personal danger. None the less, I take your remark to be a positive answer. Very well, here then are your next instructions. You are aware of course that an event is to take place at the museum next October?'

Reg stared. 'Of course – the Cellini Exhibition?'

'The Tunku wishes, first, that you acquaint yourself very thoroughly with all the internal preparations for this event, especially those relating to security.'

Reg gave a quick indrawn whistle. Mamma mia, he had been slow. Of course it would be the exhibition, the perfect opportunity for an inside job. He tried to keep his voice offhand.

'What's in mind? The sculpture, or the goldsmithery, or both? Jesus, it's not the Perseus, is it? You'd need a fork-lift and a helicopter for that lot.'

Kassim's face expressed the sarcasm of a schoolmaster listening to the ramblings of a backward pupil. 'I think we shall do better if we do not indulge in speculation, Mr Griffin. I am in the process of giving you new instructions. May I please proceed? I have given you your first order, here is the second. You are aware perhaps that the Director has at present retained full responsibility for the organisation of the exhibition in his own hands. The Tunku considers that it might be very advantageous if in some way you could get yourself involved in this work as directly as possible – without, naturally, arousing any suspicion.'

Reg sobered. He pushed away from the table and crossed his legs. 'Well, I can tell you that's out of the question. I'm a junior. Nobody in their right mind would choose someone relatively unknown like me. Besides, I suspect Caine likes exhibitions. They're his babies, as I gather, and he enjoys doing the work himself.'

Something was happening to Kassim's features. There were definite signs of movement behind the mask. Was it, could it be, the embryo of a smile?

'You are very vehement with your negatives, Mr Griffin. Surprisingly so for a man who – may I venture? – prides himself on a positive outlook. Perhaps it will be necessary for me to point out the obvious to you?'

'I can't see anything at all obvious about this idea.'

'You can't? Then permit me to assist you.'

'Permission granted.'

'You will have discerned by now no doubt that it is the *owner* of the museum who carries ultimate power, is it not, rather than the Director?'

'I suppose so. So what?'

'Very simple. If the owner has the power, it would seem a very elementary deduction that he is the person to be worked on. Would you not say so?'

'You mean go behind Caine's back?' Reg paused, reflecting. 'Well, it's true, I believe, they don't get on. I'm told by a reliable source that Ready's jealous of Caine in some twisted way, and can't keep his hands off the place. I'd also guess from my own observation that Caine isn't at his best on commercial matters. The egghead pressed against his will into the world of business, that's the sort of scenario.'

It *was* a smile. It broke surface momentarily, lopsidedly, like a swing at its highest point, finishing somewhere up by his left ear. Quite definitely Kassim would have qualified as a Dickensian pedagogue. His mastery of irony was total. A Malaysian Squeers.

The smile quickly disappeared. Kassim, Reg realised then, was preparing to go. He had closed the suitcase and was pushing it towards him across the table.

For a moment he really lost his cool. 'Look, Kassim, this is all very well. But there are a number of other matters that need discussion, and I'm going to want a contact of some kind. I can see we've got to be careful about communication, but I can't work in total darkness like this. I need to know more precisely what's on. The exhibition isn't for five months yet. I'll certainly need to ask things. I need to ask one thing right away. What's the final sum I'll be paid, and how do I know for instance…'

Kassim got to his feet.

'I have three further things to say to you. The first concerns this money here. You will bank it immediately, after this meeting, in a deposit account that has been opened for you. The name of the bank and the address of the branch are inside the case. Although it is now after closing time, if you ring the bell you will be admitted. The account is opened in the name of Alberti. If you wish, the bank will facilitate transfer of funds to a numbered Swiss account of your choosing, but to nowhere else. You will keep your present bank account, continue to use it for all daily transactions, and make no deposits except your professional earnings. I also need not add that you should avoid any large or ostentatious expenditure here in Rome, or anywhere, in the foreseeable future. Your lifestyle should remain constant. The second point should be obvious to you. Do not, for any motive, be tempted to enter these premises again or loiter anywhere near them. If you were to be so foolish, nobody would own to knowing you anyway, but the Tunku would not be pleased.'

Reg also got to his feet. 'And the other matter?'

Kassim clearly savoured his last words. He cleared his throat.

'You have entered territory where a modest fortune may be made,' he said, with fastidious hauteur. 'It is also very dangerous territory, dangerous in itself, and very dangerous if you were to make a mistake.'

'Meaning?'

'I mean, Mr Griffin, that if you *were* to make what I term a "voluntary mistake", if you were to have second thoughts about your own participation for example or if there were a breach of security of any sort, it would, shall we say, be most regrettable from your point of view. Now I will take my leave. I shall go first. Someone will come down in a few minutes to escort you to the back door of the building. I wish you good day.'

8

In a sports shirt and yellow shorts, Robert sat with Kate on their balcony, eating a late breakfast. It was Sunday, May, warm. Restless, he listened to the miscellany of church bells ringing for morning mass down in the city. Not far away a couple of rival treble-toned bells were striking frenetically like a chiming clock out of order. More distantly, from the direction of the Vatican, a deeper one boomed. Above them spread a hazy blue sky. The colony of swifts that nested under the broad eaves of the palazzo were out, madly dashing in all directions and screaming ecstatically. The air was heavy with the fume of rising pine sap.

What did such a day of promise promise him? He thought of Gabriella, began to daydream of taking her for the day into the country somewhere but, obeying the command he had given himself that day they had set up the new showcase together, quickly turfed the thoughts away. He leant back resolutely in the basket chair, and clasped his hands behind his head.

'How about tripping up to Tivoli today? In all these years we've never been to the d'Este Gardens. We could gape at the fountains, have a nice lunch, and generally behave like tourists.'

Kate was half-concealed behind a three-day old copy of the *Daily Telegraph*. She too was lightly, though as always faultlessly, dressed in well-cut trousers and a white silk shirt, her fine grey hair modishly styled.

Robert knew she had registered what he had said, but she did not move her eyes from the paragraph she was reading. Finishing it, she lifted the paper higher and began to search for another item.

'You've forgotten we're lunching with Mortimer,' she murmured, like a parent dealing with an over-eager child.

Robert remembered. Mortimer's secretary had phoned the day before and left a message: 'You and Kate come for lunch tomorrow at one. I'll expect you if I hear nothing by this evening. I have something to say to you.'

Mortimer had made Franca write it down verbatim. Robert doubted very much if there was anything of substance that needed 'saying' to him, but the wording had the ring of a command attendance? Surely it was not Gabbi again? He had thought that had blown over.

'Hell,' he said. 'I *had* forgotten for a moment. What a frantic bore.'

Kate's eyes were still zipping up and down the columns. 'It is at least a function to attend, isn't it?' she said, her reproof now overt. 'And the food will be good. You should at least appreciate *that*, shouldn't you? *He* employs a decent chef of course.'

The implications of this remark were compendious. Did she really wish to suggest that, if he had pursued the sort of 'brilliant' career she imagined but never specified, they too would have a cook to cover her disinterest in, almost her contempt for, cooking and food? Certainly her remark was designed to assert anew how dull and uneventful their life was.

For once he took the latter inference seriously. It was true he showed less enthusiasm than she did for the British Council dos, the occasional government reception, the dinner parties with the rich and titled she solicited so assiduously. But what social intercourse did he ever initiate? Almost none that was not dutiful and mandatory, arising from museum necessities. Had he really become so ungregarious, he thought, looking away over the balcony railing?

He never used to think of himself like that. At Cambridge he had had a lot more friends than Kate. Certainly they had been drawn from a wider social spectrum than hers. Perhaps he had allowed work, habit, good sense, most of all Kate's narrow certitudes, to encase him. Perhaps some effort of will was required of him, a breakout?

A breakout did not seem likely today. At elevenish began a procedure of total predictability. Kate went into the bedroom to start dressing up. Half an hour later he followed her to put on trousers which had a crease, a shirt and tie, and to substitute shoes for sandals. Then, Kate resplendent in an all-white suit, they went down to the Citroen and, riding together on the portly bench seat, began the drive out to the Castelli Romani. In the lighter Sunday traffic they soon broke free of the confines of the city and began to lap the broad and monotonous boulevard of the Appia Nuova.

Ahead loomed the dark volcanic shape of the Castelli, the white villages of Frascati and Castelgondolfo clinging precariously to the spreading slopes and, as yet out of sight, Nemi.

There was no doubt Mortimer had been right to choose this

picturesque village built inside the crater of an extinct volcano. It was a place of unique beauty. In the well of the crater was a lake with a smooth black surface. 'Diana's Looking-Glass', it was called in Italian. Apart from Mortimer's house on one side of the lake, there was little modern building, and what there was had followed the traditional style. There were no billboards.

But Mortimer's place was surely, by any standards except his own, a gross perpetration against good taste. A huge concrete structure of three storeys, only at the lower level its harsh lines broken with bougainvillaea, it was built in the shape of the front end of a liner, each storey – or 'deck', the word Mortimer archly used – set back from the lower one, so that the upper part of the building had the appearance of a white, bow-fronted chest with the drawers pulled out. The lowest, which had the widest of the three balconies and curved almost to a point to make it look like the prow, was only a few feet above the level of the lake. One almost expected to see a simulated plastic bow-wave at water-level. On the top level there was a swimming-pool.

Robert knew that Mortimer had only been granted planning permission after much twisting of governmental arms and, almost certainly, egregious bribery.

As they topped the rim of the crater he slowed the car to take in the beauty of the view below. He threaded carefully through the village street which was thronged with holiday-makers sitting at the café, buying from the ceramic and basket-ware stalls, or just strolling. Finally, turning a sharp corner, he began to descend the fertile, cultivated slope to the house.

Mortimer was obsessed by security. The drive was protected by massive iron gates kept permanently closed. As the car approached, they swung open, controlled electrically from within. 'Leathers', as Mortimer archaically called his English butler, would have been alerted to watch for them. Knowing what was expected, Robert drove under the porch. Sure enough, as he braked Leathers issued ritually from the front door in a glossy black suit. With an absurd kind of walking bow, he went round to Kate's side of the car. 'Good morning and welcome, madam, sir,' he said in his fruity voice.

Almost simultaneously, summoned no doubt by Leathers, the Italian chauffeur appeared at the run from the garage block to one side of the drive, doing up the buttons of his striped waistcoat on the way. Robert always felt like resisting this grotesque protocol. Why did cars have to be garaged? But what would be the point? He handed the man the keys and, preceded by the ludicrous Leathers, they went in.

They entered the huge hall, floored with polished black marble, relieved here and there by expensive-looking oriental rugs, and from which on opposite sides two polished mahogany staircases twisted upwards to the first floor, like two greedy arms clutching a possession. On all sides were ceramic dragons and dense clumps of dark green foliage standing in large Chinese pots of yellow and green. Below them, another broad staircase descended like Niagara to the equally vast – what did one call it? Sitting-room, living-room, drawing room? It looked most like a hotel lounge. Still preceded superfluously by Leathers, who took the stairs diagonally with a curious rhythmic sideways movement as if negotiating a steep mountain-side, they went down.

They crossed the room and went out on to the large wooden floored balcony, which was shaded by a striped awning. Sitting at a large Florentine inlaid table on red velvet chairs brought out from the house sat Mortimer and a youngish Italian couple. The man was familiar. Robert remembered. He was Mortimer's self-effacing accountant, who managed the whole of his fortune other than the museum. They had met briefly once or twice at Mortimer's office in central Rome.

Mortimer usually dressed eccentrically on these occasions. Once he had appeared in an outfit suitable for the Raj at its height, tropical khaki shorts, topee and all. Today the theme was nautical. He wore a blazer with brass buttons embossed with anchors and a navy blue, short-peaked cap. As they appeared he rose and, ignoring Robert, pounced on Kate's hand like a terrier.

'Kate, I want your advice,' he said. He led her to the edge of the balcony, which was set off with a semicircle of rampant bloom. 'Lek is tired of geraniums. She knows nothing about European flowers. All she can suggest is orchids, which are hardly practical here. You've got to tell me what I put in instead.'

Robert was left to greet the Italian couple by himself. They also had risen, rather sheepishly, Robert thought. Their name, the man reminded him was Barbone – Ernesto and Rosalina.

For a moment, as they chattered vaporously, he thought they were odd co-guests for Mortimer to invite. Usually when he and Kate came he was at pains to show off some distinguished people he had lured to his home, fellow tycoons, film directors. Last time there had been two British MEPs on a fact-finding mission in Italy. He recalled that Mortimer had 'something to say'. Clearly Mortimer had some novel financial bee buzzing in his bonnet. He relaxed, and set himself to play his part in the small talk. Another Italian flunkey arrived to ask about drinks. Mortimer seemed to have about four servants, all male.

Whilst Robert and the Barbones sought for new hyperboles with which to admire the polished surface of the lake and its setting, Lek appeared suddenly, like a cat winding herself unobtrusively round the edge of the sliding door. Robert wondered anew at her childish figure and her gift for almost total self-effacement on social occasions. What she wanted, plainly, was to join the group without fuss, but Mortimer saw her and gave a whoop. 'Ah, my jungle flower,' he said, loudly. He advanced upon her delicate frame, clad today in diaphanous yellow silk, and swept his hand round her waist as if he were the corps de ballet male lead.

'Isn't she a little flower, Ragioniere?' Ernesto gave a weak grin. 'Lek, my dear – Kate, and Robert, of course you know – but not my old friend Ernesto, and Rosalina. Ernesto and I usually do our business in town,' he explained to Kate.

Lek offered her tiny, cool hand and had it grasped in turn by both Barbones. She smiled shyly at Robert. Released, she then glided towards Kate who had not yet got a drink.

Out of the corner of his eye, Robert watched. Lek had always had a strange attachment to Kate, and Kate, touched perhaps, incongruously played up to it. It had always warmed him to see them together. It was not so often Kate did things that had no apparent social motive.

With Kate, Lek seemed to relax. After proudly giving her a comprehensive list to choose from, she went herself to get the brand of fruit juice Kate had selected.

Through drinks, and the meal – for which they moved indoors to the dining-room where a table was sumptuously laid – Robert continued to have the notion that Mortimer was avoiding him.

There was nothing unusual about this. It often happened when there were other people present. Mortimer had a sly habit, too, of addressing remarks really intended for him through statements ostensibly made to the others. But wasn't there something more than usually deliberate about the severance today? Robert had the impression Mortimer was excited.

The chef was from Bali. Mortimer had collared him on the same trip which had yielded his marriage to Lek, a Vietnamese refugee. Kate was right, his repertoire was amazing. Today it was to be Chinese food, about which Mortimer showed off his knowledge at the top of his voice.

Robert was sitting between Rosalina and Lek. When he managed to detach himself from Rosalina's description of the new bathroom she was installing in their flat and the poor attitude to work taken by the plumber, he managed to get Lek talking about her two interests, which were pop music and pets. This was a great deal more entertaining.

Lek had what she called a 'Soo' in the garden, which boasted an Angora rabbit, a tortoise, various birds in an aviary, as well as a cat. He asked after these creatures, and she told him gravely she had recently added to her menagerie a loris, which she had decided to keep in their bedroom. Though, she added with a giggle and a quick look at Mortimer across the table, she was not sure Mortimer approved of this. The loris did have 'rather naughty habits'. While she chattered happily about these, Robert wondered anew at the apparent success of the marriage, which Mortimer had openly confessed he had arranged through an agency. Though, on the other hand, was it so surprising? Would not only total feminine subservience appease and soothe Mortimer's petty tyrannies?

What was not Chinese about the meal was the replacement of tea by wine. It flowed freely. You had only to turn your head to find a white-gloved hand coming over your right shoulder and a bottle neck being thrust into your glass. Robert always drank more when he was bored. Towards the end of the meal, he realised he had drunk rather more than was politic.

Mortimer attacked him just as he was sitting back, his head tucked into his chin, in an attempt to suppress an upsurge of wind.

'Robert, your finances are not satisfactory. I would say in fact they are in crisis. Something's got to be done, and fast,' he snapped.

Robert had forgotten 'the matter of importance', and it caught him off guard. For a moment he regarded the almost neckless round head which had the appearance of a golf-ball cupped in a tee, the thin ginger hair and eyebrows, and the rather coarse, full mouth which now had a sneering twist to it. He noted again the ridiculous blazer which was nautically piped along the pockets and the lapels. He was not sure afterwards if it had been anger exactly that prompted him. It could have been genuine levity. But the words were out of his mouth before he could corral them.

'Not *another* crisis?' he said. 'I thought we'd had our ration for this month.'

He saw the shaft go home like an Exocet missile. Two orange spots bloomed amid the boyish freckles on the plump part of Mortimer's cheek. He swivelled eyes glazed with annoyance briefly round the table. Kate and Ernesto were still eating the exquisite compôte of oriental fruits. The orange spots widened into a full flush. Three servants were standing round the table like fielders in a game of cricket. He moved his head aside suddenly and, without turning, spoke to Leathers.

'Clear the table,' he said, loudly, abruptly, and with menace.

As the waiters converged and Kate and Ernesto hurriedly abandoned their unfinished food, he stood up.

'Kate – Rosalina – I hope very much you will excuse us, but Ernesto and I have business to conduct. Lek, take them upstairs, if you please.' His voice bristled with dangerous inflections.

The three women left, the servants cleared the table at breakneck speed as if their lives depended on it. While this was going on, Mortimer got up suddenly and retreated into his study on the other side of the sitting-room. He seemed to wait until the scene-shifting had been effected, then reappeared, puffing on a cigar which looked much too big for him and walking with an exaggerated, rolling gait as if he had just got off a horse. He flung Ernesto the brief-case he had parked on an armchair. Half-turning in his seat, Ernesto had to catch it against his chest.

Robert and Ernesto had not moved from their original seats on opposite sides of the table. Looking now ominously calm, Mortimer sat in his at the top. They were thus about as far from each other as they could get.

'Bene, Ernesto, avanti,' Mortimer said, waving the cigar horizontally like a ludicrous caricature of a Marx brother.

The poor man fumbled in the case and drew out papers. He took spectacles out of a case, polished them, and fitted them round his ears with both hands.

He began by casting Robert an unhappy glance. He would not, he said 'in the normal way' have wished to interfere in accounts drawn up by a professional colleague in a sphere 'which was not part of his everyday brief'. But Mortimer had asked him 'unofficially' to make certain calculations based on the last year's museum accounts, and he had naturally obliged 'as the matter was to be confidential'.

Pausing, he looked to Mortimer for encouragement. Getting none, he began at last the substantive part of his statement. Still, however, he went forwards and backwards, cautioning and qualifying. Meanwhile the dread document lay before him. Now and then he caressed it, one hand on either side of the sheaf of papers. Eventually Mortimer interrupted him, in English.

'God, you're long-winded, Barbone. We don't want a speech. What you're trying to say is, the Villa Aemelia is stagnant. On an annual basis the profit is there, just. But there's no room for contingency. A single disaster and it'll be in the red. That's the trouble with philanthropy – people soon get the idea it's a right. And to put it in a nutshell, there's a damn sight too much academic twittering going on and not enough hard business thinking that will put the gate up. Any decent museum in Europe has been thinking in proper commercial terms for a decade. You haven't, Robert. What I'm telling you is that things have got to change, and fast, or... or I shall really have to contemplate changes, changes of the sort other institutions worth their salt are making, changes that won't be to your liking.'

Denied the rest of his dissertation, Ernesto limply handed his papers to Robert. Robert glanced as a gesture at the top page, but did not begin to read. He knew what it would be, yards of unnecessary analysis with perhaps one or two minor points of some relevance buried somewhere in the middle, a labour for which Ernesto no doubt would be paid some exaggerated sum. The 'crisis', if there was one, was as always emotional, in

Mortimer's mind. He had just been on a business visit to London. Almost certainly he had been talking to someone.

Robert's small spurt of anger, if such it had been, had already gone. So, oddly, had his moment of alcoholic stupor. He now felt icily in control of himself.

'I see. What you're saying is that you want to discuss a change of policy?'

'I have no intention of discussing any policy. The financial management of the museum is your pigeon. But what I am telling you is that Cellini's got to be called off. Exhibitions don't make money, anywhere. Your last one didn't. They're ego trips for egghead curators.'

Robert went a shade colder. He could not believe this was meant. Was this really what had been led up to so deviously? Had Ernesto been summoned to make his statement as a thinly-camouflaged launching pad for this? He had better watch it. He collected himself.

'The last exhibition made a small loss which was more than made up by the sustained extra gate that ensued from the publicity.'

'That's what you say. The sums are far greater this time.'

'It's much too late to call the exhibition off. A lot of money has been spent already. Most of the exhibits have already been arranged. And Cellini's bound to be a success.'

'There's no such word as "bound" in business. Only someone as naive as you would use it. The hire of exhibits can be cancelled. The owners will be only too pleased. I've made up my mind. The Aemelia isn't big enough to handle such a risk. Increase your turnover, rationalise your costs, get up your gate, then we can begin to talk about these luxuries.'

'But Cellini *will* increase the gate. And I'm convinced the exhibition itself will make money this time. We went into it all before we started.'

'I've changed my mind. You're an academic not a business man. These accounts prove it. You'd agree, Barbone, wouldn't you, that the exhibition's an unjustified risk in today's climate?'

While Barbone did another Duke of York act, Robert paused. *Did* Mortimer mean it? He searched the intonation. The usual note of self-distrusting rhetoric was there, surely? He had to believe it was. It was the usual probing, the usual games-playing, the attempt by temporarily asserting authority to prove to himself he existed?

Whatever it was, Robert knew instinctively that something would be required of him this time, more than marking time. The rude remark he had just made ensured that a polite change of subject would not be enough. He had already been thinking that he had not given enough thought or time to the promotional side of the exhibition, which had never been his forte. He had been pondering a possible solution to this problem for a day or two. The crisis made him come to a rapid decision about it.

'The exhibition will be second to none,' he heard himself say. 'The only area of any doubt is publicity. This too is going well, but I'm going to appoint someone to do it this time, in these crucial last months.'

'What?'

'Someone with good experience.'

'Which firm? It'll cost a fortune if they're any good.'

'It's not a firm, it's a person. Someone on my staff.'

'Not Gabriella Bruneschi for Christ's sake?'

'Not Gabriella.'

'Who then? There's no one with the remotest experience.'

'The new curator, Reg Griffin. He had a good stint with Christie's on the business side, which included PR. I think he will do it well.'

'That ass?'

'I didn't know you'd met him.'

'I certainly did. In the hall of the museum the other week. Tried to make his number with me, the smarmy idiot. He *thinks* he's the cat's whiskers, I'll grant you.'

For a moment or two it remained in the balance. But perhaps Reg's uncuratorial style had impressed Mortimer, against his will. At all events, after a lot more ranting from Mortimer the hounds were called off.

'Well, you'd better make a go of it this time, Robert,' he said. 'I've made up my mind. I'm not continuing to finance an academic doddle. Your head's on the block.'

A narrow squeak, Robert thought, not unhappily, as they breasted the rim of the crater and headed back to Rome. For several minutes he had had to think that Mortimer did intend to call Cellini off.

As it was, things had surely worked out well? His decision had been taken on the spur of the moment, and under duress, but it was a good one. He had first had the idea at last week's staff meeting. He had given an update report on exhibition preparations, and afterwards invited discussion about publicity. Several people had put forward some rather amateur ideas. Reg had made two or three very succinct, professional points in a quietly confident way. He would work closely with Reg to make sure he knew what he was doing.

Absorbed in these thoughts, they were some way back before he realised he and Kate had not exchanged a word. She was immersed in an exotic-looking book of Japanese prints that Lek had lent her and had shown no interest in discovering what he had talked about with Mortimer and Barbone.

'I'm sorry you had to gulp your last lychees,' he said cheerfully. 'It was a fuss about nothing, as usual.'

'Was it?'

'Of course. There's nothing wrong with our accounts, and Mortimer was only using them as a lead-in to try to cancel Cellini. My guess is Mortimer met one of the big London state museum directors when he was there the other day, and must have been told that even they lose money on exhibitions if they aren't careful. He got a fit of cold feet.'

'With justice wouldn't you say? They aren't usually money-spinners.'

'This one will be.'

'How can you be so sure?'

'Because it's Cellini, and because it's Rome, in the autumn. And because I'm going to have Reg Griffin concentrate on the publicity.'

She looked at him, open-eyed.

'That young man?'

'I think he's very able.'

'Mortimer agreed?'

'He didn't demur.'

'And if Griffin is no good?'

'I shall soon know. If I do have to take him off, with any luck it'll be too late for Mortimer to cancel the show.'

Kate looked away momentarily, out of the window.

'You were very rude to Mortimer, and quite unnecessarily,' she said.

'I suppose I was, mildly. But what has that got to do with it? He asked for it.'

Kate paused, on the edge of returning to her reading.

'I thought you didn't believe in confrontation?'

'In the past, it's true, I've played for a quiet life. I'm not sure Mortimer can count on that for the indefinite future.'

She did now turn back to her book.

'One of these days you'll put your hand too far through the bars and get it bitten off.'

He laughed.

'We shall see. It might on the contrary be possible, with different handling, to take the bars down altogether on another of "these days". I've been thinking lately I've often been too soft with Mortimer. When Cellini proves the success I'm sure it's going to be, it could be he won't be quite so tiresome.'

Kate was reading again. Such optimism was on the periphery of her interest, he was to understand, and certainly beneath her dignity.

9

Reg did not approve of the office accommodation he had been allotted. Squashed with two others in a mezzanine area between main floors on the north side of the building, the room had one small window, a low ceiling, and did not enjoy the air-conditioning awarded the exhibit rooms and some of the other curators' offices. In the early summer heat, which he already found oppressive even with the window wide open, it was stifling.

In the normal way he would have complained to Caine. Carlo Pelucci might have put up with it for umpteen years. That was no precedent for him. But he had noticed a peculiar circumstance. At the back of the hutch was an interior window which gave on to the staircase and main hall of the museum below. He made a reconnaissance in the hall. Because of the way the light fell, you could see nothing through the window looking up at it from below. He had always known how much you can learn about almost any situation from simple, prolonged observation. He decided, on balance, not to surrender this possible advantage.

There came to be another reason for his sacrifice. After a brush with the owner of the museum in the hall about a week ago, he had decided that Haji Kassim's suggestion of working with Ready against Caine was not only impractical but objectionable. On whatever information Kassim had worked, he had made a mistake. Ready was a tricky creep, with a forest of chips on his shoulder. Any attempt at a rapprochement in that direction would be reefed with dangers. And, in his own assessment, it was a superficial judgement to think Ready ran Caine. If anything, it was the other way round. Caine's trouble was that he was too modest. His quiet manipulations did not show.

In consequence, it was clear to him that Caine was the man to cultivate, not Ready. It would be a task he would not find difficult. Unexpectedly, he found he was coming to like the man, a rare specimen in this world of graft. The afternoon after meeting Ready, an idea came to him.

He was at his desk in the room. Through the window he saw the porter, Pietro Buongusto, stroll in through the entrance doors, followed as usual by his scruffy dog. Immediately alert, Reg took binoculars from the top drawer of the desk and slid to his knees to obtain the wider view.

The hall was divided across the middle by a waist-high iron barrier in the centre of which were the two turnstiles, one on either side of Carmina Manfreddi's glass box. On the south side of the hall, between the barrier and the front door, was the book and postcard stall, which was clearly the focus of Pietro's present visit. Reg adjusted the focus of the glasses.

With an idle mien which connoted the combination of stupidity and insolence that made up the man's character, Pietro entered the stall by the door at the side. While Ingrid, the attractive Swedish blonde, was serving an outgoing visitor, and the dog, Faro, examined odours he was identifying along the wainscotting, Pietro leaned against the rear shelf of the stall, just behind the girl, making use of a toothpick. It was obvious he was making comments under his breath. Ingrid was scarcely containing her giggles. As the visitor turned away with her purchase, Pietro's hand touched her slender rump. She turned to offer her token resistance. Pietro seized the tiny wrists, and kissed her.

Reg switched the glasses to Carmina's ampler proportions. Perched high in her glass cage, she resembled an umpire at a tennis match. She was knitting. Each thrust of the needle expressed her disgust at the outrage she was being forced to witness. Of course she was outraged. Who wouldn't be by this pig of a man whose petty peculations, Reg had discovered, as well as his flagrant philandering, were as much a thorn in Caine's flesh as in anyone else's? At this moment a ready-made plan landed on its feet in his mind like a gold-medal-winning gymnast. Two targets with one missile?

The plan was one thing, however, its execution quite another. Several times in the next days favourable conditions prevailed — namely, an absence of visitors in the hall and in the two exhibit rooms off it. But the vital event that would link with this state of affairs did not take place.

An evening about a week later a couple of busloads of tourists had been and gone. It was doubtful if there were half a dozen people in the museum. Pietro had been in again for the same purpose as before and shortly afterwards, watched disgustedly by Manfreddi, Ingrid had unilaterally shut up the stall and departed. A heavy tedium had settled, as the clocks ticked their way to closing time.

If only she'd move now, thought Reg. He had been active for some time with the binoculars. There was no doubt about it, Carmina Manfreddi, embattled in her glass cage, had circulation problems in her left foot. The foot, plainly visible to him on this the inner side of the cage, on which there was a glass door, was constantly on the fidget. Sometimes she turned her foot over on its side. For long periods she took the shoe off altogether and, looking down, flexed her toes inside her stockings. Now it looked as if a crisis was brewing. Would her stalwart sense of duty falter? Would she go off to talk to one of the guardians as he had seen her do on several occasions when business was slack?

He saw her get up, consult the watch on her plump maternal wrist for the umpteenth time, and put her shoe on. 'Yes, old dear,' Reg said aloud, 'you have another hour of tedium to endure.' There was no one approaching the building. He saw her bend to peer through one of the front windows. Her favourite guardian, Alfredo, would be staked at his immovable post between the nineteenth and twentieth centuries, equally bored and ready for a chat, and her foot would gain relief.

Carmina pulled the lever that locked the incoming turnstile and she shut but, in a moment of sheer inspiration, did not lock the money drawer. She smoothed her behind with both hands and with a glance up the empty staircase came out of her hutch, leaving the door unlocked. She disappeared out of sight into the exhibit room.

The exterior door to Reg's room, and the two other adjacent ones, which were used by two part-time curators happily absent this afternoon, gave on to the landing half-way up the stairs where they turned to mount to the first floor. He had only to draw on his gloves, walk down the one flight and across the hall. His shoes were rubber-soled.

As he reached the bottom of the stairs, he could hear Carmina already in conversation with Alfredo at the far end of the room. There was no one coming down the stairs behind him, and he would not have to cross the exhibit room doorway. It would only be a matter of a second or two. He entered the kiosk.

She had the ten thousand lire notes, as he knew, stacked in the right-hand compartment of the drawer. He substituted the wooden block he had ready – with a ten note stuck on the top, it resembled a bundle of notes seen from above – and stuffed the money in his pocket.

The next stage was easy. The door under the stairs was never locked, as it led down to the male staff toilet and the small cleaning materials room where the guardians left their belongings and Pietro the white overalls he used for his evening cleaning activities. The overalls were hanging there as usual.

He was going to put all the notes into the inner pocket. On a hunch that concerned the company Pietro was likely to be keeping this evening, he put only half. The rest – a nice touch, he thought – he would anonymously donate at a later time to the museum fund.

His exit was through the door that gave on to the garden at ground level. This door, being a fire exit, could be opened by the push-bar on the inside. Within a minute he was back in his office via the inner courtyard door, to which as a full-time curator he had an electronic key, up to the first floor, and through the empty medieval rooms to the front staircase. No one saw him.

The longer the time lapse between the removal of the money and the discovery of its absence the better. He was lucky. There were no more visitors that evening. Carmina had no cause to look at the till. It was not until ten minutes before time, when the attendants began to congregate in the hall, that she thought it was time to tot up. He saw her stand up abruptly, the block in her left hand, and lift the internal telephone.

It was still touch and go. He watched Robert arrive at the double. The doors were shut, the police arrived. All the staff were asked to gather in the hall. There were no visitors left in the building. Taking his time, Reg went down to join the throng.

The two plain clothes policemen distinguished themselves. A mere hundred thousand lire or so? A turnstile cashier who had left her post to gossip – an hour ago – and no visitors left in the building? What were they doing wasting their time with such a banality? You could see the judgement written all over their faces. Robert thought they should search the building. It was possible the thief could have stowed the money somewhere, he said. You could tell he did not believe this himself. It was too clear the police would not do more than report the incident.

It would fizzle, Reg thought. There they were, the fifteen of them. Caine, Carmina – still red in the face and flustered – Gabriella Bruneschi, Pietro's wife Giulia, the secretary Franca, the ludicrous 'armour and munitions' curator Gasparotti, himself and eight guardians, and nobody was noticing the shrieking significance of Pietro's absence. Giulia had said shortly that he was 'out' when Caine asked her where he was. To compensate for his nightwatch duties he had the afternoons off.

The police were leaving. Reg was willing Carmina to pull herself together and realise the obvious, if no one else could. 'No Pietro – and isn't he due at this very moment for his evening cleaning duties?' Wasn't it possible for him to communicate this sentence to her by telepathy?

He could see she wasn't going to pick up his signal. She was too distressed. He didn't like it at all, but someone had to give the wheel a turn. He sidled up to Caine as unobtrusively as possible.

'Our ubiquitous porter conspicuously absent?' he said, out of the corner of his mouth.

Fortunately the others, minus Carmina, were dispersing. Caine had just told them to. He did not think anyone but Caine heard him say it.

Caine looked pretty blank for a moment, then doubtful at the idea of harbouring such a suspicion against an employee. But at last, he nodded. 'It's a long shot,' he muttered, 'but worth firing. I wouldn't put it past the man if he got the chance. He's been suspected of several other small robberies in the past.' He went after the police.

Through the window, Reg saw the two men hesitate, then reluctantly return.

Carmina was called forward. Had Pietro Buongusto happened to be present at all in the hall during the period when the money disappeared?

Yes, he had been present in the hall earlier in the afternoon, when the bookstall was open and its assistant present. The latter was stated with commendable point.

Was it possible that Buongusto could have taken the money when her back was turned?

Carmina did not see how, during *those* moments, which were before she left her post to talk to the guardian. Pietro came nowhere near her booth.

But, later, when she had left her post, could not the porter have returned?

He could, yes, the doughty Carmina supposed. It was possible, yes. He could have been watching from somewhere, and moved in when he saw the opportunity. Though (a fit of Catholic conscience here) she hated even to think that such a thing could be perpetrated by a colleague.

Tight-lipped and uncharacteristically sour, Giulia Buongusto was then forced to contribute that though she did not know where her husband had gone, she did not think he would be back immediately. She had agreed to do his cleaning duties for him this evening.

With a little less reluctance, the police agreed to a search. As Reg left, Caine was leading them to the door under the stairs. It was surely in the bag?

Success, Reg discovered the following morning, was fuller than he could have imagined. His timing had been impeccable, and his last-minute decision not to put all the money into the overall pocket proved masterly. Pietro would surely have needed some of the money for his evening plans? It seemed he had carelessly left the rest for further indulgence at a later date.

He had been arrested later in the evening at an expensive night-club to which he had taken Ingrid. Reg could imagine his shrill cries of innocence, his statement (for once, ironically, correct) that he was spending his own, hard-earned money, and on what deaf ears this story would fall. Had he not required a loan the year before when he was playing about with another foreign girl, he would have been reminded, and got one from Mortimer Ready?

(Robert would surely have readily given the police this information?) And had not the lovely Ingrid, who had failed to appear this morning, previously displayed an expensive standard of taste which had been stretching the amorous porter's resources to their limit? It appeared that on other evenings Pietro had taken her to several fashionable restaurants. He was to be held in custody, pending trial.

In Rome he could not expect a sentence of less than six months, which would nicely, Reg calculated, take them beyond the period of the exhibition.

This, Reg conjectured, was a third objective achieved that he had frankly not considered until this point. Whatever else he wasn't, Pietro in the company of his prehensile mongrel was a good watchman. He would no longer be a factor in any future equations.

Reg wondered if Caine would actually thank him for his part in the affair, but he did not expect a summons. When one came on the internal phone, just before the one o'clock closure, he sensed an opportunity might be at hand. He had ready two or three lines of approach if the smallest opening was offered.

It was typical of Caine's self-effacement that he had chosen for his office a dank, unairconditioned area at the back of the museum on the second floor. His own room was an enclosure of opaque glass constructed inside it. The secretary, Franca, was still there when Reg entered, but preparing to go. Caine, out of sight in his glass cage, called to him to come in.

As Reg complied, Caine rose and looked past him back into the office.

'Just off, Franca?'

Franca was taking her time about it. Caine waited until she had gone, then went to lock the office door behind her. Had the timing of this interview at the end of the morning been planned, Reg thought?

'Good, we're alone,' Caine said, motioning him to the chair opposite his. Seated himself, he frowned, picked up a pencil and began to roll it between his finger and thumb. 'I'm really indebted to you, Reg,' he said. 'Without your suggestion last night we wouldn't have caught the rogue. It was swift thinking on your part. Did you know Pietro was out with the girl last night?'

Reg shrugged. 'If he was absent, it was odds on he was. Giulia's face told a story too, didn't it?'

'It was very sharp of you. I don't know why I didn't think of it. We are all sure Pietro has stolen things before. Franca has twice missed money out of her bag. And of course Ingrid is not his first indulgence. You knew he was having this affair, I suppose?'

'He wasn't taking many precautions to conceal it, was he?'

'I suppose not. Poor Giulia. She's a good woman and deserves better. I've offered her the job, by the way, until Pietro is released. Then, I fear, if they stay together, they will both have to go.'

Definitely there was something up, Reg thought. The bouquet was sincere, intended, but he could swear the tone was giveaway somehow, secondary to something else. He had a sudden fear. Could Caine suspect something? Could someone have seen him in the hall, despite his precautions?

Caine threw down the pencil on the desk and put his hands behind his head as if he had resolved something. His face seemed to clear to its usual amiability.

'Look, Reg, I've got you up here to thank you, but there's another matter. The plain fact is I need some help with the exhibition, on the promotion side.'

10

The morning following his interview with Reg, Robert felt cheerful. He was pleased about his appointment and, even if in circumstances distressing for Giulia, Pietro, who had got what he deserved, was off his back, probably permanently. So much, he thought, for Mortimer's perverse penchant for the man. He then remembered he had not yet told Gabbi about Reg. Yesterday had been her day off.

He met her in the passage on his way to her office. He thought she looked fussed.

'Have you gone out of your mind, Robert?' she hissed at him in a low voice.

'Quite probably. What's the evidence this time?'

She turned, and went back into her room. He followed. She closed the door. 'It cannot be true Reg is going to take over publicity for the exhibition?'

'Yes, I was on my way to tell you about it.'

'But *why*?'

He sat down comfortably in one of the two armchairs Gabbi kept for visitors. 'Because he's had some experience at it, because in these last weeks we need somebody to be thinking of advertising and nothing else but advertising, and because PR has never been my forte.'

'You're doing it perfectly well, as you did for the last exhibition.'

'Thanks. But where I'm concerned it's done with an effort. Reg will perform, I guess, out of a natural bent. You heard his suggestions at the last staff meeting. They were pretty crisp, I thought, and what he said to me yesterday confirms that he's been thinking more about it. I think he'll do it better than any of us. I shall monitor him closely of course.'

Frowning, she sat on the edge of the desk and tucked her hands under her thighs. Her bare, unstockinged legs were smooth and brown emerging from the yellow cotton skirt. How young she looked.

'You might at least have told me you were going to appoint him.'

'I've just said, I was on my way. You've pre-empted me.'

'I mean told me before you did it. I didn't appreciate having to learn the news from Griffin. He's just been in here bragging about it.'

'Has he? Well, I really am sorry about that. I would of course have consulted you in the normal way of things, but, well, I had to come to the decision in a rather undesirable way. I had lunch with Mortimer on Sunday. You won't believe this, but he had asked me to lunch in order to cancel Cellini.'

'I don't believe it.'

'I think he really intended to. He must have met someone in London who fed him the idea that exhibitions are money losers.'

'And?'

'I had to think of something pretty fast. He'd also invited his accountant, Barbone, to lunch. Barbone had brought a sheaf of papers to prove how impecunious we are. I'm afraid, in the crisis, the idea of Reg doing the publicity for Cellini popped out. And it seemed to do the trick. Apparently – I didn't know – Mortimer has met Reg, and I suspect he's sniffed out that he can't pin on him the usual clichés he likes to label us with. Whatever the case, we still have Cellini pending.'

'You mean you told Ready you were appointing Reg to do the publicity on the spur of the moment?'

'Of course not. I'd already thought it out, and was intending to do it. Mortimer forced my hand a bit sooner than I'd intended, that's all. I'm sorry, Gabbi. I was of course going to put it to you first. I would have told you yesterday had you been in. But I do think Reg will be good. I suspect he's a different animal from the rest of us.'

Gabbi drew in her breath sharply. 'You can say that again.'

'You don't like him?'

'I think he's insufferably conceited.'

'You're probably right there. But at least he has some right to be, don't you think? The Courtauld, and Christie's, spoke highly of him.'

'*He* certainly thinks he has a right to total admiration. He was in here twenty minutes airing his ideas before I succeeded in throwing him out.'

'Well, at least that shows he's keen, doesn't it?'

'Keen on *what* is the question I ask.'

'What do you mean?'

Gabbi made an impatient movement of her head and looked sightlessly out of the window. How unconsciously beautiful she was, he thought, especially when annoyed.

'Unless I'm much mistaken, the man is making a pass at me.'

Robert was pulled up abruptly. 'Surely not?'

'I'm not totally blind to male practices, you know. To a man of his type, the fact that a woman is married – quite apart from the fact that she may be a hundred per cent immune to his charms – is of no consequence whatsoever. He imagines, I'm quite sure, that he's God's manna to womankind and that we shall all feed on the bounty in our hearts with thanksgiving.'

Robert swallowed. 'He's got a nerve if it's true.'

'He's already asked me twice to have a drink with him in the Veneto. And now he wants me to drive him round the city tomorrow, during museum time, to inspect publicity hoardings. It's another gambit of course but, in his carless state, he made it sound like my duty to help him.'

'You refused?'

In a panic, Robert saw the flush that ignited momentarily on her cheeks before she turned away to hide it. She was attracted to him. Of course she was attracted with a husband like hers and when subjected suddenly to Reg's vibrant personality beamed at her so guiltlessly. London came back to him, the meal he had eaten with Reg in that Baker Street restaurant, their conversation about the film, and women. 'I prefer them one at a time myself,' he had said. How had he failed to realise this would happen?

She was pretending to rummage in a file.

'I told him I wasn't sure, that I have work to do, and that you might not agree to us both going off anyway.'

'Which he accepted?'

She did not answer. She found the file she was looking for, and took it to the desk. 'He said he would ask you,' she said at last.

Robert's mind raced feverishly in several directions at once. What was she up to? Was she covertly asking his advice? Did she really want him to say she should go, for museum reasons, which would provide a respectable cover for her real feelings?

An idea came to him, like the thought he had had on his return from London about her helping him with the new Etruscan showcase.

'I've got a super solution. What you want is an alibi, isn't it?'

She looked at him fiercely. 'I certainly do.'

'Well, you know I've got my annual visit to Tarquinia tomorrow with the Irish Convent School girls. They terrify me. There's a nun coming, but last year they ran riot in the village. You wouldn't consider coming, would you? It really would be a help. I'm sure the girls will behave if you're there, and I can leave Gasparotti in charge here for a few hours.'

He scrutinised her face. Did it show disappointment?

'Super,' she said, still with a note of defiance.

'You'll come?'

'I'd love to.'

Robert strove to keep himself on an even keel. She had accepted his offer entirely because of Reg, he kept reminding himself. Yet he spent the day in a state of nervous excitement he could not quell. Several times he caught himself daydreaming, and had to wrench himself away.

That evening Kate had a long story about her publisher with whom she had lunched. The publisher had made a number of suggestions for her new book. She listed them now at length. He found himself not listening. When they went to bed and Kate was soon asleep, he could no longer keep himself from thinking of Gabbi. He lay awake imagining himself listening to her telling him how unsatisfactory her marriage was, how she had always been in love with him. He imagined them leaving the party at Tarquinia, going to a hotel, making love.

He could not be in love, he told himself the next morning for the umpteenth time as he sat beside the jolly and garrulous Sister Angela in the front seat of the bus. She was discussing Ulster and its troubles. While with one ear he listened to her vigorous, galloping brogue, he endlessly turned over the facts of the matter – that Gabbi was thirty-one and he was forty, that neither of them was the sort for divorce. And even if he could contemplate such an amputation, how could he imagine it would enter Gabbi's head? She saw him no doubt as of another generation, and as her boss.

Yet, because Gabbi had come on the trip, he knew the day was transformed for him. How did he explain that?

The sun, sparkling on the Tyrrhenian Sea they were travelling beside, seemed to open before him a new vista of what life could be. And all the time he was acutely aware of Gabbi behind him, talking and laughing with the girls whom, as he had guessed would be the case, she had immediately won. While the nun broke off for an instant to search for something in her bag, he turned briefly to look. She was sitting at the back. The two girls in front of her were kneeling on the seat to face her, two more were standing in the aisle, intent on missing nothing. He had another spasm of joy.

He made himself concentrate on Sister Angela. He liked her. Smelling voluminously of lavender, and exuding Irishness from every pore and every cadence of her humorous, light-hearted voice, she was castigating the seedier side of what she called 'the Irish soul'.

'You know what our real trouble is, Dr Caine, don't you?' she said. 'It's the gab. We talk ourselves out of everything constructive, and into brawls. James Joyce knew it. I daresay Shaw, too. That's why they left the country. They knew they wouldn't write a word if they stayed. They'd have spent their genius in the Dublin bars. And look at me here now, at it again – and I've *left* the blessed shores.'

How charming she was. Her quick, excitable laugh delighted him. Was it the sexual sacrifice nuns made that accounted for the humanity and energy so many of them seemed to have to spare? And how, he thought, could a nation that had produced this ebullient, balanced woman also have spawned the IRA?

They went first to the museum in Tarquinia. Like most museums founded more than twenty years ago it was haphazard, the objects simply moved like furniture into the rooms to occupy the space, with no idea of telling a story. But by knowing the layout of the place as he did, he was able to give some chronological as well as a geographical clarity to his remarks. He did not plod round, but selected objects in order as he needed them. This involved doubling back sometimes.

He doubted if the girls knew much about the Etruscans, if anything. His idea was to leave them with one or two definite impressions, and not overload them with facts. He wanted to get across what a distinctive culture the Etruscans had, so different from that of the Romans, yet how varied it was from region to region, and from one end of their period to the other.

Perhaps because they did not trudge round, he seemed to keep the girls with him. When he moved them on, they followed eagerly, competing to be up at the front. There were only one or two stragglers. As they built up some knowledge, he was able to involve them with questions.

'Now where have you seen this before?' he asked a bright-looking, younger girl, as they looked at a fine black-ware vase.

'It's Greek, is it – Athenian?'

It was the perfect lead-in for what he wanted to say about the connections between Etruria and the Ancient Greeks. The pot was not Greek, but a copy made at Velletri in the sixth century BC. He pointed out some of the differences.

He had really feared the girls would misbehave and disappear, as they had last year. Most were well-heeled seventeen-year-olds, probably more at home in the wealthier Roman discos than under the iron discipline of a convent school, of which they would view this excursion as an extension. But they behaved impeccably. Half-way round, he whispered to Gabbi and the Sister that the two of them might like to peel off for a coffee.

'Oh no,' the Sister said loudly, so that all the girls heard. 'We're just as enthralled as the girls.'

She looked at Gabbi, whose nod was convincing. He felt absurdly pleased.

He did not overpress his luck. When they had been going for just over an hour, he cut it. There was little point in a lecturer lapping his auditors and arriving alone at the finishing post. He suggested a Coke-break before they tackled the tombs.

The girls descended on the two cafés in the small square like a flock of migrant birds. Some girls, together with Sister, went off in search of postcard and trinket shops. Sister said she wanted a card to send to her brother – 'a property king,' she explained, 'who needs constant prompting on the existence of culture.' Robert found himself drinking iced lemon-juice with Gabbi. The sun was hot but as yet unoppressive.

'You know you were so good,' Gabbi said, as soon as they seated themselves. 'I'd no idea you're such a good teacher. You managed to transpose into their key so easily, and without distortion, without condescension, and with such enthusiasm. I couldn't begin to do it with my stuff. I really enjoyed your talk.'

At the tables surrounding them there was a jabber of teenage noise and laughter. He felt young and happy, and now, suddenly, breathless again. What had happened to him in the last twenty years?

He looked at Gabbi, and a tremor passed through his body. For several seconds he allowed his eyes to feast on the brown skin of her arms and throat, the tensions of her sensuous mouth, the full breasts that were so high and proud. He wanted her. He wanted to undress her, to make love to her, to relax those tensions of hers, and his own. Was it possible? She could not be happy with Giancarlo.

Their eyes met by mistake. She must see his naked desire?

For an instant she held his look. He saw the confusion, the quick flush of recognition on her cheeks. Then her hands flew to the coffee cup, her head dropped, so that her hair fell forward, partially covering her cheek. She raised the cup with both hands to her lips.

They sat in a heavy silence, Robert in an agony of suspense. What had he done? What was her response? Then Sister Angela appeared, peering for them on the other side of the square. Gabbi saw her and immediately began to wave vigorously. The nun approached and sat with them. Gabbi talked to her, almost turning her back on him.

His spirit died. It was true then. The truth was she saw him as a fusty old museum director, pushed around by an empty-headed tycoon and an elegant, disappointed wife. What he had imagined to be her pleasure in his company was an act of charity, no more. And what he had allowed her to see in that one rash moment had assaulted and insulted her.

In the tombs he felt no inspiration, though the girls were no less interested. They kept him going by their questions. Did they not notice that it was another man talking to them?

They had a late, snack lunch they had arranged in one of the cafés which had a large vine-covered area at the back. The three of them were about to sit at a table together when a couple of the older girls came and asked Gabbi if she would sit with them. With a rueful glance backwards, she went. She was glad of course to escape. He lunched alone with Sister.

After lunch there was a further opportunity for the girls to roam the town. Miserably, he went off by himself, pretending he wanted to look at a church. When he got back, he was the last to clamber onto the bus. Sister Angela and Gabbi were already occupying the front seat. In his absence they appeared to have struck up a strong liking for each other. He sat alone on the seat opposite. His isolation was symbolic, he thought.

For most of the journey he tried to make himself read. Once he looked up and gazed sightlessly at the sea. Ashamed of his mental betrayal, he tried to think more kindly of Kate, today bustling about somewhere in the marbled precincts of ancient Rome. Weren't they really a pair? Surely, somewhere was a formula that would help her to recognise that they were?

But he could find none of the usual expectation he felt when he had been away from Kate. He glanced quickly sideways. Gabbi was still deep in animated conversation with the nun. The sight of her, so free of his mental entanglement, stabbed him like a knife. How could he have imagined that she could ever return his feelings?

They dropped the girls and Sister Angela at the school. The driver would have taken him and Gabbi home. He declined the kind offer. The traffic had wound itself into the usual early evening chaos. He had a sudden resurgence of pride. Somehow he must return things to normality. After all, nothing had been said. Somehow he must let Gabbi see that it had been a moment of aberration, to be forgotten.

'You knock off. We'll take a taxi,' he said to the driver. 'I'll drop you off, Gabbi.'

They went first to Termini. In the back seat together, he made himself chatter about commonplaces, though he felt hot and tired.

Gabbi did not say much. A good deal of the time she stared out of the window, away from him. He felt diminished, superseded, but he kept going. At last the taxi curved into the pavement. The man waited, without turning his head.

Gabbi did not move for a moment, then suddenly she turned to him, took his arm with both her hands, and kissed him on the cheek. 'Thank you, Robert. Thank you for asking me. It was a very special day, you know. And you're a super boss, a super man.' Before he could collect himself, she was getting out of the taxi. He watched her trim, tall figure receding, with her rather jerky, vigorous walk. She did not look back.

Uncertain what she meant, he was about to tell the man to proceed to the Borghese, when he saw Reg standing by the paper-stall twenty yards ahead. He had apparently just bought a paper and was studying the front page, but Robert had the impression that he had just moved his head very sharply down to the print. Was it his illusion, or had there also been a quick look of amusement on his face?

11

He had surely done as well as could be imagined, Reg thought? Caine had formed an inner working committee of three for the exhibition with himself and the gorgeous Gabbi, which made him privy to a lot more besides publicity arrangements. But the weeks were passing. It was now August, and an earsplitting silence was developing from the Tunku's direction. Every day he expected the renewed voice from the clouds. No voice came. There was just, daily, the stifling heat and the exigencies of the publicity job he had taken on. There were other disturbing events.

Reg had in no way allowed himself to relax on the higher matter. Robert had modified the security system as a result of the theft. Not only had he had a lock put on the door under the stairs, but the cupboard door in the basement area which gave access to the loose cash safe, and more relevantly, the alarm system switches, had been strengthened and fitted with a newly patented magnetic lock, certainly beyond his powers to pick. Giulia did not want the responsibility of setting the alarms and locking up which Pietro had always done. Carmina was entrusted with the keys of the kingdom.

The changes raised no great obstacles. In some ways they made matters easier. It had not taken him long to realise that the security weakness of the museum lay in the crucial hour after closing, before the alarm system was activated. This was the time when cleaning took place, and it was important that the cleaning routine, especially the movements of Carmina, who was surely now crucial in the new arrangement, were minutely reobserved. On several evenings he stayed on after closing time at six. This was easy enough to justify with his extra workload.

The pattern seemed clear. Giulia was a lot more methodical than Pietro had been. Pietro had often arrived late, Giulia arrived punctually at six every evening. Giulia and one of the outside women did the ground floor, one on each side of the building, the other two the first floor in a similar fashion. All of them started at the back and worked forward to the front hall. With little variation, so far the operation had always been completed at the latest by five past seven.

On the fifth evening of these soundings, Reg decided he had accurate information. At about five to seven he went down, carrying his brief-case, and as usual stopped to talk to Carmina.

She was in an expansive mood, and began to talk about Carlo Pelucci, his predecessor. Carmina had a generally low opinion of curatorial staff, and Pelucci, it seemed, had some priority for her scorn. No doubt he was a scholarly man, she conceded, and she had never been one to detract from the value of learning. But he was, alas, a bachelor and a recluse who could think of nothing but his work.

'Do you know, I'm not sure we exchanged one word during all the years he was here? He'd walk right by you as if you weren't there.'

With one ear Reg was gratified. It seemed he might by implication be an exception to Carmina's censure of learned bachelor curators. It was important that he maintained good relations with her. With his other ear he plotted the positions of the four moaning polishers. They were all into the last rooms now. It would be another classic finish.

One by one the machines switched off, and shortly the women began to come into the hall. The three non-resident women left their machines by the door under the stairs, and departed through the front door. Giulia appeared last.

Carmina had graduated from listing the shortcomings of the unfortunate Pelucci to the circumstances of his disappearance, which was not, she adjudged, so unexpected to her as it had been to others.

'I myself am quite sure he committed suicide,' she said loudly, as she unlocked the stairs door and stood aside for Giulia to descend the steps with the first of the machines. 'After all, what had a man like that got to live for?'

'I'm not so sure about that, Signora Manfreddi,' Giulia said, dextrously winding a length of flex between her palm and elbow. 'He may not have spoken to you, but he talked to Pietro all right. As a matter of fact, they often went out for a beer together.

'Now my days here are numbered, I can speak out. In my view, there's more in Pelucci's disappearance than meets the eye. Pietro was with him the evening before he went missing. Pietro said he was perfectly normal when he saw him, certainly not contemplating killing himself. Pelucci also told Pietro he wasn't going walking in the Abruzzi after all that weekend, as he'd been planning. He'd had an invitation.'

Carmina was not friendly with Giulia. She had already made it plain she included Giulia within the curtilage of her husband's crime. But this was too succulent a morsel. Her eyebrows lifted.

'An invitation, what invitation?'

'From a stranger apparently, who came up to him in the street. Something about some statue he wanted Pelucci to look at. He was going to be paid a lot of money for his pains.'

Reg chipped in. 'But why didn't you say all this at the time, Giulia?'

'We didn't want any trouble with the police. It was no business of ours.'

Giulia would say no more. Understandably, her manner had become clipped since her husband's arrest. She wiped her hands lightly on her overall.

'Well, that's all then for tonight, Signorina Manfreddi. I'll be off. You'll be wanting to lock up.'

Reg had of course several times considered the general question of violence, including the ultimate violence, in connection with himself and others. He had considered it first that night in the Tunku's mansion in Kuala Lumpur. Was that aristocratic Malaysian face capable of killing? In the kind of split-second, intuitive way one decides on such matters, he had thought not. Ruthlessness, yes, an entire lack of sentimentality, yes, but not, surely, the dimension of murder? Above all, looking back, he had had the notion that Raschid might be a kind of a games-player. It was not exactly public-school games he played perhaps, but they would be games played to finite, predetermined rules, games which were terminated with a silver cup on the mantelpiece – or rather, a masterpiece above it.

But it had never occurred to Reg to question Pelucci's disappearance. He had left it, as Caine had described it to him at their first meeting, as an unsolved mystery. With the disturbing news Giulia had just given, could he continue with this wishful thinking? Even if he was right about the Tunku, how much of the day-to-day tactics did he leave to his subordinates, to Kassim for instance? The stark question faced him now. Had Pelucci been murdered to create the vacancy? And if Pelucci had been murdered, was he, who might very soon be not only redundant but a walking file on Raschid's potential criminality, similarly expendable?

Two other events which followed in rapid succession increased his unease. He had very early discounted the idea that Pietro was the Tunku's sleuth. Pietro was too stupid to keep his thoughts off his face, and Reg had been aware in early May that he was being rather spasmodically followed. At different times he had identified three faces. This was not unexpected, especially since the meeting with Kassim in the Galleria Ottavio. It was also almost certain that his flat and the telephone in it were bugged. He had not even bothered to look. But he got back one evening to find the place had been systematically done over. He always left the skylight open for Attila, whose movements were irregular. If he had food remnants within the animal's gastronomic repertoire, he left them on a plate in the corridor. The intruder had shared the skylight facility.

There was nothing for an intruder to find in his flat, but it seemed excessive. What did the Tunku and his minions expect to unearth, his police papers under a floorboard? It was heavy, not at all the delicate touch he had come to expect.

The day afterwards, he had an appointment at RAI to do a radio commercial on the exhibition. He left the museum, then realised he had forgotten the script. Returning to his office, he caught the guardian, Alfredo, in flagrante delicto. He was standing by the desk, as if he had just had time to shut the drawer he had been searching.

Alfredo had an alibi. He said he was collecting up the fire-extinguishers for the man who had come to check them. Wasn't there one in this office, he asked? There was a maintenance firm visiting the premises that afternoon. Reg had noticed the van outside. But, since he had been in the museum, the nearest extinguisher to his room was at the top of the main stairs. Alfredo must know this as well as he did. Also, why had the man shut the door? He had to be the internal sleuth.

Just what were they after?

Reg did the broadcast, badly. He could not keep his mind on it. Emerging from the radio building into the heavy late afternoon heat and glare, he was still thoughtful. He was only half-aware of the black Mercedes that moved out of the car park and followed him. It drew level, still moving, and the back door opened.

'A lift, Mr Griffin?'

It was Haji Kassim. He felt the now familiar light zephyr of fear prickle his neck. Was this it then? Should he run? Half a second's reflection prevented him. Run? Where to? One might as well say one wanted to get off halfway down the Cresta Run.

The Mercedes seemed to possess some spatial quality of lubrication which allowed it to penetrate the dense traffic without friction. They wove their way smoothly towards Termini and, circumnavigating the station, settled for the Tiburtina, going north-east. He and Kassim sat together on the back seat. Kassim's head was turned away from him. He had reverted to his original state of chronic speechlesness.

Reg could not live with this. Speech, it had been demonstrated at their last encounter, was not beyond Kassim's powers. He had managed whole blocks of it. And silence, like plaster of Paris, hardened if you left it.

'Where are we going?'

The dapper head did not turn, and remained silent.

He was convinced there had been a change of plan, and that they had decided he knew too much. He had at first imagined for some reason that they would take the coast road northwards. Was it one of those Italian political scandals he remembered, a corpse found on a beach up there somewhere, just south of Civitavecchia? The driver had Boulder-Head's physique, also bald, with three bulges of flesh on the neck.

At least he was wrong about the venue. They seemed to be making for Tivoli. Then, passing the Villa Adriana, they turned off to the left and began to wind upwards into low, well-cultivated hills. They passed through a village, and took an unmade road, little more than a track, which wound through orchards.

They crested a shallow summit and a densely wooded valley came into view below, which apparently had no habitation. They began to descend and were quickly engulfed by the trees. At the foot of the valley they crossed a bridge over a sizeable stream. The road now was in worse condition, and even the Mercedes made heavy weather of it. Suddenly, ahead, standing in a small clearing of trees, Reg saw what appeared to be a semi-ruined castle, with an area of unkempt gravel in front of it. The road seemed to end here.

They drew up in front of a restored tower, which had curtained modern windows set into the stone. Beside it was an obviously modern reconstruction using one of the original walls. The rest of the castle lay in heaps, rising here and there from overgrown bushes and trees. At the foot of the tower were massive, unpainted, wooden doors with large iron studs. A smaller door cut into them opened, and out stepped Boulder-Head.

Boulder-Head opened Kassim's door, not his. Reg was left to follow them like a faithful dog. They entered a dim baronial hall which would have pleased Osbert Lancaster. It was complete with a menagerie of tusked and whiskered taxidermy. There was a regulation fully-armoured warrior standing with a halberd and managing to look, as armour of this sort usually did, peculiarly helpless, a fan of pistols high on one wall, and on the floor a spreadeagled tiger-skin. Malaysian? Was one to assume the snarling head was a welcome?

Somehow Reg expected the procession would continue up the fine medieval oak staircase ahead, but Boulder-Head peeled off, and Kassim led the way through a side door which opened into a modern apartment. Reg was left in a carpeted, heavy-curtained, and ornately furnished sitting-room. On Kassim's departure, a deep silence fell.

Across one corner of the room was a grand piano. Reg approached. Whether he was about to see Raschid he could not be sure, but at least there was no longer any doubt who owned the place. On the gleaming walnut wood stood a forest of framed photographs, including a very recent one of 'the latest'. A lady he guessed was the discarded Princess Elena also figured, less centrally, and there were several other informal shots of what must be other members of the family. He recognised the Sultan. Raschid himself did not seem to figure. Magisterial modesty?

Then he noticed a rather less prominent, framed snap behind the Sultan. He picked it up. It seemed to have been taken some time ago, at an archaeological dig, Etruscan to judge by the large vase. He took in the three figures in the foreground. The man holding the vase was Robert. Beside him was the Tunku, on Raschid's right Mortimer Ready.

'You have an eye for the relevant,' he heard behind him.

Reg put the photograph back on the piano. Raschid, relaxed, in shirt sleeves, had entered soundlessly. He trudged across the room, stood beside Reg, and took up the photograph again in both hands.

'Yes. This was taken in 1976, at a new find in Velletri. Mortimer was behaving as if it was all his doing, as usual. He tried to muscle in on all the publicity.'

Reg was already feeling some relief. He could not imagine his end could be that near with Raschid showing this degree of amiability. But all he could do was gape.

'You mean you know Caine and Ready personally? You know them, and are about to rob the Aemelia?'

There was a rare occurrence. Raschid smiled. His fierce medieval-warrior features were transformed. 'Once again you pre-empt me, Griffin. You do certainly dance ahead. But your words are not strictly accurate, are they? It is not myself who is going to "rob the museum", as you put it so picturesquely, it is you, is it not? Shall we sit down?'

There was a tantalising delay while the drinks ceremony was enacted. There was no bell-pulling. The Tunku did the serving himself. Settled, Raschid crossed his elegantly trousered legs.

'I must first apologise for kidnapping you like this. However you will appreciate, I am sure, the need for precautions at this time. We approach a critical phase.

'But now, the very agreeable part of our conversation. Kassim will have passed on to you some weeks ago my preliminary congratulations. I now have further laurels to bestow. You have done, if I may say so, exceedingly well, far beyond my best hopes. I confess I am but partially informed on how you managed to manipulate yourself so artfully, and crucially, into Robert Caine's confidence, though I suspect your part in the removal of the obnoxious porter, a very fortunate circumstance incidentally, was involved. But it is a quite astonishing achievement in so short a time.'

He took a small sip of his orange-juice. 'I am more than delighted to tell you that, in consequence of all this, the time has come to take you fully into my confidence. My instinct about you has been proved right. Are my instincts also correct in telling me that you're rather enjoying your role? I do hope so. The best operators, I've always found, are those who function with a certain innate insouciance and pleasure.'

Reg nodded, barely perceptibly. Insouciance was not a word he would have used about himself at the present. But he looked Raschid fully in the eyes, slowly blinked, and waited deferentially. The Tunku was screwing one of the rings on his fingers.

'To business then. The exhibition starts three weeks next Monday. I'll let you into a secret. My interest was aroused some eighteen months ago when I first heard that a Cellini Exhibition was to be mounted. But I doubt if I would have taken things further had I not heard, in the early spring, that your director had obtained one particular object. Indeed the late decision taken on this object has caused me to act a lot more precipitately than I would have wished.

'"A particular object", yes. You have noted my phraseology, and you are no doubt wondering which one? The selection of exhibits is quite outstanding, don't you think? Some half a dozen of them certainly. But of course there is the one piece of pure paramountcy, in my opinion one of the half-dozen great master-pieces of the world. Cellini's Perseus is a great work, so is the Cosimo bust, the Escorial Crucifixion and the others. But it is Cellini's skill as a goldsmith that makes him one of the greatest figures of history. I'm sure you will know at once what's in my mind?'

There were only a couple of possibilities. Reg plunged.

'The Vienna Salt-Cellar?'

'Naturally. I was sure our aesthetic judgements would coincide. Well then, let us adopt British military manual procedure. We have the information, let us proceed to method. I have no doubt, following your last meeting with Kassim, that you already have some ideas of your own on this matter?'

Reg settled himself more comfortably. He was sorry the Tunku did not seem to know the full story about Pietro. But maybe it was pleasant to know that his sleuths could miss a trick or two. The money question was also not yet straight. But they were now on home ground.

He began to unfold his plan for entry and departure. To him it was simple. Have the estimable Carmina hijacked for the evening. Someone else would have to do this. He thought the seclusion of her own flat would be the safest venue for this operation. With her keys, it would be possible to immunise the security system and all electrical circuits. If it was to be a question, as the Salt-Cellar would be, of breaking open an air-pressure-protected showcase, that would be the difficult and dangerous part. He thought it would mean a certain element of smash and grab, which meant he would need other help outside the building.

But some time before he got to this, he knew Raschid's attention was wandering. He stopped. For a moment there was silence. Raschid was gazing at an ivory Buddha sitting on the mahogany sideboard. He smiled again.

'I rather thought you might come up with something like this,' he said.

'You don't think it works?'

'Oh, I think it would work all right. For an ordinary operation it's the obvious thing. Keys, a breakage, and a get-away. But this is not quite an ordinary operation, Griffin. You are not ordinary. I might flatter myself by thinking I am not entirely ordinary. Your suggestion, sound as it is, I'm afraid leaves out the all-important aesthetic quality. We must remove all banality. The Salt-Cellar is one of the most exquisite objects on this earth. Its removal must be effected in an equally exquisite way. There must be no trace of how the getaway was made. We must think of you, and your future. You must be in a position to report for work the next morning to add your astonishment to everyone else's.

'I think the latter would be an especially nice touch, would you not agree? I cannot imagine you would enjoy having to lead the rest of your life in obscurity, even as rich as you will be.'

Reg's look asked the question arising from this. Raschid picked it up at once.

'Ah yes, your remuneration. You are naturally interested in that. How nice to do business with someone so straightforward. I have been thinking of a quarter of a million pounds, payable immediately into the numbered Swiss account I gather you have wisely opened. There will be a further, equal, instalment on completion.'

Part Three
~ ~ ~ ~ ~ ~ ~ ~ ~ ~ ~

Part Three

12

Kate Caine had not slept soundly until the early hours of the hot, late-August night. When she woke in the morning she was in no hurry to get up. She lay trying to resurrect her pleasure in last night's dinner, given in her honour.

She had never thought too much of the heterogeneous group of classical archaeologists who made up the association she belonged to. They seemed more interested in their own triumphs than in those of others, and least of all in the general advancement of knowledge. But last night the 'celebration of her success', as the Chairman had put it, had seemed genuine and had not contained any of the usual element of jealousy. Could it be perhaps because following as she hoped she always had in her father's footsteps, she had always ridden above small gossip and tittle-tattle?

Of course it was, she thought fiercely, and they were at last registering the fact. And her book on the villas *had* indeed contributed something very solid to the common endeavour of their profession.

Yet why could she not fully celebrate her triumph? She realised that throughout her thoughts about last night she had been half-listening to Robert getting breakfast. She had heard the coffee-grinder, the clatter of the grill as he made toast, and finally now he called briefly to her as he carried the tray through on to the balcony.

Damn him, she thought. Why should she allow him to spoil her success? And what were her recent thoughts in his direction worth anyway? When had she ever allowed herself to deal in doubt, supposition, and secondary source information? If his present mood had any significance it was a reflection of some worries he had about the Cellini Exhibition. In his usual state of seigneurial reserve, he was concealing them. Why couldn't he admit to difficulties as other people did?

She roused herself, put on her housecoat, and went out on to the balcony. The sun was filtering in powerful shafts through the upper foliage of the pines that surrounded them. She put back her shoulders, drew in a long breath of the already warm September air, and sat in the basket chair.

'I think I'll spend the morning down in the Forum,' she said. 'It's an indulgence, but with the book finished, I feel I've earned it. There are a number of things I'd like to look at. I'll take my camera. I do actually need a good shot of the Vestal Claudia's plinth for my new monograph on my chisel-width theory, so it won't be entirely a swan.'

She launched easily into further aspects of this idea of hers. Her point was that chisels seemed to vary in size through the period. Chisel marks could thus be used as corroborative evidence in dating. That Robert seemed less than attentive, she refused to allow to worry her. As with many undemonstrative, academic Englishmen, you could sometimes think he was mentally sporting the oak, when in fact his listening faculties were perfectly alert.

She was surprised, however, when he suddenly interrupted her in an unusually brusque way.

'Do you mind, Kate – this morning?'

It was as if she constantly bored him with details of her work. 'Mind?'

'I'm sorry, but I just can't take in what you're saying.'

She blinked.

'Is something wrong?'

He did not answer. Now she looked at him he did look a bit under the weather. She seized a piece of toast and began to butter it. 'You're worried about the exhibition, I suppose. Is that it?'

'No, not especially.'

'What then?'

He picked up his cup with both hands and held it in front of his face in a slow brooding way she had always disliked. 'Nothing, really. It's just a bit early in the morning.'

She was furious. The incident annoyed and, worse, alarmed her to a degree that was surprising. Whatever else Robert was, or wasn't, he was almost never rude to her.

She dressed at a leisurely pace. By the time she was ready, Robert had gone downstairs. She was going to take the Citroen down to the Forum. She knew one of the attendants, who allowed her to park by a gate. Though she had asked Robert to leave the keys for her, he had forgotten.

Angrily, she searched the pockets of the suit he had worn yesterday. They were not there. She seized the intercom phone. Franca could jolly well bring them up if he had them. As usual there was something wrong with the machine. She would have to go down.

This was doubly annoying. She never liked to go into the museum if she could avoid it. She always used the lift and the courtyard door for her exits. And she was dressed in her working clothes, a garment which resembled a boiler suit. She did not care to be seen in this garb by people like Franca. But she was certainly not going to change. It was already late if she was to finish before closing time.

What an unkempt warren the museum was behind the public rooms, like the area behind a stage. The musty smell that always seemed to hang about – was it damp plaster? – assaulted her as she came out of the lift on the second floor. No carpets of course on the wooden floors, and there were long bare walls, high ceilings harbouring black dusty cobwebs which were never swept, huge doors, and rooms much too large for their present purpose. It gave her the impression of a derelict house in which rather undesirable people were squatting.

She entered Robert's office. Franca half-rose in the semi-deferential way she had. Nice enough girl, at least always polite to her, but what a sight in the usual pleated tartan skirt and a none too clean and creased cream blouse. Robert wouldn't notice of course, let alone pull her up for it.

'Is Robert there?'

He obviously was, in the absurd makeshift frosted-glass cubicle. She heard voices through the half-open door. She swept in. It was the Bruneschi woman with him. She was kneeling on the chair, which she had drawn up beside Robert's. The two of them had their heads together over a plan. Both heads came up in tandem as she entered. It gave her the most disagreeable sensation, as if she were an intruder.

'You've got the car keys,' she heard herself bark.

Robert scrabbled in his trouser pockets, then in his jacket hanging on the back of his chair. Meanwhile she was aware of the woman, still kneeling there, suspended, waiting for the tiresome intrusion to come to an end.

113

'We're just working on the final layout plan for Cellini,' Robert said.

She made no reply, and walked straight out.

Driving, uncontrollably her thoughts flew back to that day three months ago when Robert had gone to Tarquinia with the convent girls. The nun had rung the next day to thank him and she had answered the phone. The nun also wanted to thank Gabriella Bruneschi 'who had been so helpful with the girls, and who was such a delightful person'. Robert had said nothing about Gabriella being on the trip.

At that time she had dismissed it. It was typical of Robert to indulge in such petty concealment. He was, she had known for a long time, attracted to the woman, but the idea that he was having an affair with her, even contemplating one, was laughable.

She had to consider that she had been totally wrong. Gabriella, of course, was quite capable of having a go if she saw an opportunity. You could see at a glance that her marriage to that Communist idiot was on the rocks. She had seen it a long while before. At work in the Forum, she just could not get that scene out of her mind – Franca there, the door open, but the expression on their faces, engrossed, intent on the matter in hand, intimate, *established.* Had Robert been unfaithful to her? Was he, despite all she thought she knew of him, leading a double life?

She could not, still, believe it. He was incapable – not of the act. She supposed most men were capable of that, given the opportunity. But of the degree of duplicity he would have had to practise. As the morning wore on, and she became immersed in her work, the oscillations steadied. There was nothing substantial on which to base such a fanciful thought, she reprimanded herself. It could only be some curious emotional eruption of her own that had caused it. Tonight, when he came up to the flat, it would be the same as it always was.

It seemed to be. Her nerves calmed.

The next day she decided to turn out the sitting-room. She put on a pair of Bermudas and set about it. By mid-morning she had the heavy work done. She thought she would make herself a cup of coffee. Passing through the hall, she saw that Giulia had brought up the letters. Most were for Robert as usual. One, unstamped, unaddressed, was for her. It had 'Mrs Catherine Caine' neatly typed on the envelope. Mystified, she took it into the kitchen. She read it while the kettle boiled.

The two sentences were also typed, in the centre of the page.

'Are you aware of your husband's infidelity? If not, await a further communication, which will supply the proof.' It was signed, *'A well-wisher'.*

13

Two adjoining rooms on the first floor at the top of the main staircase had been set aside for the exhibition. Their normal contents had been put into storage ten days before the opening. The various showcases were then delivered, the screening and panelling was erected, and the electricians got busy wiring up the special systems that would be necessary.

For general security they relied heavily on the three systems that had been operative for several years, the passive infra-red body heat sensors which operated in all the public rooms, the hall, the staircase and in the courtyard entrance lobby, pressure pads at strategic points where there was carpeting – principally on the front and back staircases – and a contact-breaking apparatus for objects of exceptionally high value. To satisfy the demanding researches of the lending museums, they had hired as well very expensive, especially constructed showcases which operated on an air-pressure system. The cases were airtight, and the pressure inside the glass was different from that outside. If the glass was broken, the increase of air-pressure would trigger the alarm system. In addition, Perseus, The Crucifixion, and other major statues would be wired.

Robert felt as confident as it was possible to be that with this gadgetry, and the huge window grilles with which the Renaissance had supplied all the ground and first floor windows, any night intruder would be up against it. To replace Pietro's tireless patrols, the police were providing a permanent presence outside during the closing hours. The one contingency against which no defence could be raised was an armed and ruthless incursion by day. Here the only positive factor was their position in the middle of the Borghese Gardens. It would take any vehicle, with no traffic to hinder it, at least two minutes to escape into the city round the park, and the Aurelian Walls would limit and funnel their exits on one side. The staff had been instructed not to resist an armed attack, but at the earliest safe opportunity to set the alarm off with one of the manual switches placed about the building. This alarm not only set off the bells inside and outside the building, but linked directly to the police.

Most of the items for the exhibition had been timed to arrive within a day or two of the opening. This reduced the security risk, and caused minimum disturbance to the daily life of the museum. Perseus was almost the last of the deliveries. It came on the evening of the penultimate day, after closing time, when the exhibition was ready. Its arrival was, as it were, the *coup de grâce*.

Robert thought the fewer people present the better. Gabbi had an appointment, so he asked Reg if he would stay on and help him supervise the hand-over of Perseus from the courier and the transfer of the crate from the vehicle to the exhibition rooms. As with the other larger objects, by prior arrangement the courier had the van drive to the back of the palazzo and into the court. The museum's electrically-operated fork-lift took on the crate, and by way of the service lift and the exhibit rooms on the first floor, conveyed it directly to its position in the inner of the two rooms.

The fork-lift gently lowered its load, the men from Florence fussed over its final positioning and removed the crate, the electrician connected the already-fitted security system and tested it. At last the fork-lift hummed away back to the lift, their own storeman and the visitors departed. Reg closed the inner door of the farther room with the additional locks and bolts which had been fitted. For a moment Robert stood with him at the vantage point between the rooms from which the whole exhibition was visible.

The first room was dedicated principally to Cellini's work as a goldsmith and to his life and personality, about which so much was known. On the walls to right and left as they entered were two pictures, Alessandro de Barbière's 'Goldsmith's Shop from the Palazzo Vecchio', which communicated powerfully the spirit of energy and endeavour that animated the Italian Renaissance, and Vasari's round 'Cosimo I and his Architects, Engineers and Sculptors', in which Cellini's white, bearded head appears.

Visitors were advised, having looked at these pictures, to gyrate in a clockwise direction. In the first stand there was an introduction to the diary – selected facsimile pages in the original handwriting, each intended to illustrate an aspect of Cellini's character. There were English and modern Italian translations. Other languages would have to rely on the polylingual brochure or on a verbal commentary delivered through headphones.

Other stands in the room dealt with the earlier and later Florence periods, the sojourns in Rome and Paris. From a considerable choice, they had the best of the number of medals and seals, among which were the magnificent Clement VII medal, with its reverse of the Allegory of Peace, shown by means of a mirror, and the gold Scudo of Paul III. Maximum use had been made of lavish mounting and lighting, which Gabbi had supervised, and explanatory notes had aimed at aesthetic comment as well as factual information. The centre-piece of this room was the glorious masterpiece, the Vienna Salt-Cellar. It was mounted in its own case.

By the door into the second room they had the bronze relief of Perseus Rescuing Andromeda, showing the transition to sculpture, and the second room was entirely the statues. In the centre, handsomely lit and dominant, was the huge bronze Perseus from the Piazza dei Signori, which it had been such a coup to obtain. So as not to steal any thunder from the bronzes, Gabbi had had the other masterpiece, the stark white marble Crucifixion, mounted in an alcove against a background of black velvet with strong lighting.

As they stood together, Robert was aware of the poignancy in their instinctive silence. They had all been working so hard in the last weeks there had not been time to ponder beyond the immediate tasks. Now everything was in position there was nothing to do but wait, and admire.

'It's strange,' Robert said reflectively, 'that these works have probably never rubbed shoulders like this before, not even in Benvenuto's lifetime.' Reg nodded. 'It's like a family reunion after many years of separation. I wonder what the artist would think if he could be here?'

'He wouldn't be,' Reg said. 'We'd never have put on the show if Benvenuto was alive. He would have asked too high a price, and you wouldn't have been willing to pay it.'

'You're right. No one quite wields the Medici power and wealth these days. If the prince said yes or no, that was it in

Cellini's day. It was the prince's price, or nothing.' He paused. 'Cellini would be pleased, though, don't you think? He had a villain's vanity.'

'Villain?'

'A villain and a genius.'

Reg shrugged, but Robert was sure they shared similar thoughts, as he felt they did on most subjects. And was it his imagination, or did Reg seem a little less casual and confident than when they first met? He was gazing at Perseus, but there was an imminent look on his face as if he was about to say something.

Robert waited, but Reg remained silent. He thought of asking him up for a drink, but then remembered Kate's mood. She had been more than usually remote in the last week or two, to the point almost of offensiveness.

He had told Carmina he would lock up when they had finished. Reluctantly, he made the move to go.

They went down to the front hall together. Robert felt a redoubled wish that something overt should pass between them. Their entirely extroverted relationship had grown in the six months they had been working together, and the other matter had not developed. Gabbi must have been wrong that day. Reg had shown no sign of flirting with her, which somehow made his own decision about Gabbi easier to bear. Before he locked up, he had first to let Reg out. By the door he put his hand on his shoulder.

'You know, if the exhibition is a success, a good part of it will be owing to your efforts. You've really contributed enormously since you've been here, and not just on the publicity for all this. I hope you know how grateful I am.'

Reg lingered. If Robert had had to make a bet, he would have said he was pleasantly embarrassed. Then, in a gruff voice, he said a curious thing. 'You have to go for things you want in life.' With this he gave an odd curt nod, turned away suddenly, and departed.

Robert watched him as he descended the steps and strode purposefully across the forecourt. For a moment he felt sorry for him without knowing why. An oddball, as the Courtauld professor had said, at once attractive and elusive. Perhaps, when the exhibition was over, and when the moment was ripe, he would be able to do a little sympathetic probing.

Robert went back towards the security switches under the stairs, but for a moment stood in the centre of the hall. The staircase gave a massive creak as the evening warmth ebbed. Around him he felt the brooding presence of the museum, as if settling itself for the solitude of the night. Next week with any luck the turnstiles would be spinning and the place would be swarming with people. The thought was exciting, but reminded him of his onerous responsibility. He went once more over the security arrangements. Could he have missed anything?

Well, he thought, he was committed now. There was nothing more that could be done with the money available. The lending museums had been satisfied with the arrangements. The national indemnity schemes would cover any losses or damage if, Heaven forbid, anything disastrous happened.

He continued to the security room under the stairs, opened it with the cylindrical magnetic key, and threw the switches. He returned to the front door. There was only a minute's grace before the alarms became operative. Because of this, he had to go round the outside of the building to get to his flat. The sensors protecting this rear door to the museum, though linked to the main system, could be independently neutralised for sufficient time to go up to his floor.

The exhibition was to be opened by the Minister on Monday morning at a reception for invited guests. Robert was worried about Mortimer's role in the occasion. Mortimer had said no more about cancelling, but about three weeks earlier he had made a panicked telephone call about security. This was typical, and in line with his opposition to the exhibition. But since then they had not spoken. He had not been in for a preview of the exhibits.

It was not until Saturday morning that the secretary called to say he would be at the reception but did not intend to make a speech. This could not be trusted. Mortimer had been known in the past to arrive at such functions with an unannounced speech in his pocket which upset all the timetabling. And as often as not he made a gaffe that offended someone.

The Rolls drew up a good hour before the guests would start arriving, when Robert was in the middle of an interview with a

Corriere reporter Reg had arranged. He had to cut it short to give Mortimer a tour. But Mortimer seemed in a good mood. Dressed in a bright blue suit and a red tie, he was almost jaunty. 'Fine, fine,' he kept saying, as they went round. 'All excellent. Everyone must have worked very hard. If this doesn't pull them in,' he said twice, 'nobody is to blame.'

There were no more references to burglaries and hold-ups, no snide remarks about exhibitions in general, and he confirmed that he would be keeping a low profile at the reception. 'No, it's your show, Robert. You take all the bows. You deserve them.'

A curious, very unpredictable man. Did it not confirm that it wasn't worth taking seriously anything he said?

The barrier, and Carmina's cockpit in the hall, had originally been made removable so that the hall could be usable for functions. It was the obvious place for the reception. Canapés and wine would be circulated from the bookstall by the waiters, and speeches could be made from the stairs. The latter would add, Robert thought, a rather British touch of informality.

By the time the Minister was due, the hall was full. It looked as if pretty well everyone who had been asked had come, and no doubt several who had not been, accurate scrutiny of invitation cards at the door being difficult in the throng. Robert had no illusions. He knew from long experience of Roman ways that the large turn-out was largely luck. None the less it was pleasing to see so many, when people had worked hard on the reception. The publicity would be good, both for the exhibition, the cost of which had of course frighteningly exceeded their original budget, and for the museum generally.

The Minister was late. At any moment Robert expected one of those electrically-communicated hushes when everyone starts looking at everyone else and a collective unease spreads. The obvious thing was to release the food and drink. But this he was loth to do, mindful of a recent occasion at the British Council when the goodies had been allowed to precede a lecture and half the audience had vanished before it began.

At the crucial moment a stir by the door indicated salvation. The large black limousine had glided into the forecourt. Robert struggled to detach himself from a Cellini 'expert' who lectured at the Dante d'Alighieri Institute and who was now lecturing him.

By the time he had fought through the crowd, the Minister, accompanied by two very mafioso-looking bodyguards, had mounted the steps and Mortimer had pounced on him. Mortimer's behaviour continued to be exemplary. He almost effaced himself. 'Well, Minister,' he said after a short chat, 'I know you will want to talk to Robert. I'll leave you in his expert hands.'

For once too, Giovanni Battista Palomero had decided to act as someone who was not acting. 'Robert, I'm so glad about this,' he said in a natural tone of voice, not searching over his shoulder as he spoke as he usually did. 'The Aemelia deserves a success. I'm sure the public is going to respond to your magnificent initiative. It is a much-needed exhibition.'

Palomero did his stuff admirably on the stairs, beginning with the words, in English, 'Friends, Romans and countrymen,' which got a laugh at least from the British contingent, and from a few Italians who wanted to show they had read some Shakespeare. Robert kept his own speech short. He thanked the Minister and the people who had made the exhibition possible, then gave most space to talking about Cellini and how fortunate they had been to gather together so much of his major work, and such a representative selection.

The waiters were released, and had a hard time fighting their way through the mass of guests snatching at their trays from all sides. Battista was handed a glass of champagne, and met some of the staff whom Robert had asked to come up. Needless to say he fastened on to Gabbi, the most attractive woman present. Robert doused the involuntary geyser of jealousy that spouted. Had he not decided, in the interest of his own dignity if nothing else, to end all that?

The din of voices became deafening. The food and drink seemed to disappear in minutes. Quite a number of guests were already gathering at the foot of the stairs, barely retained by a length of rope and the two guardians he had posted there. Robert thought it was time to lead Palomero upstairs. If they did not go soon they would be fighting their way up with the mob.

As they reached the top of the stairs, Robert relaxed. If the Minister was jostled now it would not matter. He would surely only be impressed by the animation? Of one thing he was sure, that the exhibition was the finest ever mounted on this artist.

They had excellent coverage, with pictures, in all the important newspapers, but at nine the next morning Robert was down in the hall. Things looked depressingly as usual. An old man in a black beret came in looking round him furtively as if he might be assaulted. It was not clear he even knew there was an exhibition. He was followed by a nun and a group of young schoolchildren who did know, then a steady trickle. Robert did his best to reassure Carmina, the two men he had put on the door, and the other two on the stairs whose job was to check and tear the tickets, all of whom were loyally worried. They couldn't expect it to get into spate on the first day, he said. Then he went back to his office.

At eleven there was a frantic call from Carmina. She needed help, she said excitedly. He rushed down. The hall was thronged, and a queue was beginning to build up. Already it extended through the front door, down the steps into the forecourt. He could see the car park was filling, with a line of cars coming in. Carmina was coping perfectly well, and the queue was moving reasonably fast, but Robert called in another of the guardians from one of the back rooms to help take the tickets on the stairs, and himself opened up the window on the other side of the booth and released the brake on the second turnstile. They were at it non-stop for an hour and a half. There had never been so many people in the museum at one time in its history.

On the next day the queue was forming before the doors opened. The press took up the excitement. The perfunctory notices on inner pages of the first day became front-page stories. Robert engaged extra staff. It was quite beyond their wildest speculation. Money poured in. On the second day five thousand people went through. And they were not only visiting the exhibition. The whole museum was thronged. It was as if the public had just discovered it.

On the third day he took Gabbi and Reg out to a celebratory dinner. Kate excused herself. They had a lot too much to drink. Gabbi said they – generously she actually said 'he' – had pushed the Aemelia into the first division. Would tourists, and tour companies, ever be able to leave it out of their itineraries in the future?

Robert felt an unfamiliar but solid exhilaration. He was aware his feelings had a source beyond the gate numbers. Perhaps they had nothing directly to do with the exhibition at all. Would things ever be quite the same for him again? Mortimer's behaviour was symbolic, he felt. Mortimer had slipped away before the end of the reception and had not even said goodbye to the Minister. Since then there had been radio silence.

An immodest thought occurred. Mortimer had always been a sensitive power barometer. Had all his recent doubts about himself been groundless? Was the truth the reverse of what he had thought? Could the exhibition prove to be a turning point in their relationship? Had it really been that simple?

And if things were to be different with Mortimer, could that mark a profounder change in his life in other ways? Would it change things between him and Kate somehow? If it did, he thought, he would always pay silent tribute to the young man whose appointment to the staff had seemed to be the starting point of his renaissance and, indeed, whose contribution to the exhibition itself had been so considerable.

14

Reg woke in a sweat of terror. He was being guillotined. Boulder-Head, stripped to the waist and wearing a black mask, had been busy hauling up the blade. His throat was on the block. In the crowd was Tunku Raschid, shaking his head ruefully.

He realised the crash was not the blade severing his head, but another clap of thunder. It was almost dark in his bedroom. He sat up with a new, waking fear, and snatched up his watch. Thank God, it was only mid-afternoon. But he felt dreadful. He got up, and sat on the edge of the bed.

His first clear thought was that he would have to call it off, and that was not unpleasing. It could be suicide in this weather. This was not to mention the fever that had attacked him, today of all days. He would need every ounce of his strength and mental alertness.

And yet underneath these considerations, he was already making corrections. If he did not go tonight, when would he? Kate's being in the building he could just about risk – if his plans for her removal did not work out. But not Robert's. And Robert's diary showed only three definite evening engagements during the whole exhibition period. The first evening he had had to abort. This was the second, and half the scheduled period of the exhibition had run.

He stood up and tried his legs. They worked – just about. He went into the bathroom, took off his vest which was wet through with sweat, and washed. He put on a dry shirt and the rest of his clothes, and went to the terrace window. The rain was bucketing, but there seemed to be a thinning of the cloud towards the south-west. As he stood there, he was conscious of a slight improvement in the light. Yes, definitely, there was clearer weather only a few miles away, and it was approaching the city. He had told them that morning it was on, in spite of the forecast. He would have to attempt it.

For a moment, fear seized him again. It was madness risking his neck. Or, if he kept that intact, his youth – inside an Italian prison.

Was it worth it? They had tested the suit several times, the pressure tent, the rest of the gear, but in other, simulated conditions. What did *they* lose if practice did not match up to theory and the alarms went off like banshees?

He would rather have done it his way, the way he had suggested to Raschid. He was more at home with locks – even magnetic locks. The pressure-case in which the Cellar stood could have been dealt with by smash and grab. It was true that Raschid's method left less chance of his being identified, but if he succeeded with it, would he really be able to brazen it out? He would almost certainly be a prime suspect, even if he left no traces. What sort of an alibi did he have? The museum knew he had gone home with a temperature, and the concierge downstairs had seen him come in, seen his grey face, and heard his croaking voice. But the police were not going to be greatly impressed with that. It would be Düsseldorf all over again, with less on his side, and a great deal more at stake. If by some lucky chance he did not finish up in the Queen of Heaven Prison here, it might well be Brazil instead, or some other God-forsaken extradition haven.

He forced himself to think of the alternative. He conjured again that vision of academic life – years in libraries, academic gossip, decades of hack teaching. He thought of the quarter of a million already snug in the Swiss account he had opened, the further quarter that Raschid had promised on completion, and what he would be able to do with it. He thought of the golden masterpiece, those two magnificent reclining figures, Neptune and Tellus, God of Sea and Goddess of Earth, the miracles of colour and movement round the base. Above all he thought of the excitement. All the impetus of his nature impelled him. How could he not do something as dynamic as this? Into what downward vortex of psycho-complexity would he be hurled if he withdrew? He would be condemning himself to that ever twisting, outer-spatial limbo in which most people so amiably turned. He knew that could never be for him.

The rain ceased suddenly, leaving the drains gurgling. He went out on to his small terrace. A bar of bright yellow light had appeared to the south-west. Definitely the storm was over. The squalling winds were dropping. They would, hopefully, be replaced any minute now by a persistent breeze from a constant point of the compass. When that happened, it had to be on. He forced himself to eat something. He was going to need it.

Soon after six, the kitchen curtain began to stir in the open window. Before he could have a second thought, he pulled out the aerial of the short-wave radio they had given him.

'Trajan. Trajan calling. Over.'

There was a pause. Could Kassim's man have thrown it in for the day, seeing the weather? That would let him off. But after a few moments there was a pregnant crackle.

'Trajan. Cato here. I hear you. Over.'

'Trajan says green. Over.'

The voice came – promptly this time. 'OK. Over and out.'

He climbed out of the skylight, crossed the roofs to the hotel, which was the last house on the block. He was prepared to have to force the roof door, but the laundress who used the washing lines on the roof had left it open. He descended in the service lift he had reconnoitred, and walked out, unseen, through the delivery door which gave on to a side street.

He knew that one of the trickiest parts of the operation was getting into the museum during the hour after closing, when it was still daylight. There were the four women, and almost certainly both Caines. If he was seen by any of them he would have to abort. He walked up the hill, having decided not to take a taxi. He did not want drivers coming forward, eager for insurance bribes. As he walked, he realised the breeze had dropped a notch or two and a ground mist seemed to be forming. Already long shrouds were slowly rising from the ground and threading between the pines. What would this mean?

Keeping out of sight, he approached the front of the building. The light was on in the hall. He could see Carmina in her box. It was gone half-past six. Giulia and her colleagues would be well away from the back of the building now and working their separate ways back to the hall, one in each wing on each floor. He began to move round the house, still keeping in the trees. The danger now would be the Caines. Robert's appointment was at eight, but it could not be certain what time he would leave. If he chose to come down when he was entering, that again would be cards. Although there was hardly any wind, thank God, at least the mist was thickening nicely.

The Caines were not on the balcony. Nevertheless, to be safe he went back to the side of the building before he broke cover. The police were nowhere to be seen. They did not come on duty till later. In the short time it would take him to cross the grass, he would be in full view to Giulia or her colleague working on the first floor if either happened to look out of the window. But with any luck they would be concentrating on their polishers.

He made the wall, and kept close to it as he doubled the corner. He could not now be seen by the Caines unless one of them came out and leaned over the balcony. He went into the court, entered the building through the courtyard door with his electronic key, and in a few seconds was up the back stairs to the first floor on the south side. He had decided before not to use the lift, in case the Caines heard it. He made his way through the medieval exhibit rooms towards the front of the house.

The first-floor cleaners were just finishing. Ahead of him, he heard the woman on this side clamping down the stairs with her machine. The other seemed already to have gone down. He followed her, stopping half-way down the first flight, where he was still out of sight from the hall. The downstairs women were also finishing. From their voices he could plot their positions, and Carmina's, below. Things were following the usual pattern. He heard the three outside women leave. Giulia was apparently still putting away the machines under the stairs. She came up then to tell Carmina she was finished, and also departed. He heard the rustle of Carmina's keys as she made for the switch cupboard under the stairs. He would have several safe seconds to nip across the landing to his room.

He made it comfortably. Through the interior, back window of the office that gave on to the hall, he saw Carmina emerge from under the stairs and make briskly for the front door. He saw her locking it from the outside. He was in, as far as he knew, unobserved. He drew a chair to the outside window of his room.

He saw the police arriving and deploying below, then Robert leaving in his car at 7.45. He pulled out the radio and reported. The next phase was going to be the most agonising – although, he

128

noted with satisfaction, the mist was thickening further. He could now only see the ground immediately below, and only the upper half of the pines. Another hour and the whole building would be engulfed. If Kate did not go out, he thought he would definitely risk the operation anyway.

But would she take the bait? Of one thing he was as sure as he could be. She had not, as he had guessed would be the case, said anything about his note to Robert. The grim expression she had worn since reading it had not modified, neither had he picked up any vibes from Robert on the two or three occasions he had seen him with Kate. Once he had caught her looking at him oddly. He had grinned back at her, and she turned away quickly. Did she suspect him of sending the note? Why should she? And it would not matter especially if she did. If it ever came out he would simply deny it.

To while away time he played patience on his desk. As he played, he imagined Kate up there in the flat, the phone ringing, his voice, which he had recorded for Kassim – and had taken care to make unrecognisable. He reckoned it was a fifty-fifty chance.

It was just after nine when he heard the car in front of the building. On his hands and knees he could just see through the hall to the forecourt. Out of the mist, he saw the brief loom of the headlights. They went out, flashed twice, then remained extinguished. It was the signal that it was the Tunku's man, posing as a taxi. So, Kate had phoned for a taxi and they had picked up the call on the line they had bugged. If they had gathered the name of the taxi firm they would have phoned it to cancel the taxi. If not, the taxi was to be intercepted and paid off by one of the Tunku's men in the second car down the road. Either way, it seemed to have gone smoothly. The police had not apparently noticed the car arrive. All to the good. What a shower they were. He returned to the outside window. In a couple of minutes he saw Kate briefly as she hurried along the unmade road below. She too seemed to be unobserved by the police. No other car came.

He heard the door of the parked car slam, and the engine restart. As the noise of the vehicle died away, Reg drew a long breath. Apart from Giulia, who was slightly deaf, he now had the place to himself.

Again he took out the radio. This time he signalled, 'Trajan, yellow,' to indicate Kate's departure.

Kassim's operator acknowledged, and used none of the code words that referred to wind speed and direction. This meant wind factors remained feasible, as they saw it at least. At this point the whole back-up function would be activated. He unlocked the cupboard and took out the suit, complete with the in-built oxygen pack and the carbon-monoxide waste bag, the aluminium bridge, and the pressure tent. He unzipped the suit and began to put it on.

The suit entirely covered his body. It had fitted soft shoes, and its outer surface, like that of the pressure bell, was electrically warmed. The system was fitted with a thermostat which switched it on and off whenever the suit varied more than a degree centigrade from the temperature of the surrounding air. This was well within the tolerance allowed on the infra-red sensors. Reg waited for the red light on his right sleeve to go out, then put on the light attached to the headgear, switched on the oxygen, pulled up the waste duct over his nose, closed the head visor, and finally donned the gloves. He had now to breathe in through his mouth and out through his nose.

He was shut off from the outside world. He heard the faint purr of the oxygen supply and the labour of his own breath. He felt the isolation deep-sea divers must experience. Thank goodness Robert had decided to put the exhibition on the first floor. He did not want this thing on for long with the vents shut. It was like being steam-cooked in his own body heat.

On the short journey up to the exhibition room there were four pressure pads, three of these under the stair-carpet on successive stairs in the flight that led from the mezzanine to the top landing. The bridge was just wide enough to span them, for which he was grateful – doing a leopard-crawl up the slippery banister was not his idea of a joke with this gear on. The fourth pad was on the first-floor landing, which was also carpeted to the wall, across the entrance to the exhibition room. This, as he had already realised, was going to be tricky, encumbered as he was. He could not use the bridge until the door was open, and he could only just reach the lock while keeping his feet out of trouble.

On the Friday before the exhibition opened, when most of the major exhibits had been scheduled to arrive, the museum had been closed. Robert had left him in charge for three hours with no one present except some of the guardians. Not only had he been able to arrange for the delivery of his gear during this period, posing as a Cellini exhibit, he had also had the time, through the driver of the phoney security vehicle, who was one of Raschid's men, to get a copy cut of the key to this door, with which Robert had entrusted him until his return.

He got the door unlocked, checked the thermostat on his wrist. All was well. The light was out. This was going to be the moment of truth. The stairs and landing had not been within the arc of any heat sensor. As the door opened he would be exposed to one and would know whether theory fitted with practice. If it didn't, he was to run for it. The second car would be two hundred yards down the road. He gently opened the door. There was a crack like a pistol shot.

He realised a moment later it was the parquet floor, which had chosen this moment to express itself. A merciful silence followed. He placed the bridge and, stepping carefully across it, entered the room.

His light glinted on the gold and silver medallions. As he approached the end of the room, through the open door into the second room, for a moment it illuminated the ghastly stare of the Medusa's severed head, gleamed darkly over the helmeted Perseus who held the head aloft, and a bead of light ran up and down the horizontally-held sword.

Robert had wondered if Cellini would have approved of the exhibition, Reg thought momentarily. More relevantly, would he have approved of this operation, of Raschid? Of course, if it had happened to suit him. 'A villain', had been Robert's description of him. Was he not three times in prison, once for murder? They didn't go in for effete niceties in those days.

Reg made a silent salutation to the dead artist.

His concentration fixed on the Salt-Cellar standing magnificently before him, with just the glass case between him and its liberation. What was it worth – ten million, twenty? It was anyone's guess, as it would never be for sale. Where would the Tunku put it? Would he display it openly in that salon sometimes, like the Frans Hals? How did these felonious collectors operate? Were they content to gloat in secret, or did they display their ill-gotten gains to each other? He was sorry that he would probably never know.

What he did now know for sure was that this was not the first time the Tunku had entered the field of grand larceny. Quite apart from those empty spaces on his study wall and the details of the Amsterdam robbery which Razzy had sent him, Reg had had the impression all along that he had been included in a practised team. Almost certainly, somewhere, perhaps in the Sultan's Palace, was an Aladdin's hoard of treasures, of which this, perhaps, would become the centre-piece.

He unhooked the bell-tent from his waist, to which it was fastened for ease of carrying. The thermostat light on his wrist was still comfortingly out. Placing the tent alongside the display case, he unzipped the side, stepped inside it, and draped the tough fibreglass material over his head. The zip could be operated from both inside and outside the tent. He used the inner zip lever to close the tent.

He pulled out the lightweight telescoped metal rods in the four corners, which tightened the envelope and held it steady. With the tent standing securely, he unzipped three sides of the three-foot square on the side of the tent facing the showcase, and put in position on the showcase glass the four strips of material, adhesive on one side, magnetic on the other, that would marry with the electromagnetically-activated tape fixed round the aperture on the outside of the tent. He opened the cover of the small box, housed in a pocket on one wall of the tent, which contained the minute battery of the magnet, and switched on. Holding the material taut with outward pressure by means of two finger loops sewn into the fibreglass, he pushed it towards the tapes on the top side of the aperture and felt the sharp tugs as the tapes engaged. With downward as well as outward pressure, he did the same for the bottom side. This had the effect of also securing the two side pieces.

Now he was ready to inflate the inside of the bell to rather less air pressure than he would require for entering the showcase. He pressed the button that controlled the compressed-air unit. In a few seconds, the canvas pulled taut. The junction tapes that joined it to the showcase held. He switched off.

He had tried out the apparatus in the Tunku's castle under Kassim's supervision, and it had worked perfectly. But that had been with another showcase with another pressure system. Would it work now? He was getting hot. Sweat was pouring down his back and gathering along the elastic of his underpants. His pulse rate must have gone up to a dangerous level. He feared he would pass out before he had finished the job.

He drew from his pocket the retractable metal ruler which opened out into a square of the exact dimensions required, and which had rubber suckers that gripped the glass. With the greatest care, he attached it to the glass. Next he returned to the pressure-control gear, set the dial beside it to the exact pressure inside the case and pressed the button again. As the pressure began to rise he felt the discomfort in his ears. The light went off to indicate parity with the showcase pressure. He drew out the glass-cutter. With strong bold strokes, he made the four incisions.

He unfastened the small sucker grip that was attached to the inside of the canvas beside the window. He placed it against the incised portion of the glass and gave a sharp tug. The glass came back sweetly, and uncracked. There was a spare piece of glass fitted inside the tent, but it was infinitely preferable to use the same piece he had cut out, whose dimensions could be guaranteed to be accurate. For a moment, intent, and now relieved at his success with the glass, he did not notice that the pressure-operated alarms remained silent.

Realising that they were and that so far his luck was holding, he paused several moments to rally his strength. Then he lifted the Salt-Cellar into the tent. He took off the protective covering from the eight instantly adhesive, mitred glass strips, and placed four of them, one by one, round the aperture on the inside of the showcase. He had cut the aperture accurately. The mitred corners of the frame joined firmly, and the four sides overlapped the square on the inward side by a good inch. He replaced the severed panel, which was now held from falling forwards into the showcase by the frame and, holding the glass in position with his left hand, fixed the other four strips to form an outer frame on the outside of the case. For safety, he additionally taped the four sides. He reset the pressure-control dial to the room level, pressed the button, and set himself to endure again the pain in his ears.

At last the red pressure-gauge button winked out. He unzipped the tent. The glass frame held. He put the Cellar outside the tent, deactivated the magnetic seal that joined the tent to the case, retracted the corner-stays, repacked the shrivelled material into its carrier, and reattached it to his waist.

The Cellar was heavy, but liftable. As he carried it to the door, a surge of fever returned. It was like a tropical hothouse inside the suit. He felt a violent wave of nausea and faintness.

He recrossed the bridge, put the Cellar on the landing floor, returned to take away the bridge and to shut the door. Then he collapsed. He opened the visor of the head-dress just in time. He sat, gasping, for fully half a minute.

There was still silence inside and outside the museum. Recovering somewhat, he then relocked the door, folded the bridge, attached it to his belt for easy carrying, and prepared to mount the three floors to the attics. There were no more heat sensors to negotiate and he would not need to shut the visor again, but he would need all his strength.

That Friday before the exhibition, he had stored the rest of the gear in the attic, some twenty yards from the roof door. He had to use the bridge again on the steps up to the door, where there was another pressure pad, then he was able to step out into the welcome cool of the mist. He placed the Salt-Cellar on the lead floor of the flat central area between the two sloping roofs, and went back to fetch the gear, which had been neatly packed into one case. He unpacked the balloon envelope of the Cloud-Hopper, the chair-harness and cylinder, the flying wires and clips, the burner, and the especially constructed, light metal box which would hold the Cellar and hang from a strap round his neck. He thought of the police again, prowling below. Surely, in the deathly quiet they would hear something?

On his reconnaissance of the roof, Reg had discovered the museum air-conditioning duct, right in the middle of the flat area. To maintain an even temperature for the museum exhibits it was on night and day, and it could be used for the initial cold-filling of the envelope. It would be totally silent, and would eliminate the necessity of an inflator which he would otherwise have needed. He positioned the envelope near the duct and spread it out to leeward on the sloping tiles. Next he attached the burner to the chair-harness. With a length of nylon rope he anchored the chair to a firmly-bedded iron bar he had also reconnoitred – it seemed to be the remains of a flagpole tripod – and fixed the releasing mechanism of the rope, so that he would leave no trace behind him. Finally he pulled the envelope over the duct, keeping the input vent of the envelope open with the two metal rods that were stowed with a clamp to the burner.

The filling would take three or four minutes. He glanced upwards. The wind had backed to the south. The mist was moving, but painfully slowly. With any justice, he would get a knot or two more higher up, but he would need at least five to clear the city to the north. The single propane cylinder gave an hour's flying time. What if he came down in the suburbs to the north of the Tiber? He imagined the scene, waiting half an hour perhaps before Kassim's men got to him.

The envelope began to lift and roll, and his imaginings were abruptly severed by a more immediate anxiety. Normally, even for a Cloud-Hopper, one had at least two hands for launching. Though he had practised several times alone, and it was comparatively sheltered here between the chimney stacks, the rolling, even in a slight breeze, could quickly get out of hand. That duct really had been a brainwave of his. It was one less item to manipulate.

He had to get the timing exactly right. As the rigging stirred and the vent opened almost fully, he climbed into the harness and secured himself on both sides with metal clips, at the shoulders and thighs. He lifted the Cellar and felt its weight on the strap round his neck. Finally, he drew out the radio from his interior pocket and made contact. 'Trajan. Trajan calling.'

The reply came faintly, but thankfully there. 'Cato, receiving, over.'

'Trajan. Red.'

'Cato. Go.'

He waited further seconds in the humid silence. Then the radio-tripped, diversionary sirens began, fixed into trees on either side of the building. They began with a low growl and grew to a full-throated wail. With any luck they would keep the police busy for long enough, and make enough racket to cover his ascent. As he fought with the balloon to keep it stable, he was dimly aware of whistles below. At what seemed a calm moment, he plunged. He pulled the lever. The pilot caught, and the burner went.

Kassim's burner was the best on the market and relatively silent, but in the noiseless mist, even against the sirens, it sounded as if someone had opened the door to hell. If they heard it, or Giulia, despite her deafness, and they realised what was going on, how long would it take them to break in downstairs, mount the stairs, and find the roof door?

Minutes seemed like light years. Then at last the envelope began to lift. He let out a few feet of slack on the anchor-rope. The seat began to leave the ground. He went with it, and as his feet left the ground and dangled, he gratefully felt the transfer of the weight of the Cellar from his neck on to his thighs. He watched the thermometer fitted to the top of the burner above him. The needle passed through seventy, eighty, then ninety degrees centigrade. He had thought about a hundred would be the mark, ten more than usual. He made a final setting on the electronic navigational aid strapped to his wrist, and released one end of the anchor-rope from the clip. He watched it snake under the bar without fouling, and felt himself sharply levitate.

In a few moments, as if rising from the sea like some mythical creature, he broke through the mist into clear moonlight and began to drift northward as the balloon climbed.

Though he had had only two practice sessions in the Monti Sabini some miles west of the Tunku's castle, the balloon was relatively easy to handle – easier than the gondola-types he had flown in at the university club – but the breeze remained alarmingly sluggish, even at two thousand feet. He went up another five hundred. There was a slight improvement, but he guessed it was still only just over three knots. It was obvious he was not going to clear the city. But the good news was that he could see both the radio mast and the Hilton Hotel rising clear of the mist dead in line with his direction. If there was no wind change, he should be able to come down somewhere short of them in the Foro Italico region at the foot of the hill on which they stood, one of the areas they had decided on as feasible and which they had awarded a code name. This was an advantage. None of them wanted an explicit landing fix going over the radio. He only hoped he would not land on one of the sloping roofs of the Olympic stadia, or in the Tiber. But even this would be a great deal preferable to going on and finishing in the labyrinthine suburbs to the north.

Twenty minutes out, he decided. His course had been steady. He could well use the spare propane a Foro Italico drop would give him. In this mist he might well have to go up several times before he found a flat space. He pulled out the radio and made what he hoped would be the penultimate contact. Kassim had assured him their frequency was not listed as being in official use in Rome, but there was always a chance of somewhere like Fiumicino Control doing a scan and picking up something.

'Trajan. Trajan, picnic – Fido,' he announced.

'Fido' had been the Tunku's contribution – the F and I for Foro Italico. Raschid had been in a skittish mood that first evening at the castle, with his English upbringing ironically apparent. 'Picnic' meant a landing.

He had confirmation of receipt. There was a different operator now, he noticed. Not unexpectedly, when he thought about it. He would not be dealing with headquarters now, but with one or more of the three cars which, hopefully, were fanned out somewhere down there in the mist, tailing him.

There was a calm period in which he realised how ill he was. The fever was back, and a throbbing headache. If he came through, he would get back to the flat and sleep for a week, he thought. To take his mind off the self-pity, he thought about Robert. If Robert got the boot because of the theft, he would be sorry. He did not deserve such treatment. If Robert did not get the sack, he would stay on at the museum for a time. It would be a necessity anyway, until things had cooled. It would not be a total bore.

The flashing light of a helicopter half a mile to the west brought him out of his reverie. It was on a divergent course, Reg noticed thankfully, but the incident realerted every flagging nerve in his body. He checked altitude on the digital clock beside the pilot light and, deciding to drop a thousand feet, reached for the 'red line' that controlled the vent on the top of the envelope. He cursed himself for not making more careful observation on his ground reconnaissance of the relationship between the Hilton and the sports complex. His impression was he was a little too far to the right.

He dropped another thousand. The mist was thicker here. At five hundred feet he was nearly into it. At the museum he had been free of it at two hundred feet or less. He felt a sudden drop in the temperature, then after a few seconds it rose again. Could it be the river he was passing over? He decided to risk it and went down. In seconds the moonlight was switched off like a light and he was in the gently swirling nothingness.

He kept one hand on the burner, the other on the red line, and stared downwards between his legs. He dropped to two hundred. Still, nothing. He remembered the tall apartment blocks just beyond the Foro. He kept a look-out ahead now as well as down. At any moment he could smash into the side of one of them.

This factor made him take the plunge. At fifty feet he saw what seemed a low building directly ahead of him. He gave a five second burn and cleared it. Immediately he pulled the plug on the balloon.

He had overdone it, and the ground came up suddenly at him in a rush. He stretched his head forward, kept his legs bent at the knee, and clutched the steel flying wires just above his head like a parachutist. At the moment of impact he tried to hoist himself upwards to lessen the shock to himself and to the Salt-Cellar and, simultaneously, to turn the seat so that he fell sideways. He fell heavily on his left side and felt a piercing pain in his ribs.

For moments he lay gasping and in agony, jerked and tugged by the settling balloon. Then he realised that whatever he had landed on was hard and red. The mist thinned for a moment, and he saw beside him a tennis umpire's chair. He realised in some marginal region of his mind that he must be in the tennis club where the championships were played, and that he needed to get out of this harness fast. In agony, he managed to unclip the burner, and to relieve himself of the Cellar. Lying on his uninjured side, he listened. There was not a sound except a drip somewhere. He pulled out the radio and made contact.

'Trajan. Fido. I say again, Fido. We have picnic.'

138

There was a garbled noise the other end that sounded like a wild western shoot-out.

'A red shale tennis court. Several together.' He threw caution to the winds. 'For Christ's sake hurry.'

He must have passed out. He came to, shivering, though he knew the air was still warm. There were figures busy about him. They seemed to be collecting the envelope and the rest of the gear. The Cellar, he noted, had vanished.

He groaned. 'Hey,' he tried to say. 'I've at least one rib broken, probably an arpeggio.'

He thought he said that. The next thing he knew was that he had sticking plaster across his mouth, that he was being turned roughly and agonisingly on his back. Then he knew nothing.

15

Among the strong precepts on which Kate based her life was the idea that one got on with things. She tended to think that people who did not, and who examined their motives and those of other people, were shilly-shalliers. Implied in this was the idea that there were a number of matters one did not talk or even think about.

She would have had no difficulty in diagnosing the origin of this trait. In her teens she had had a strong relationship with her father, whom she had deeply loved and respected. But she had learnt that there were certain matters he would always remain silent about. She did once ask an oblique question about Mother, whom she also loved in a different way, but who, always immensely busy, seemed to her sometimes to be inexplicably and possibly unjustly on the outside of that close companionship she and Father shared. He simply changed the subject. Had he heard?

Another later attempt taught her that he had heard perfectly well. It was intended she learnt that there were certain subjects in life which, like old wrecks or submerged reefs, were marked with a buoy, to be left as they were, circumnavigated. She came to accept this with all the other wisdom she learnt at his feet.

Robert's less than fully explicit account of his day in Tarquinia with the convent girls some months ago, and now the anonymous note, would normally have fallen into this category of dismissal. Smut, calumny, faithlessness could surely be atrophied by a simple absence of attention? But she had caught herself out in an inconsistency. The normal way would have been to mention the note en passant to Robert, or simply to thrust it into his hands. She would have adjudged even an examination of his face at the moment of disclosure an unwarranted prurience on her part. But she had done no such thing. She had done nothing, and each day that passed made it less likely that she would do anything in the future. Yet she could not forget it.

The thunderstorm that had crashed about the city for most of the day had unnerved her. She usually liked storms, but today the venomous flickering of the lightning and the reckless aggression of the thunder had seemed like a personal siege. The storm must have circled. It seemed to go and return several times. In between, there were drenching bouts of tropical rain, like long periods of retribution following violence.

Now at last it had stopped. In the late afternoon, yellow sunlight had bloomed for a period behind the retreating black clouds, raising the temperature and the humidity. Just before dark a dense mist rose from the ground, obscuring what would have been clear moonlight. She went again to the sitting-room window and drew aside the curtain. It was thick, white, and viscous. She could not see the pines. It made her think of Eliot's line – 'the fog, that rubs its back upon the window panes'. She was alarmed from a new direction. The mist was dead, isolating. Battered by the storm she now felt washed-up, middle-aged, abandoned, forgotten.

Robert had gone to a museum directors' dinner. The prospect of an evening alone stretched ahead of her like an abyss. She walked listlessly about the flat. She went into the kitchen, intending to boil herself an egg. She decided she was not hungry. She went back into the sitting-room to read, but soon put the book down. The words were lifeless and meant nothing to her. Some mending perhaps...

While she sat there, transfixed with inertia, the phone shrilled, as if it were an emergency.

She jumped up. She said 'pronto', and there was an odd pause as if someone had got a wrong number and was deciding to put the phone down without speaking. 'Pronto?' she said again.

There was a click. 'Tonight's the night,' she heard. 'Go immediately to the Val d'Oro restaurant in the Appia Antica. Your proof is sitting there.' The caller rang off.

She stood, stunned, the receiver in her hand. 'Who are you?' she said, fruitlessly tapping the cradle of the phone when the line was already dead.

It had been an English voice, male she thought, but muffled. The tone was dead-pan, expressionless, somehow electronically scrambled. Obviously it had been recorded.

It was undoubtedly someone up to no good, someone maybe who wanted to break into the flat. She remembered the wording of the note she had received. 'Await a further communication which will supply the proof.' It was unsophisticated. Most likely of all it was a teenage prank.

She quite decided she would not go. Of course she would not go. She switched on the television, though she had no intention of watching. It was noise she wanted. The mist had muffled all sound outside, like snow. She could not hear the usual distant roar of traffic.

She got out her mending bag and plunging her hand into a pair of tights searched for the hole. She could phone Robert, she thought. This would have a dual purpose, to tell him about the call, and to check that he was at the dinner. But she realised she had not taken in the name of the restaurant where he was. She was only certain it was not the Val d'Oro. Then she considered phoning Gabriella Bruneschi. Her home number must be in the book. If Gabriella answered, she would not need to say anything, and this would prove the call was not genuine. But she did not do this. Vaguely, she thought the call could be traced. She certainly would not do *that*.

Finally, in a minor fever, she began to think she might go. She could take a taxi. She would only be out for an hour or so, and she would set her mind at rest once and for all. He would not be there. She would prove that it was malice, or a hoax.

Suddenly, she got up and dialled a taxi firm. She told them to have the car wait outside the museum. They said it would be ten minutes.

She went down, making sure to reactivate the alarm at their end of the palazzo when she reached the ground floor. She ceased then to think of anything except her objective. She hurried round the building, walking on the grass, glad of the mist that no doubt was protecting her from being stopped by the police and from having to tell a lie. The taxi was already waiting in the forecourt with its lights off.

The man said nothing as she got in and gave the address. He started the engine, put the lights on, and moved off. The mist was so thick they had to crawl. But as they moved down the hill towards the Piazza del Popolo it cleared a bit. The street lights appeared and visibility was marginally better.

The restaurant was some way down the endless Appia Antica,

outside the town, and it took longer than she thought it would to get there. But at last they arrived. She told the man to wait.

The restaurant seemed to be part of a club. It had a pool. Standing beside it, she could see into the well-lit dining room. There was only one diner. The waiters were in a huddle. But she had better make sure, she thought, and she did not like the taxi driver observing her like this. She slipped inside.

As she stood in the doorway, confirming what she had seen from outside, the head waiter approached.

'Cerca qualcuno, Signora?'

Robert was not there. An enormous relief swept through her.

'Yes,' she said, wanting almost to embrace the man. 'I'm looking for my husband. Something urgent has come up. I thought he might be here. His name is Dr Caine. Has he a booking for this evening?'

Clearly, bookings for this evening did not abound. But they went together to a large book propped on a lectern, lit by a shaded strip light. No, there was no booking in the name of Caine.

Kate sat back in the taxi and closed her eyes, chiding herself happily for her stupidity. She could go back and no one need know she had been out. If she bumped into the police she could think of some story.

It was only after twenty minutes she realised the mist had thickened and they did not seem to be going in the direction of the Borghese Gardens. None of the buildings they were passing was familiar. Was it possible the taxi driver was lost? She asked him. He was leaning forwards, peering into the gloom. She got a grunt for an answer, and remembered that from her brief glimpse of his face at the museum she had fancied he was not Italian. Probably an ignorant immigrant. Well, let him sort it out, she decided. There was no meter, and she would pay him a reasonable fare for the distance to the restaurant and back. He would ask a passer-by and find the way eventually. She was in no hurry.

16

Robert was bored. Neither of the two people he had hoped to see had come to the dinner. He looked helplessly round the table at which he would be imprisoned for another hour or two.

Opposite him Demerero, spearhead of the Historic Monuments lobby, was holding forth about the latest Government proposals to extend the much needed Metro through what would inevitably be, whatever part of Rome you liked to choose, what Demerero called 'the priceless seams of antiquity'. His ardent listeners fed and flattered his ego with smaller pieces of outraged sentiment. Robert felt a traitor. As an antiquarian, he should surely support them? What would he have felt if someone wanted to drive an autostrada through one of the Etruscan sites? And yet, in this case, inasmuch as he had an opinion at all, it was weighted towards the needs of the living. He objected to the automatic elitist high-mindedness, the enjoyment, for its own sake, of the manipulation of power. How outraged really was Demerero? On Robert's right sat Ludini, the Vatican Library man. He was complaining of the failure of the rich Vatican Treasury to put funds his way, while priceless books mouldered on his shelves.

Were they a cornered breed, Robert asked himself? All of them seemed to be on a permanent whinge about something. Was culture on the run in an economy-mad Europe, pursued by the Furies of materialism? Probably. But then, except at rare times in history such as the Renaissance, when art and the material world had briefly enjoyed such a miraculous marriage, had that not always been so?

The success of the exhibition might be making him feel smug, he thought. Well, why not? Was not the exhibition a perfect example of how academic excellence could be made to march hand in hand with popular enthusiasm? Thanks be, very largely, to Reginald Griffin for the latter, and to himself for finding, and promoting, him.

He had to endure three long speeches, and two hours, before he could decently slip away. It was nearly eleven, he saw. He wished he had not come, not the least when in the street outside he found the mist had thickened. It could be quite difficult up in the Borghese, where street lighting was sparse. The thought crossed his mind that it was just the night someone might choose for an attempt on the collection. He should not have come out.

It took him twenty minutes to get through the city centre. Figures, other car lights, emerged, floated briefly, and receded in the white, silent world. He had never known a mist as dense as this in Rome, rare as mist was at all. Crouching forwards, the windscreen wiper ploughing, he crawled, his eyes on the curb, all his faculties alert. Once a pedestrian lurched into the side of the car.

When at last he turned into the museum forecourt, he was aware of a blue light flashing. Approaching, he saw that it was a police car. A figure came up. It was a policeman, presumably one of the people on guard duty.

'Identity?'

Robert ignored the usual indifferent surliness of Italian police. 'The name's Caine. I'm the Director of the museum and live here. Is everything all right?'

The man examined his driving licence without giving an answer. At that moment another figure emerged. It was one of the officers. Robert had met him. He said something to the man, and Robert got back his licence.

'Everything's all right, yes, Dr Caine. No cause for alarm. We've established it must have been a hoax.'

'*What* was a hoax?'

'About two hours ago someone let a siren off, out there in the trees. Our men immediately closed on the entrances as planned in the event of anything suspicious. But of course there was nothing. It took us some time to locate the siren in the mist. It was nailed to the upper branches of a tree, with its own battery, and radio triggered. Either someone's idea of a joke, or the beginning of something that didn't happen. I'm doubling the guard tonight.'

'A siren?'

'Yes. Ordinary factory type.'

'It couldn't have been a diversion of some kind?'

'That was our thought. We've searched the exterior of the building thoroughly. There's nothing amiss, and certainly nothing came out through a door. All the window grilles are intact.'

'You haven't been inside?'

'No call to. It meant breaking in the front door and triggering the alarms unnecessarily.'

Robert relaxed, until he remembered Kate.

'My wife – did you contact her?'

'We telephoned. There was no answer.'

'But she's in. She's been in all evening.'

'We contacted the lady in the ground floor flat at the back. She too said she thought Mrs Caine was in, but that if she wasn't she had probably gone out with you.'

'But I told Giulia Mrs Caine would be in this evening.'

The policeman shrugged. Robert's anxiety was reborn.

'I'd be glad if you would come up to my flat with me to make sure my wife is all right. It's most unlike her not to answer the phone. I'm sure she hasn't gone out.'

As they came out of the lift, Robert could see the hall light was on in the flat. He fumbled for his keys and felt an unpleasant brush of fear. There were three locks, one a Yale type, and two stronger, turn-over bolts. If Kate was in, almost certainly the bolts would not be drawn. She had an indifferent scorn for would-be intruders. He tried the Yale first. It did not open the door. Panicking, he rolled back the two bolts.

He rushed in. Lights were on in the kitchen and the sitting-room, but Kate was not there. He went into the bedroom and switched on the light, thinking she might be asleep. The room was empty.

As he stood with the police officer in the sitting-room, baffled and alarmed, they heard a noise outside. They had left the front door open. They both realised it was the lift. It had been summoned from below and had begun its descent. They looked at each other, and the officer drew out his portable radio. At that moment one of the men below called him.

'Mrs Caine has just returned in a taxi. She's coming up.'

They waited for the ponderous ascent to be completed. The doors stirred and opened. Kate appeared. Robert stepped forward.

'Kate – are you all right?'

'Of course I'm all right. I got bored and went to the cinema. Good evening, officer. Everything all right here?'

Robert had an unpleasant feeling that it was not. He asked the policeman to accompany him downstairs to check that all was well in the museum. The man agreed reluctantly. He plainly thought his time was being wasted.

17

The woman hummed as she bent to the metal tub beside her on the flat roof-top. She took pegs from her mouth and hung the clothes in a lengthening, miscellaneous string. After the storm the day before, the September day had dawned without blemish.

Yet before she went down, a faint anxiety she had felt returned to her. Tucking the tub under her arm, she went to the parapet. He was still there, lying on the rough grass bank just by the first arch of the bridge, where the junkies usually slept. She had seen him first from the flat. Something about the position he lay in had caught her eye, awkward somehow. It reminded her of one of those modern paintings of Christ on the cross. The limbs and joints were not right, sort of back to front. She turned away quickly. Poor devil, sleeping down there without cover in that filth. The police, or the Government, should do something.

Later she went out to shop. She didn't have to go along the river bank, the back way was quicker, but it did occur to her that she should check if he was still there. He was.

On her way back with a full basket, she came the same way and he was in exactly the same posture, motionless. She looked around, but there was not a soul to consult, let alone a policeman. It was not a populous part of the city for pedestrians, and it would be a waste of time trying to stop one of the cars flashing past. In two minds, she thought she should go down. If he were ill or drugged she could get help. Maybe if he were hungry she could give him a bit off the loaf.

She could not see him as she went down the steps beside the bridge, which were on the far side from where he lay. She negotiated the steps with care, sideways. The basket was heavy and her legs not good. At the bottom she paused to recover from the effort. What a stink the Tiber had after the summer.

Then she walked under the arch and saw him.

'Oh, my God,' she said aloud, and crossed herself.

He wore jeans and a shirt, stained horribly with blood round the neck and shoulders, and, surprisingly, gloves. He was lying on his stomach. One leg seemed to stick out almost at right angles to the other, unnaturally. Then she noticed that what she had thought was dark hair was a seething ball of flies. *There was no head.* At that point she put down the basket of shopping and ran.

Two hours later – the Roman police did not hurry to incidents of this sort, particularly in this locality – it was established from examining the underclothes that the headless corpse was probably British. A St Michael label was found on the neck of the shirt, which a cosmopolitan detective recognised from a recent Marks and Spencer shopping spree in London. If this information was correct, it was mildly annoying. Foreign deaths usually caused more bother. Consuls could get active. Political questions could be asked. Suicide became murder, murder conspiracy.

Later in the day, when investigating the theft of the Cellini masterpiece from the Villa Aemelia, the police learnt that a British employee at the museum was missing. This made the body a great deal more interesting. The apparent murder was elevated into quite a different category.

Part Four

~ ~ ~ ~ ~ ~ ~ ~ ~ ~ ~

18

'I feel it's the least I can do for the poor blighter,' Robert said. 'If that ghastly corpse really is Reg's.'

Kate was at her electronic typewriter. After all these years she had never learnt to type. Her two single fingers, protruding from clenched fists, hung predatorily over the keyboard. She made sharp, stabbing movements like a bird taking grubs. She continued working. 'You still doubt it, do you?' she said. Her tone was derisory.

Despite this, he went on. For God's sake, he needed to talk to someone. 'The body was certainly his stature. As I say, I identified the watch and signet ring they'd found, and his clothes.'

'And the glass-cutter in the pocket, the particles of glass you say forensic identified as identical with the glass in the display cabinet?'

'I know. But still I couldn't be absolutely sure. What I can't understand is why anyone wanting to kill him would go to the ghastly lengths of severing the head. If Reg stole the Salt-Cellar and they killed him in order to wrest it from him as the police are suggesting, why shouldn't they allow him to be identified as the original thief?'

'I should have thought the police gave an adequate explanation of that.'

'Mafia brutality? An example of some sort to others not towing the line? It's just possible of course. But it all seems a bit glib to me. Or, rather, too complex.'

Kate was staring at the page of handwriting she was copying. 'If I were you I should let sleeping dogs lie,' she said.

'What do you mean by that?'

'What I say.'

'How can I leave things when I'm not absolutely sure that body was Reg's?'

She got up to lift down the dictionary from the shelf above. 'Because if you mess about, you're likely to get yourself into bigger trouble than you're in already.'

He gaped at her. 'What on earth are you saying, Kate? What trouble am I in?'

'You appointed the man, didn't you?'

'Of course I did.'

'I don't know why I trouble to advise you. But if I were you, I shouldn't bother about a funeral. Let someone else take care of it.' She found the spelling of the word she was looking for, snapped the book shut and put it to one side. 'Look, if you don't mind, I've got to finish this.'

What had got into her lately? Her mixture of innuendo and casual aloofness maddened him. 'For Christ's sake, Kate. A young man who worked for us – whatever he did – may have been slaughtered. Is that all you can raise, your shoulders?'

She levelled a pale stare in his direction. She looked, he thought, just as her father had when freezing off someone he thought was taking liberties with his eminence. 'I do find it difficult to get excited about a felon of this magnitude, certainly, dead or alive.'

He felt himself flush crimson. 'Reg...' he began.

She smiled thinly. 'Was rather a friend of yours, wasn't he?'

'I liked him, yes.'

'That of course was obvious. You seemed to be alone in your partiality, however.'

'I wasn't the only person to like him. Anyway, a funeral has nothing to do with liking. It's a question of common decency.'

'More common than decent, in my view.'

He was furious. Her inferiority complex, for as such he now openly enunciated it to himself, based on her father's struggle to gain social as well as scientific recognition in another less egalitarian age, seemed absurd and anachronistic. 'You know what's wrong with you, you're still carrying round your father's burden,' he found himself saying. '*His* acerbity and social prickliness I could understand. Yours is just a wilful habit you won't let go.'

Kate straightened her back. At least he had exploded her into a reaction. 'Habits we're speaking of, are we? You talk of acerbity. Couldn't we also speak of complacency and sloth?'

He teetered on the brink of total explicitness. This standing issue between them had been thought, hinted at, but never spoken.

For his part, this was because he had always believed that however clear one might be about one's attitudes in private, the overt is revolution, revolution is overthrow and annihilation, and it is at the slow inner levels where really constructive changes are made, over long periods – planned changes, under constraint.

His instinct now was to withdraw. But he had a vision of Reg's living face, grinning humorously, urging him on. He remembered how Reg had talked of 'women', always in the plural like that, as a deep-sea fisherman might speak of swordfish to be hooked and reeled in.

But for no apparent reason, his mood changed abruptly. He realised he did not want to quarrel with Kate. Ironically, at the moment where it had become possible to do so, he felt only an indifference to her, even perhaps a distant sympathy. Probably, he thought, she could not help herself. His anger evaporated. Instead, as if stepping suddenly from a chrysalis, in spite of the appalling situation he felt an unexplained lightness.

'I have perhaps been complacent,' he said.

'Pathetically so.'

'That also has become a habit over years.'

Her look puzzled him. Was it one of triumph or of terror?

He left her to her article. Leaving aside other considerations, he was too busy to lock antlers with her. Their conversation had been the result of a few minutes' break in the middle of a frantic morning. He had just had to get out of the office.

In addition to the fuss the theft had caused – police, the press, the Italian Ministry, the indemnity officers – because of the considerable increase in the gate the notoriety had brought about, he had managed to extend the exhibition a further week. He half-wished he had not. For himself and several of the curatorial staff, the afternoon break disappeared. He was working fourteen hours a day non-stop. Coffee, sandwiches, and soggy, greasy, paper-wrapped pizzas were delivered at intervals to the offices. In the evenings he seldom got upstairs until nine. He had been eating, falling into bed, sleeping fitfully, until it all started again.

But his conversation with Kate decided him at least about the funeral. He came to accept that the body must be Reg's. He had been guilty of wishful thinking to imagine it wasn't. Reg had pulled a giant con, probably from the start, and he had been gulled. He may as well recognise it. But he still could not accept that it had all been cynicism. You can't fake personality, and the memory of Reg's apparently uncomplex, guiltless humour lived on untarnished. As soon as he had a moment, he would arrange things. He told the police of his intention. They made no objection. Forensic had finished their post-mortem.

The exhibition ended, and the last exhibits safely left the premises. No relative of Reg's had come forward in spite of world-wide press coverage. Robert mentioned at a staff meeting that he was organising the funeral as there appeared to be no family and that, in spite of what Reg appeared to have done, he thought the museum should pay for it.

The announcement was met with silence. But he did not think there was any hostility, merely an indifferent relief that the matter was being dealt with by someone else. Gabbi more or less confirmed this when he asked her afterwards.

'They've got used to your doing the decent thing for them,' she said. 'If you'd said, "Tip the bastard in the Tiber," they'd probably have been up in arms about it and become high-mindedness personified. As it is, by silence, they get it both ways, don't they? They don't commit themselves to any sympathy for Reg, and can't be accused of lacking humanity.'

'Will any of them come to the funeral?'

'It depends on how you word the notice. Urge them, however you say it, and they'll come, and grumble behind your back. No urging, and they probably won't. Of course, they're now all saying it was predictable, that they always thought there was something odd about Reg.'

'As you did.'

'I didn't mean in that way. I simply objected to him trying to get off with me. And he had the sense to take no for an answer.'

How typically fair-minded of her, Robert thought. It would have been so easy for her to take an I-told-you-so attitude. She had done nothing of the sort. In the busy weeks before and during the exhibition he had succeeded in muting his feelings for her. How could he do otherwise when any repetition of what had happened at Tarquinia would lead to his overt humiliation? Now, her sympathy reawakened all his feelings.

He wanted to ask her if she would come to the funeral, but all he said was: 'I'm not pushing the staff. They can come or not.'

Which was probably why it was only himself, and the concierge of Reg's block of flats, who accompanied the English parson in the Anglican Church of Rome one chilly afternoon in early December, plus the undertaker and his posse of pall-bearers, and an unknown male figure who sat at the back. Was he a professional mourner or a necrophile? Robert and the Signora sat in the front pew.

Out of the blue Gabbi arrived, and sat on the other side of the Italian woman. She smiled at the woman, but would not catch his eye. Gabbi was not religious and as far as he knew never went to mass, but did she feel embarrassed and out of place in an Anglican church?

The clergyman's unfussy white surplus – so preferable, Robert thought, in a not very logical access of Protestant sentiment, to the lacy, rather girlish garments of Italian priests – appeared in the gloom of the altar area. He came forward to the brass railing, his hands together and pointed outwards from his chest like a child learning the breast-stroke. A light switched on in the organ loft, and the instrument stumbled unwillingly into action. A stir behind them indicated that the coffin was on its way.

The Reverend Giles Perkins was a decent man, Robert thought. His attitude to funerals might not be so different from his own, a kind of sweeping-up of the glass after a catastrophe. Perhaps too it was a simple act of humanity, an affirmation of respect for the dead and, when there were bereaved, sympathy for them.

Gabbi had not come in her car. Like the Signora, she had used public transport. The three of them went to the cemetery, some distance from the church, in Robert's car. Perkins had his own. They followed the hearse at a dignified pace.

At the graveside, they had part two of the service. All three of them threw dust to dust. There was just the one wreath, Robert's which, like the funeral, he had decided to pay for himself. He had also put his own name on the tag, not the museum's, in view of the ambiguous response from the rest of the staff.

When it was over, Perkins apologised and said he had to rush to a parishioners' tea-party. Robert asked the Signora if she would like some coffee. Perhaps they could find a café? She declined. She said she did not care what Reg had done or what he had been mixed up in, he had always been very decent to her and understanding of her problems, and she had wanted to pay her respects, even though it was not a Catholic burial. She pulled down the black, heavy-knit shawl from her head to its usual position over her shoulders, and went off, even refusing the lift Robert offered. He was left on the deserted pavement with Gabbi.

He knew in this moment that his resolution through the summer had been useless, and that what he felt swept aside all his other thoughts of that afternoon. The surge of emotion which he had so many times shored himself against and successfully resisted, came again with renewed force.

The last vestiges of autumn had gone in recent days, and it had turned wintry. Gabbi was wearing a brown coat, tied at the waist with a wide belt of the same material. It was still fashionable, and she looked good in it, but she seemed to have had it a long time. How often did she spend her money on herself, he wondered?

'It was dignified, wasn't it?' she said in a quiet voice. 'I can't say, as you know, that I desperately liked Reg, but when death comes I suppose one approves of some kind of a ritual, of whatever kind, whoever it's for. I'm glad I came.'

Her thought about funerals, so close to his own, made him want to grasp her hand, so small inside the black leather glove. Perhaps he would have done, but he became aware of a figure in a dark overcoat carrying a battered brief-case, approaching behind them. It was the man he had noticed at the back of the church. He must have followed them in another car.

'You are Dr Robert Caine?' Robert nodded. 'The name's Storti.' He spoke in Italian. A card was produced from the breast pocket of a rather shabby dark suit and held out between fingertips yellowed with nicotine. He kept his eyes lowered. *'Giuseppe Gustavo Storti. Avvocato,'* Robert read, in thin sloping print.

'You will perhaps pardon this intrusion, at a time which must be distressing to you. But I thought…' He glanced significantly at Gabbi. 'I may speak freely?'

'Go on, go on.'

'I did see the small announcement in the *Daily American* and I thought this occasion, which I guessed you might attend, would be as good a one as any to make contact, given the need for discretion. I presume this lady is, er, Mrs Caine?'

'No. No, she's not.'

Storti looked confused. 'Oh, pardon me, pardon me,' he muttered, flushing. 'Then I should certainly not have…'

'Carry on, there's no difficulty. Signora Bruneschi is a senior colleague. You can speak freely.'

Storti was still thrown by his gaffe. 'Perhaps, Dr Caine, in the circumstances, we should make an appointment to meet somewhere else…'

Robert succeeded finally in allaying his fears. The three of them went to a small bar in the next street. They sat at a table with a pink plastic top at the back of the narrow room. The waiter brought them coffee.

'My mission concerns, as you may have guessed, Signor Reginald Griffin.' He pronounced the English name with difficulty. 'He came to see me some time before his unfortunate and violent death, in order to make his will.'

He paused, for the effect to register.

'Now I explained to Signor Griffin that there are two ways of making a will in Italy. Either, as you are no doubt aware, you can make a public one before a notario, which is registered, or a private one, in handwriting, which does not require a lawyer, not even witnesses, though these are preferable. As there is always the possibility in the latter case that someone challenging the will can say it was made under duress, or that the testator was of unsound mind, I told him that most people choose the former method. However, Signor Griffin made it clear that he did not much favour the public will. In fact he indicated that he wanted the will to remain as secret as possible. I thought at the time there was some family reason for that. I explained that in these circumstances the best thing was for him to list his wishes clearly, date and sign the document, and if possible find two witnesses whose discretion he could trust. There was no need for him to engage my services.

157

'To cut a long story short, he did not in the end choose the private will. He repeated that he wanted his will to be as secret as possible, but he also did not want there to be any difficulty in the way of the beneficiary if this could be avoided. What I had said about the difficulties that can arise with private wills had obviously impressed him. He decided he wanted the public version after all.

'As I was at this stage imagining I would myself draw up the document, I then began to question him about the nature of his assets. It became clear that, "such as they were" – those were the words he used – the assets were in Switzerland. There were, it seemed, some funds in a bank, and some other documents in safe keeping. I imagined they might be share certificates or something of that sort.'

Storti paused. His own rhetoric seemed to have encouraged him. He gently and unnecessarily brushed the sleeve of the overcoat that hung loose over his shoulders.

'I come now to a peculiar circumstance. I cannot explain to you why it should have been so, except that I suppose I have acquired over the years a certain nose for the quirks of human nature. And though I liked Signor Griffin – one has to say he had a most engaging personality, does one not? – I had a very definite sense all of a sudden that I was dealing with someone who might involve me in trouble. Maybe it was the very fact of a young man making a will in this way. At any rate, I found that I had a quite positive wish to extricate myself.

'As it happened, I had a legitimate way out. The assets are in Switzerland. Probate is always likely to be difficult in that country. A Swiss lawyer, I thought, would serve my client better. He would know the ropes in his own country. And I did know of one, a certain Herman Gosser. Herr Gosser is a man I have dealt with from time to time in connection with commercial transactions between our two countries. It also chanced that he was in Rome when Griffin came to see me. I recommended him. Griffin accepted. By means of a telephone call, made while Griffin was still there, I arranged for the two of them to meet.

'I did not, however, completely free myself from association with my client. Griffin was about to leave when he had a further hought. He was anxious that, as he lived in Rome, if he were to die it was possible a Swiss lawyer would never know about it. He asked me if, in the unlikely event of his death, and if I happened to hear of it, I would carry out for him the errand I am at this moment engaged upon. It seemed a strange request, and not very orthodox. I also thought that I might be as unlikely as Gosser to hear of his death. But he was so insistent that I agreed. He paid me, in cash and on the spot, a great deal more than I wanted for my advice.'

Once again Storti stopped. He glanced to the right and to the left as if the walls might have ears, and leant forwards. 'It is because of my agreement that I am talking to you at this moment. I imagine from the, if I may say so, rather puzzled attention you have awarded me, that you have not heard anything from Gosser?'

Robert felt himself staring at Storti as if he were a mesmerist.

'No.'

'Then I suppose this at least bears out the necessity of my client's precaution. It is my duty to tell you, Dr Caine, that I have every reason to believe Signor Griffin has made you the sole beneficiary of his will.'

Robert's surprise and alarm prevented him from replying at once. Storti now became brisk. He handed over a postcard with the Swiss lawyer's name and address written on it.

'There is a final point,' he said, in a more minor tone, as if they had departed now from territory where he felt at home. 'I do not know what you will make of this. But as we were shaking hands at my front door, Griffin made a final request of me. He asked me to tell you that – I think I quote verbatim – it was "not only assets" he bequeathed to you.'

Storti had finished. He was clearly relieved. Bending forwards, he finished the coffee in the minute cup. He dabbed his mouth with the paper napkin, and threw it on to the table.

The full implications of what he had revealed struck Robert. What on earth had induced Reg to do this? Was it a practical joke? And if the police knew of the legacy, however small, what construction would they put on it? He had a desperate need to retain Storti, who was now standing up.

'Signor Storti, please, will you have a brandy with us?'

'You are kind, but I think not, if you will excuse me. I have discharged my duty, and must confess to feeling relief at having done so. When I undertook to help Signor Griffin, I had of course no notion that there would be such an outcome. You will appreciate, it is not something a man in my position likes to be publicly known.'

Robert also rose. 'I too had no idea... and this legacy...'

'Quite so.'

The bony hand was stretched towards him.

Robert knew that any attempt to explain his predicament would be fruitless. He took the hand. There was faint pressure, and the man was off. He did not look back as he went out of the door.

19

Gabbi had taken her coat off in the steamy heat of the bar. She sat pensively when Storti had gone, her arm resting on the table, fingering the spoon in her saucer. The fire that Robert had tried to douse burst out anew and engulfed him. He was aware of his voice, as if it were someone else's. 'Well, this is an amazing development,' he heard himself say, dully, tamely.

She nodded, almost imperceptibly, her eyes downcast.

He could not have said how or why, but suddenly he knew that she was aware of his feelings, knew that for her, too, the subject of Reg and all the new questions Storti's revelation raised, were for the moment of secondary importance. Behind the bar a new consignment of coffee was slapped into the chrome machine and a long scalding noise ensued. He took her hand, tinkering with the spoon. She looked up, and simultaneously her fingers tightened on his. He saw that her eyes were unamazed, miraculously understanding.

'Gabbi, you know what I feel?'

She smiled. 'Yes, I do.'

'How long…'

'Since the day in Tarquinia at least.'

'You've known all this time?' She nodded. 'And…'

'And it's the same for me. It's not going to go away, is it?'

The racket from the bar ended abruptly, and it was as if they had emerged from a long tunnel into a new country, a new climate. After the long journey, there had been a sudden glimmer in the darkness, then an explosion of full daylight, spring where there had been winter.

They paid the barman, left the café, and walked holding hands to the car. In the car he wanted to embrace her. Somehow, it did not seem right. Instead he gripped the steering wheel. He needed to. His hands were shaking.

'Shall we go to a hotel, now?'

She nodded, and turned her head away.

They drove in silence like two condemned people. He remembered a small hotel in the Zono Africano, off the Via

Nomentana where he had once put up a visiting lecturer. It had seemed modern, clean, quiet, and he was sure they would not remember him.

He felt embarrassed at the desk when he asked, in English, for a double room and signed 'Mr and Mrs Lawrence' in the book. Gabbi stood quietly beside him as he wrote. Did the male receptionist guess? Probably. He did not ask about their luggage. If he guessed, he displayed the Italian genius for tact.

'Enjoy your stay in Rome,' he said in English, as he took back the biro and handed the porter the key.

The three of them mounted in the lift, in silence. In the room the porter threw open the shutters, switched the heating on, and did not wait for a tip. Robert gave him one. The door closed. They fell into each other's arms.

In a minute or two she pulled away, and began to undress. The chilliness of the room relieved the tension. The radiator was clicking. Laughing, they tore their clothes off. Gabbi ripped back the counterpane and plunged with a squeal into the cold sheets.

'Come in quickly, it's arctic,' she cried.

In spite of the tension, their love-making was miraculously together.

They slept for an hour. Robert woke first and knew that everything was different. He felt a physical peace he had never before experienced. It was a sensation of floating, and yet at the same time of being profoundly attached to the earth. He saw through the undrawn curtains that daylight was almost gone. An orange neon light winked on and off on the building opposite, cheekily. He raised himself on his elbow and looked at Gabbi, turned away from him. He pulled a salient of her brown hair behind her ear, and whispered into it. 'In flagrante delicto.'

She woke quickly, twisted her head, and in a snap of the light he saw her smile, slow and beautiful. He had never seen her smile like this before.

'In flagrante delicious,' she said. 'What time is it?'

'There's no such thing as time, not until we decide there is.'

They agreed they would spend the night in the hotel. He saw the question in her eyes. She was all right. She had told him that

Giancarlo was away at some conference. For Kate he would have to invent a story.

'I'll phone Franca,' he said.

Franca would still be there, he thought. He had to be at Velletri in the morning. He would think of something. Franca could pass the message. He did not care.

They had dinner in the hotel restaurant. The place was almost empty. There was an elderly couple who probably lived in the neighbourhood and were eating out, three lone males dining singly. The waiter ignored the other diners and hung about their table. They were worth fussing, it seemed. Lovers perhaps on a honeymoon? They abandoned the pretence of speaking English. The man discovered Robert was English, and told them at length about a summer job he had had in Bournemouth.

At last he left them alone with their *abaccio al forno*. Robert would not think of Kate, and complications, not tonight. Now it had happened, he felt no regret. Later he would think about her, and Giancarlo, as they both must. He gave himself to the muted wonder of the present, his miraculously rested body, Gabbi's face opposite him in the light of the candle on the table as if it had always been there.

The room lighting was subdued, a couple of wall lights, the candles on the tables, and in the centre an illuminated tank of fish. He watched the fish, little striped tropical creatures. They hung in the water, mouthing, then darted off into the reeds. The only noise was the low murmur of the older couple's conversation, the clatter of cutlery on a plate, the steady procession of oxygen bubbles in the tank.

He remembered the events of the afternoon, the funeral, Storti, the robbery. He tried to concentrate on them, to re-engage with them, to decide what to do about the will.

Gabbi looked up. She put down her knife and fork onto the plate and regarded him humorously, her hands under her chin. 'Deep thoughts?'

'Very superficial, unimportant thoughts trying to muscle in.'

'Why not let them?'

'They don't have the motive power, not right now. My subconscious doesn't seem to realise that since about four o'clock I'm not at the same address.'

'You're thinking about the will?'

'It can wait. It will wait. Everything can wait. It's all secondary now. I love you, Gabbi. I have a feeling that's going to be top of my ratings for the rest of my life, if you'll allow it to be. It's only curious, isn't it, that it took a tragic funeral for us to find each other?'

Or was it, he thought? Just for a moment Reg's grinning face appeared momentarily in the shadows of the room. Would not Reg have approved?

20

Since the night of the theft Kate had lived in a state of suspension. Her body functioned. It slept, walked, fed, performed household duties. She continued to do her work. But it was as if she could watch these activities from outside herself. She was not part of them.

The two hours she had spent in that car had been a nightmare. At the beginning, she had been so intent on her mission she had not questioned it. The car had no meter, but after leaving the restaurant it had seemed to her the man was genuinely lost. Then, when she ceased to recognise the streets, she was scared. God knew where they got to. She fancied they milled for an hour and a half or more in the suburban maze to the south-west of the city. She tried several times to make him get out to ask the way from passers-by, but he kept on driving, head down, peering ahead, ignoring her.

Was it a kidnap? Should she get out when he stopped at a light and run for it?

Finally, she resigned herself. The man did not seem to be up to anything his incompetence did not explain. Eventually he would get her back. She tried to concentrate on the positive result of her mad excursion. She decided that if she did not get back before Robert she would say she had gone to the cinema because she was bored. It was unlikely he would question her. She had done this once before when he was out.

When the theft was discovered, and the next day it became clear that Reg Griffin had carried it out, she realised he had probably sent the original note and made the anonymous call. Robert had not been with the woman at the restaurant, but Reg must have realised Robert was having an affair and used his knowledge to get her out of the building. All her suspicions about Robert were back.

She realised her evidence could be useful to the police. But the more she thought about it the less inclined she felt to do anything. Why hadn't she said all this before, they would say, when the policeman was there? Why had she lied about the cinema? She would have to reveal her suspicions about Robert. That was out of the question. Griffin was the thief, and he was dead, for whatever reason. What use would her evidence be? It was much better to leave things as they were.

On the afternoon of Griffin's funeral, Robert said he would be back about four. She decided she would force herself to go on with the article she was doing for an American archaeology journal. But at half-past four, when she had not seen or heard the car come in, she could no longer concentrate. She went down to the office. From Franca she learnt, with an innuendo added, that Gabriella Bruneschi had made a last-minute decision to go the funeral as well. So Franca also knew, or guessed? She returned, disturbed, to the flat.

At seven, when the museum finally closed, he was still not back. Going through the hall, she saw a note on the mat.

It was Franca's handwriting. *'Robert telephoned to say he will not be home tonight,'* Kate read. *'They want him on site at the Velletri dig early in the morning. He says he will spend the night in a hotel there.'*

Why, first of all, had Robert phoned Franca, and not herself, when he knew she was in? And why had Franca not used the intercom as she usually did when there was a message? And if the phone had broken down, as it sometimes did, and Franca had had to come up, why hadn't she rung the bell and told her about it?

She decided this time she would phone Gabriella Bruneschi. She could legitimately pretend to need information about some medieval engravings of ancient Rome which she had thought might illustrate her article. Gabriella would probably know where she could find them. She rang the flat number. There was no answer. At eleven she phoned again with the same result. Should she phone the hotel at Velletri he usually used? Something prevented her. What would she say to Robert if he was there?

The fever of thoughts came back. She could not sleep. The next morning she went down to the museum offices again. She marched into Gabriella's room. She was sitting at the desk doing nothing, just staring into space.

'Ah, I wonder if you can help me with some information.'

The brazen creature was insolently nonchalant. There was a

copy of the engravings in the museum library, she said, not moving. In the middle of saying this, she reached for the phone, trying to pretend that her mind was on more important matters.

Kate's fury overflowed. 'I did phone you at your flat last night,' she said tartly. 'You seemed to be out.'

Gabriella began to dial, her face a mask. She tucked the phone into her chin and began to rummage in the drawer for a pad. Her call was answered. 'Pronto – Luigi?' she said. 'Perdona – un momento.' She put her hand over the speaker. 'Is that all you want?' she said to Kate, a great deal too politely.

Kate swept out. They despised her, laughed at her, all of them, not only this young trollop. Museums, how had she ever agreed to associate herself with anything so banal and dreary? She cancelled two appointments she had that morning and went shopping in the Condotti. She bought a very expensive winter suit.

After this, she felt temporarily better. Perhaps she would not even bother, she thought, at a summit of indifference. Why should she sink to the plebeian level of petty questioning, like a cheap lawyer? She returned to her former frame of mind. If he was carrying on, let him do so until his pathetic antics reached their predictable end. She would give it six months, if that, before the woman grew bored. She had probably quarrelled with that red idiot she lived with. Robert could be no more than a fill-in while she looked for a replacement.

But when she heard Robert's key in the front door that evening she knew she had again lost control over herself. A thought surged up of him touching that brown, beautiful skin, of his lips on the attractive young mouth. Her frenzy was back.

'Comfortable night?' she monitored herself saying, as she entered the sitting-room. He was standing by the window sifting his letters. He murmured something unintelligible.

'The Nekropolis, was it?' Again, a noise. 'I said, did you stay at the Nekropolis Hotel as usual?'

'Er, yes, yes.' He held up one of the envelopes and said something fatuous about someone having forgotten to put a stamp on and the post office having missed it.

She went into the bedroom, shut the door, and phoned the hotel. Robert had not stayed the night there.

She waited until they were seated in the kitchen eating dinner. 'Why did you say you stayed at the Nekropolis Hotel last night when you didn't?' she said clearly.

His startled head came up like an animal's from grazing. She was able to observe with an anaesthetised detachment the exact process he went through. Panic, the thought of a further lie, resignation, finally a cornered resolve. He was, she thought, as transparent to her as a shrimp, and as insignificant.

'I am in love with Gabriella Bruneschi,' he said. 'We spent the night together, in a hotel.'

'So what's new?'

'It is, for the record, the first time.'

'Don't compound your lies, Robert. It is really not necessary. As with most things you do, you are not very good at them.'

She watched for a moment of exhilaration, the look of blankness on the amiable features she had once thought handsome. How could she have so deceived herself? She opened the book which she had brought on purpose for this moment. She could already feel something a lot colder and stabler moving into her deepest consciousness. Was her period of doubt and oscillation over? Was her own life, so ruined by the terrible mistake she had made in Cambridge twenty years ago, now to be restored to her, clean and dignified, and aloof from the petty treacheries of a man atrophied by a privileged birth, too weak to go for success, who had turned out to be a failure?

There were one or two other actions she might want to take, she thought, as she ran her hand down the opened seam of the book. Actions that would give her the greatest satisfaction, and which only some unjustified residue of loyalty had prevented her from taking before. Were not these actions now her duty as a citizen? She began reading.

21

The museum had closed for the day and Gabbi had gone, with the rest of the curatorial staff. They had decided to give no more publicity to their new lives than was necessary, and they travelled in to work from their new flat in two cars.

Robert went back to his office to wait until the cleaners finished. Now he was no longer living on the premises, he did not like to leave until he had seen the place locked and secured.

He dreaded the hour ahead of him, when anxieties, he knew, would creep out of their corners. He found it difficult to work. The terrible loss of the Salt-Cellar weighed heavily, and tonight his mind was full of Reg again. He wanted to be able to condemn Reg. What was he doing allowing any consideration to mitigate the enormity of what Reg had done? Reg was a duplicit, cynical conster, a criminal of the first category who deserved his fate.

Yet he could not condemn Reg, not as simply as that. He half-expected that at any moment Reg would saunter in in his casual, humorous way to discuss light-heartedly some aspect of publicity, as if nothing had happened. Would he be so surprised, would he be angry, if he did? Wouldn't he principally be relieved to find him still alive?

Accusation, conviction, so totally and so unjustifiably changed people's perspectives of the condemned. Whatever they have done, criminals remain people, don't they, essentially no different from what they were before? Whatever he had plotted, Reg remained the same man he had known, found amusing, and liked. Wasn't it the case, as perhaps with so many people who break the law, that it was only in the one, possibly reformable, aspect that he was deviant? The Courtauld professor had spoken vaguely of 'some tragedy' in his past. He could not entirely believe, still, in the brutal finality of his end. He saw again the white corpse on the marble slab he had had to identify, and had to wrench his mind from the memory.

But another worry at once took Reg's place in his mind. During the business of the day, he could forget Kate upstairs in the flat.

Now, in the silence, broken only by the distant sound of the hoovers, he felt her presence above, accusing him, despising him.

He did not, at base, scruple about her. Nobody could ever accuse him of having leapt into Gabbi's arms. It was Kate who over the years had, piece by piece, dismantled his affection for her, so why now should she be indignant at being freed from a man who was apparently so little to her taste? Yet he feared to meet her. Why was that? Did she wield still, by remote control, some authority over him?

He feared that in these stark, vulnerable minutes at the end of the day she would descend and loose upon him a rage that would be ugly, human, and inconsistent with that undoubted prickly dignity of hers which paradoxically he could still admire. Did Gabbi, too, he wondered, experience such dreads in these tender early moments of their miraculous love? Did she fear the inevitable return of Giancarlo, who had been so conveniently at some conference in Paris since the day of Reg's funeral? In fact, how stable was their happiness? How would it prevail against the accumulated weight of the past?

At last the phone tinkled, and he heard Carmina's co-operative voice. They all knew of course. Franca, the orthodoxy that ruled her life so brutally assaulted, had hardly been able to look at him in these last few days. Carmina's urbane and maternal understanding was comforting. 'We are all ready now, Dr Caine,' she said, in her flawed English, every inflexion of which nonetheless communicated her sympathy and approval.

He suspected she had never cared for Kate. Absurdly relieved, and thankful for Carmina's loyalty, he went down.

As he got into his car and drove off, he felt the pressures lifting. Physically, just being in the museum with Gabbi untouchably in the room next door had become oppressive. Perhaps they would leave, he thought vaguely. Perhaps they could find other jobs, start afresh, have children, maybe in another country?

They had seen the flat advertised in the *Daily American*, the English-language Rome newspaper. They went to see it, and both immediately liked it. It was in an idyllic position on the Aventino, and belonged to an employee of the United Nations Food and Agricultural Organisation, who was away on a field mission for six months. The flat was small. On the top floor of a large five-storey house, it had probably originally been either a laundry or servants' quarters. But it was completely encircled by a large terrace packed with flowers in pots. Above was a large monastery with a deep bell that tolled sometimes. In its garden, which they looked down on, were huge glossy magnolias, in which it was said nightingales sang. It was horribly expensive. But what was cost when the flat would be their honeymoon?

Gabbi's car was already in the garage. How could he have lived all his life without love, he thought? His worries fell away as he ran into the building like a teenager. She was waiting for him as he came out of the lift which opened with a key directly into the flat. Feeling a surge of reckless happiness, he swept her up into his arms.

'Ten hours without kissing you is like a famine,' he said, emerging from their long embrace.

They sat with iced Martinis amid the white roof-garden furniture. It was only February, but on mild days like this one could feel warm enough. They laughed at themselves.

'Fancy me sitting here,' Gabbi said. 'What's that song of Noel Coward's – mad dogs, an Englishman – and one renegade Roman woman added – out in the midwinter freeze. I'm a traitor to my country.' Then, remembering something, she jumped up and went inside. She came out with a large buff-coloured envelope.

'I forgot. This came for you just after I got in, by special courier. I had to go down to sign for it.'

The envelope had his name on it in a flowery, sloping type that was instantly recognisable. His spirits fell. He slit the heavy paper that was nearer to vellum. The short note was scrawled in Mortimer's untidy handwriting on a card which had the Nemi address printed in embossed gold lettering at the top. *'I want to see you here tomorrow. Ten o'clock sharp.'* It was not signed.

He had been expecting some kind of communication. Mortimer had been unpredictably silent about the theft. Since the brief telephone call he had made on the morning the theft was discovered, they had not spoken. Mortimer had made a sour remark about exhibitions and how they always led to trouble of some sort, told him to bloody well sweep up the mess he had made, and put the phone down.

He handed the note to Gabbi.

She put it down, frowned, and picked up the envelope from the table, turning it over. 'How the hell did he know our address?'

'A very relevant question.'

'He must know about us. I wonder how?'

'It's not difficult to imagine, is it? He heard something, and spoke to Franca probably. She'd have enjoyed giving the details.'

'And you think Mortimer sends the letter here just to let us know he knows?'

'It's possible.'

'What do you think he wants to talk to you about?'

Robert shrugged, and looked away to the monastery.

'Robert, you're not telling me something. What is it?'

Was he worried? Yes, of course he was. He must be emitting vibes and Gabbi was picking them up.

'It'll be nothing substantial, as usual.'

'The theft? He hasn't said much about it, has he?'

'What can he say, apart from the fact that I appointed Reg? He *will* say that, but it's not going to get him anywhere. Our security was passed by the indemnity people, and the exhibition has been a roaring success, thank God.'

By tacit agreement they dropped the subject. How could they let Mortimer intrude on an evening like this, Robert asked himself rhetorically? But an uneasiness remained for both of them. It would not be resolved, he thought, until they knew what it was. The weight he had felt at the museum had moved back in.

Nemi was blacker than usual. A set sky of high pumice-coloured cloud arched over the unruffled ebony surface of the lake. Was the goddess Diana angry, reflecting her dark mood in her looking-glass? As Robert tipped the Citroen over the brink of the road that descended precipitously from the village, the absurd house stood lifeless, its awnings furled, its flagstaff buntingless. Somewhere in there was Mortimer. What did he do when he was at home? He

172

was always so busy and bustling. It was difficult to imagine him at ease, doing nothing.

The outer gates were open. He drove straight up to the house and parked. No chauffeur appeared to garage the car, no Bertram Leathers teetered from the porch. This had never happened before. Had the electronic eye in the gate fused? Faced with a closed front door, he had to ring the bell.

There was a long wait. At last there was a noise. Bolts were being thrust back on the inside of the door. A large figure he had not seen before confronted him, wearing a grey-striped shirt and a green baize apron.

He did not appear to be too bright. He stared blankly. 'I've come to see Mr Ready,' Robert said in English. Mortimer had always insisted his Italian servants spoke good English. The man obviously did not understand. '*Signor* Ray-ar-dy,' he substituted.

Something registered. The man stood aside for him to enter. Robert waited in the hall while the door was rebolted. Was Mortimer expecting the Mafia, or had they arrived?

The man disappeared. Not quite the Leathers touch of being shown to a seat. Abandoned, Robert went down the stairs to the sitting-room and sat in one of the huge, soft leather armchairs which gave you the feeling you were being swallowed. Sunk into the ample depths, you wondered if you were still visible.

Minutes ticked by, marked audibly by two clocks, a grandfather in the hall taking its time with a measured second-a-time clonk and an expensive modern contraption with a see-through glass case and a frenetic tick, sitting on top of a Louis Quinze chest of drawers – Mortimer's usual historical miscellany. Otherwise the house was totally silent.

A door was wrenched open and Mortimer's rapid footsteps were audible on the marble floor of the hall above. He appeared at the top of the stairs, and was apparently surprised to see Robert below. 'You've arrived?' he said, red faced. 'That man has the brain of a chicken.'

'He certainly believes in keeping your front door shut,' Robert said as Mortimer descended. 'Why all the bolts? Are you expecting a siege?'

Mortimer did not answer. He looked somewhat harassed, Robert thought. 'We'll go in the study,' he said, marching in that direction. He snatched open the still-drawn curtains. Further evidence of recalcitrant flunkeys?

'Leathers on holiday?'

'I've sacked the lot.'

'You mean the entire ship's company?'

The witticism was lost. 'Bloody disloyalty. At least three of them were involved.'

'Stealing?'

'Buying and recording cassettes for Lek. It was Ludo, the chauffeur, who was doing it, but Leathers knew and connived. When I confronted him, he tried to organise all the others into a trade-union stance. So I kicked the lot out. Ludo I can understand, but not Leathers. The man had got too big for his boots. People who work for me need to know I give the orders.'

Cassettes for Lek? What on earth was wrong with that? It was tempting to probe. But Robert knew better. Anything to do with Lek was a no-go area, and there was no point in provoking more trouble. He sat in one of the armchairs, of a less carnivorous variety than those next door, and waited. Now that he was actually in the presence, he decided he had never felt more relaxed.

Mortimer was certainly in a fuss. He went to the mahogany desk and began rummaging in one of the trays on the tooled-leather top. Then he opened drawers and began feeding the paper into them, snapping them shut as if each one settled an old score.

Perhaps he needed soothing. Robert decided to say nothing about the theft until Mortimer raised it. 'I've had the final exhibition figures,' he remarked casually, as the paper-sorting reached an optimum level of aggression. 'They're on the way to you. They're much better even than we expected. I think everything's in now and there's good daylight between debit and credit. Something like six hundred million lire. The brochure did particularly well.'

'I'm glad to hear it.'

'The extra week made a great difference.'

It was clear something was coming. Mortimer was pretending to have found something of interest in the bottom drawer. He bent to scrutinise it, almost out of sight. Then he banged the drawer shut and sat back in his chair, rigidly, as if he were wired for execution. The paper-sorting act, as Robert suspected, had been a cover. 'Migliore's been here,' he snapped.

'Who's Migliore?'

'The detective in charge of the investigation. Hasn't he been to see you yet?'

'Oh, him. I'd forgotten his name. He was buzzing around the museum for a day or two after the theft – rather ineffectually, I thought. He was there when I went to the mortuary, too.'

'I wouldn't call him ineffective. I got the impression he's rather on the ball. Not someone I'd like to be on the wrong side of.'

'Well, are you?'

Mortimer flushed. 'Of course not. But what was pretty clear, and what I want to talk to you about, is that he thinks *you're* implicated.'

'Does he now?'

'It's no good taking up your usual casual attitude over this, Robert. I had a hard time defending you. He grilled me relentlessly about your past. Naturally I said you've been a reliable and honest director and the rest of it.' Mortimer turned his head aside, as if there were something offensive. 'Of course, it's a question of the keys.'

'Keys?'

'To the security system. There are three sets, aren't there? Manfreddi has one – and I have to say I think you've been most ill-advised to trust that woman after her performance over the Pietro business – and you have the other two. It's obvious what happened. Whatever her protestations, Manfreddi has been careless again. But Migliore isn't ruling out the other possibility.'

'That I was in cahoots with Griffin and hired him the keys for the evening?'

'Precisely.'

'And I suppose he thinks I then decapitated him and have the Salt-Cellar stashed under the floorboards somewhere?'

'It won't get us anywhere if you're flippant. The point is you're a suspect. The fact has to be faced.'

Robert still felt entertained. 'In that case, perhaps you are, too. Perhaps you and I are also in cahoots.'

'Kindly be serious. Can we return to the keys? If it wasn't you, and Signora Manfreddi wasn't careless, what *is* the explanation?'

175

Robert frowned. He had spent a lot of thought on this.

'I have of course talked to Carmina, and I'm as convinced as it's possible to be that she hasn't been slack over the keys. Every evening on returning to her flat she hides them, so that if she goes out she won't risk someone taking them out of her bag. *Because* of the other incident, she has been triply careful. She's an extremely loyal and efficient person. Another possibility is that the safe was cracked, where I keep my keys. But I am the only person who ever opens it. The safe records electronically each time it's opened. It hadn't been touched since the last time I used it. Anyway, I'm the only person who knows the combination, and I memorise it. I'm convinced the thief had some way of neutralising or bypassing the security system without using the keys. The police know, or guess, how he bypassed the air-pressure case in which the Salt-Cellar was sitting. He must have had another method to deal with the heat sensors and the pressure pads.'

'That's pretty far-fetched, isn't it?'

'This was not an ordinary theft.'

Mortimer made an impatient movement. With a rather arch gesture he tucked his chin into his neck and brought up his fingernails for inspection.

'There is another matter. I presume you don't know Kate's been here. Yesterday.'

'Indeed?'

'Look, what you're up to in your private life is your business, not mine, though I must say I'd never have dreamed I'd have *this* situation to deal with. Kate came to ask my advice.'

'About our marriage?'

Mortimer ignored the question. 'She came, first, about the flat, which I told her she can keep without rent for the moment, though I'm not sure I won't charge it to you as you're no longer living there. She also came to me about the theft. Migliore's seeing her today, apparently. She knows he's going to ask her about your relations with Griffin. She wanted to know what I thought she should say.'

'That's an easy question to answer, isn't it?'

'Is it?'

'She has only to tell the truth.'

'Hardly as simple as that from what she told me.'

'What did she tell you?'

'That, like Migliore, she isn't convinced that you, and this girl you're infatuated with, weren't in with Griffin from the start.'

Robert gave a sniff. 'You can surely guess the reason for her making that insinuation?'

'This is no laughing matter, Robert. Whatever the truth may be, Kate isn't sure of your innocence. Of course she has very hurt feelings, and no doubt she's bitter. But I didn't get the feeling she was acting simply out of anger. Kate isn't the sort of woman who would ever perjure herself to that degree, or sink to any level of vindictiveness. I'm sure, whatever I said to her, she's likely at least to hint to Migliore what she suspects. You can imagine how he'll interpret what she says. And with your own wife against you, you're in deep trouble. If Kate were called in a trial she'd be very impressive in the witness box. She wouldn't volunteer her evidence. The lawyer would have to drag it out of her. Her status as an injured wife would stand to her credit, not the reverse.'

Robert became aware that something was not being said. What was Mortimer up to? This was not the usual discussion, in which Mortimer gave vent to his pathological self-doubt in the form of criticism.

'What are you driving at?' he said.

Mortimer had at least the decency to look guilty.

'I think you ought to resign, and clear out of the country. If you are charged – even if you aren't, *whatever* the outcome – it's not going to be good for you, and it's certainly not going to be good for the museum. At very best you're going to be seen as negligent. There was the Pietro business, and now the slackness over the keys. The best thing you can do is cut your losses.'

'There was no slackness over the keys.'

'It will appear as if there was.'

Robert looked at Mortimer in amazement. He thought he observed a change. The bombast was missing. Was it possible that for once this was no ploy, that he really meant it? Was Mortimer really prepared to sacrifice him after all the years they had been together? No wonder there had been all this silence over the theft if this was what he had been cooking up.

'Well?' Mortimer prompted. 'You'll do the sensible thing?'

'Of course I'm not resigning. For a start how do you think *that* would be seen by the police? It would be tantamount to a confession of guilt.'

'I'm confident I could present it in another light. You felt, in the circumstances, it was the best thing for the museum, and so on. Your relations with Kate, and this woman, could be used as a motive as well.'

'Do you really think I'm going to do that?'

'It makes sense. Do you want to endanger the reputation of the museum more than it has been already?'

'Of course I'm not going to resign. There isn't a shred of evidence, either of my involvement or of my inefficiency.'

'Migliore can make things very nasty indeed if he sets about it.'

'How?'

'Robert, I'm not going to argue with you. I can see it may not at first be possible for you to see clearly. But after reflection I'm sure you're going to view things differently.'

'I'm not leaving just to get this man Migliore off the silly hook he's made for himself. If he's really making this charge against me – and even that isn't plain, policeman often hint at things without meaning them – let him bring the evidence and show it to me directly, not via a third party. I'm sorry, but resigning is the last thing I shall do. If you want to sack me, go ahead, and give your reasons in writing. I tell you, if you do, you'll risk a charge of unfair dismissal.'

Mortimer stood up and marched to the window. He stood with the fingers of his podgy pink hands gripped and tensed behind his back as if he were Mr Atlas about to demonstrate his dorsals.

'You're a fool. You've always been a fool. But now I think you've lost your marbles. You chuck over a charming woman who has helped you all through your working life for this slob of a lefty slut, whom I advised you to get rid of months ago. With your conceited, blasé, academic complacency you have just presided over one of the biggest art thefts in Europe for years, carried out by a man you appointed in the most irresponsible way, and you have the neck to sit there as if nothing has happened. I warn you. If you stay in Rome and are arrested, I'll not lift a finger to help you. You can stew in prison for the rest of your life if that's what you want. I was offering you a decent, sensible way out of the fix you've got yourself into. I was even going to offer you a sum of money to tide you over. Now I'm damned if I will.'

The tirade was vintage. It lasted all the way up to the hall, to which Robert led the way. In the hall, the rhetoric was suspended for a last attempt.

'You're still telling me you won't do the sensible thing?'

Robert smiled. He felt calm again. 'You're forgetting one small fact. I don't happen to be guilty of any criminal act. I appointed a well-qualified man who turned out to be a high-class villain, something anyone might have done. That's all.'

Mortimer bellowed for the servant, who came at the run. As the man fiddled with the bolts of the castelline door, there was a further avalanche. There was talk of firing and lawyers.

In the village at the top of the hill, Robert looked back. The house was as it was when he'd looked at it earlier, dead and motionless. The water of the lake was unruffled, the day as indeterminately still. 'Col weather', they called it, didn't they? A space between two weather systems. It was a good metaphor for his situation. The elements would decide future events. Let Mortimer stampede, and see where it got them. For once he was not going to try to manipulate him. It was a restful thought.

One thing at least had been decided by his visit. He was not leaving Rome just yet. If he ever went, it would be under his own steam, not under duress.

22

Carmina Manfreddi woke at seven as she always did almost to the minute, and lay preparing herself for the effort of rising. She remembered it was Sunday.

The thought was not pleasing to her as it usually was, and for a moment she could not think why. She loved Sundays, when she lingered over her coffee, read the paper, cleaned her small abode, and visited friends. Then she remembered.

She lay on in bed, hoping she might doze off again. But there was no chance of that. The details of that interview with the policeman came flooding back, as if they were only held at bay by sleep.

How offensive he had been, accusing her practically of lying about the keys. She had denied all his insinuations of course. But he was so insistent, she had for a moment begun to wonder if she could have been remiss, as indeed she had been in leaving her place when the money had been stolen from her till back in the early summer. Was she getting old and missing things? Had she allowed her bag out of her sight at the museum, or in a shop on her way home, giving someone the time to take an impression of the keys and put them back? She was sure she had not been careless, and she did not think these types of key could be copied in this way. But because she hesitated the policeman had been even more convinced she was at fault.

Things weren't the same at the museum, she thought. First Pietro, now this terrible business. It wasn't surprising Dr Caine had looked for solace in a more sympathetic direction than his wife. She feared for him. It seemed to her sometimes that, like so many decent people, he was vulnerable in these violent days. She wished there was something she could do.

Hearing the cats yowling, she got up, put on a housecoat and went into the kitchen. They knew she was late, pacing about, butting their backsides on her legs and the furniture, looking up at her accusingly, snapping and hissing at each other. For a moment, as she screwed off the tin lids, she ceased to love them. Nature was raw and ugly when its needs were not satisfied. She turned the meat out on to the four plates, brushing one of the animals roughly off the sink where it had jumped up.

They ate in their usual ungainly way, their heads on one side, gulping the food greedily. But when they had wolfed their plates clean and, licking their whiskers, began more amiably to look for somewhere to sit, she was able to love them again. As she sipped her own coffee, she watched them. Lea had as usual leapt up on the window-seat and with one leg stuck up in the air was cleaning her belly fur. Little Simone, the most affectionate, hopped on her lap, settled, and began to purr – great ratchets of vibration she could feel in her legs.

It was then she remembered Giulia. Now here was something she could do, not to help Dr Caine exactly, but an act of decency – and it would contribute to filling her day. Pietro was out of prison and had found work and other quarters. He could not be allowed back of course. Giulia was moving out of the museum today.

She had felt guilty about Giulia for some time. She knew she was a good woman and it was not her fault she was saddled with a man like that. Since Pietro had gone, Giulia had done the cleaning work quietly and efficiently. Carmina knew she had for too long ignored this fact and kept up a superior distance, trying to blame Giulia unjustly. She decided she would go up to the museum. She almost certainly would not be very welcome during a removals operation, if she were welcome at all. But she would go and say goodbye, to put the record straight.

Feeling better for having something positive to do, she set about her normal tasks, dressed for mass, which she would go to after leaving the museum, and at nine set off into the damp, balmy morning. She caught the bus halfway down the acacia-lined road of semi-detached villas.

There was a small removals van in the court of the museum. Two men in white coats were loading a sofa. Carmina had bought carnations from the kiosk in the Piazza del Popolo. She felt foolish knocking on the open door and holding the green paper that swathed the flowers. Supposing she got a snub?

There was no answer to her knock, so she went in. The place was bare. Giulia was sitting disconsolately in the kitchen, the two children at her side. At the sight of her standing in the doorway, she half got up.

'I've come to say goodbye, and to give you these,' Carmina said quickly, holding forward the bunch.

Giulia looked nonplussed. She took the bunch as if it did not belong to her. She laid it on the table, sat down again, and took a handkerchief from her pocket. She held it over her mouth as if she were going to be sick.

In a few moments she recovered herself. She took up the flowers again and looked at them.

'Thank you, Signora Manfreddi,' she said. After a pause she added, 'There's no coffee. It's gone, with the other things.'

Carmina shook her head dismissively. What did coffee matter at this stage of things? She sat in the remaining chair. She felt immensely awkward and out of place, and sorry. She had never been in this flat, she realised, in all the years.

It should not be like this with a colleague, she thought. After all the time they had worked together in this building, it should be easier. It was her fault. They should be able to be personal – two women talking naturally together.

But she could not manage this. She could not refer to Giulia's position and her obvious distress, only to impersonal matters like the museum, and with a consciousness of their relative status.

'It's a sorry business,' she remarked, 'this theft, and the terrible death. Did you have to talk to that policeman?'

'Yes.'

'He has his own ideas and won't listen to anyone else's, that's my view.'

Giulia did not answer. The little girl was needing comfort. Giulia took her on her knee and drew her cheek to hers. The boy was listless, running his finger along the edge of the plastic table top.

'Strange it was Griffin,' Carmina persisted. 'I have to say it, I liked him. You would never have guessed, would you? Greed for money, I suppose. Though it didn't get him very far, the poor soul. Some ruthless gang must have been using him.'

There were thick seconds of silence. The two men appeared.

'This is to go?' one of them said, eyeing the table and chairs.

Giulia seemed to take a grip on herself.

'Will you take that cupboard first?' she said. 'That's ours.'

When they had shuffled out with the piece, Giulia looked Carmina in the eye. 'It's all the same to me now, Signora,' she said. 'It's not going to make any difference to my life. But you still work here. You've got a position to maintain. I'll tell you one thing. Griffin isn't the only one who's been doing things he shouldn't. There's another here, still here.'

'You mean someone on the curatorial staff?'

'I mean Alfredo Ludic. I've never said anything. It wouldn't have done any good if I had. Pietro was quite capable of taking that money but he didn't, as it happened. He was with the girl that evening from the moment they left together earlier in the afternoon. In my opinion it was Griffin who took the money and put it in Pietro's overalls pocket to get him out of the way. But if it hadn't been him, and you hadn't been talking to Ludic at the time, I'd've said Ludic was a good second choice for the job. I've never thought much of him. Shifty.'

'Shifty, you say? I must say I hadn't noticed?'

'Going up to the roof. What business has he got up there?'

'The roof? What do you mean, Giulia?'

'The week before the theft. Signor Caine had asked me to tidy up a bit in the conservation room on the third floor. Down he comes while I'm up there – down the staircase from the roof. You should have seen his face. He wasn't expecting to see me there. He had to think quickly. Said something about fire-extinguishers being his responsibility and he thought there ought to be one up there. But I knew he was lying. He's not Italian of course. Croatian or something. In my view he was Griffin's accomplice.'

Carmina remembered Giulia's information about Pelucci, which she had also kept to herself. 'But didn't you tell anyone?'

'What's the point? It wouldn't have saved Pietro. They would have said I made it up. You don't get justice in this country, and I've nothing concrete. I tell you now, though. You can make what you like of it. Tell Signor Caine if you like, now I'm going. I've nothing against him. He's always been good to me.' She pushed the girl off her lap. 'Well, this is it, apparently.'

The men were returning. Carmina also rose. She did not know what to say. Giulia took up the flowers. 'Thanks again for these,' she said. 'Decent of you to come specially.'

Carmina wanted to say a lot more, not about the museum or the theft but about Giulia, and her own regrets. It was not possible. Giulia was going in the van. It was sad, unavoidably sad. Obviously Giulia did not like the move. She had been here ten years, had her children here.

Carmina stood outside while the van moved off. There was no point in waving. Giulia was shut in the back, sitting on the sofa.

23

'You'll pardon me, but it seems you've changed your tune.'

'I don't think so.'

'At the morgue you were unable to identify the body as Griffin's.'

'I couldn't for sure, no.'

'But now you appear to think otherwise. You have buried your ex-colleague with the rites of your Church.'

Robert bridled. He had decided Luigi Migliore was going to be unpleasant from the moment he emerged from the lift. He must keep ice cool, he thought.

'Griffin disappeared. The other evidence – his watch, the ring, which I was able to identify – points to its having been Griffin's body. The court assumed it was. But I haven't changed my neutral views on the actual body. If I had to identify it again I would say the same thing. I presume the police want me to be accurate?'

Luigi Migliore delicately plucked an eyelash. 'Quite so, Dr Caine. And of course at that early stage you did not wish to accept that a member of your staff, whom you had appointed, was a criminal, did you?' Smiling faintly, he began to range the small sitting-room with his alert eyes as if any object they encountered might be mentally pocketed and used in evidence.

He had wanted to see where he and Gabbi were living of course. This flat was the last place Robert would have chosen for the meeting. But Migliore had phoned at eight, only an hour ago, and insisted. The only good thing was that he had persuaded Gabbi, despite protestations, to go to work. He did not want her involved.

The man continued, 'No, from the point of view of who *carried out* the theft, there has only been one candidate from the start. Even if we hadn't found Griffin's body the morning after the crime, this case had all the hallmarks of an inside job. The method was simple. Apart from the entry to the actual showcase, it was a matter of keys – the key to the door under the stairs, and the magnetic key to the switch cupboard. Thanks to your trust in him,

Griffin somehow acquired copies of both. He entered the premises after you so conveniently left them for your dinner party, and simply helped himself. He let himself in through the front door, just as Signora Manfreddi does every morning, turned off the security system, and did the job, probably with a sophisticated portable pressure-chamber, and certainly with the simple glass-cutter we found in his pocket.

'He reset the system and departed, again through the front door, with the loot in his arms. His friends were waiting in a car down the road. His only risk was bumping into our patrol outside. But he had chosen a good evening for his escapade, hadn't he, with the mist as thick as it was? And no doubt the siren diverted our men's attention for the vital moments of his departure. His mistake was not to realise that, having accomplished his mission so neatly, he had outlived his usefulness. Rather sad really, a gifted young man like that. You must feel that yourself... having been responsible for his appointment?'

Here it came. There was a change in the atmosphere. Migliore's tongue appeared, and turned upwards against his upper lip. 'I think it might be worthwhile if we indulge in a little history, Dr Caine, the history of your relations with this man. You will agree that, right from his appointment in London, Griffin commanded, shall I say, your spontaneous confidence?'

'He won my confidence, over a period, in certain directions.'

'I would prefer to suggest he had it from the very start.'

'What are you implying, Inspector?'

'I refer to that part of your statement which describes the events in London – in, er, April, was it not?' Migliore glanced at the clipboard on his knee. 'You appointed him, if I read you correctly, off the street as it were.'

'I met him by chance, in a cinema. He handed me my raincoat, which I'd left under my seat.'

'A very decent act, but does it merit the instant bestowal of a major curatorial post? You've no doubt reflected that he might well have followed you to the cinema, and engineered the apparently casual encounter? You've said he knew you?'

'By name. He'd read, or knew about, some of my books. And I think he said later he'd heard me lecture.'

'And he knew you were Director of the Villa Aemelia?'

'Er, I think he did. He'd lived in Rome while doing work on Bernini, so that wasn't so surprising.'

'And so you appointed him. Just like that.'

'Of course it wasn't just like that.'

'Will you explain, Dr Caine?'

Mortimer had not exaggerated. Robert swallowed, much too visibly he was sure. 'We got talking in the foyer. It was raining hard. He had no coat. I think it was I who suggested we had a drink together.'

'Which he readily agreed to?'

'He agreed. We actually had a meal as neither of us had eaten.'

'A meal. And talking to him, you discovered he was a Renaissance expert?'

'Yes.'

'With precisely the speciality of the curator who disappeared, and whose post you were seeking to fill?'

'Not precisely, but nearly.'

'Didn't that appear to you as a remarkable coincidence?'

'Yes, it did, rather.'

'Indeed. So you offered him the job to celebrate it?'

'Naturally not, not just like that. I didn't appoint him until the next day, after a formal interview and after I'd checked on his credentials.'

'His credentials being?'

'Professionally very good degrees, and primarily the fact that the Courtauld Institute, a leading British art history college and part of London University, had offered him a fellowship.'

'Tell me, if you'd been in his shoes, and had been offered the choice between a fellowship in a prestigious university and a junior curatorship in a private museum, which would you have chosen?'

'What I would have chosen is hardly relevant. Griffin chose a museum. He said he wanted to do museum work and wasn't keen to be a don. It was a perfectly understandable preference and I accepted it, as did the Courtauld.'

'I see. And character? You no doubt gave some thought to this side of things – a young man who was going to be a colleague in a largely expatriate community?'

186

'Naturally I gave thought to personality.'

'You liked Griffin?'

'I'd seen a number of candidates, in Rome and in London. None of them had greatly impressed me. Griffin did. He not only knew his subject, I thought he had a certain humour, a maturity, and a worldliness, qualities that are not always paramount in our profession.'

'He certainly had worldliness. That was very perspicacious of you. And you no doubt checked with the police?'

'Police? No, I didn't.'

'A pity. For if you had, you might have gained further evidence of Griffin's "worldliness". You will say, no doubt, you had no knowledge of a certain incident that took place in Düsseldorf a month or two before your interview, in which Griffin played the leading part, alleging that a very dubiously authentic but highly insured piece of Fabergé jewellery he was delivering to a buyer had been stolen from his hotel room?'

'I knew nothing at all about that.'

'Really. An expensive omission of yours, wasn't it?' Migliore was looking at his notes again. 'Pelucci, now. Carlo Pelucci. Let us turn to the matter of your former employee. It was established that Pelucci probably took his own life, was it not? I have been reading the files. "Morose, self-critical, lonely." Those are the words you used to describe him, you'll recall. Indeed, as far as I can discern, the official view of his character is largely one established by your evidence.'

Robert stared in disbelief. The destinations of Migliore's odysseys were becoming obvious.

'I gave those views at the inquest, certainly. They would be corroborated by anyone here.'

'*Not* by everyone, Dr Caine. Not by your ex-concierge for instance – a very delightful lady incidentally. According to her, her husband had amiable and frequent sessions in bars with your "morose" ex-curator. Did you know that?'

'No, I didn't.'

'Then I expect you won't know, either – or you will claim you don't know – that on the day before his disappearance Pelucci told Buongusto he wasn't going to walk in the Abruzzi mountains, as you stated was his intention, but was to meet someone who had accosted him in the street and offered him a large sum if he would value a picture.'

'I never knew that. Giulia Buongusto…'

'The lady, it seems, was frightened of telling anyone about it. She feared repercussions. I do have to wonder *what* repercussions.'

'Inspector, are you suggesting…'

'I'm not suggesting anything yet. I'm asking questions. And what I'm proposing is that it's perfectly possible Pelucci was murdered to create the vacancy which Griffin so swiftly filled. You'll admit that?'

'"Admit"?'

'Allow, concede the possibility?'

'It's possible, I suppose.'

'But it didn't occur to you before this moment?'

'No.'

'It seems to me that for an intellectual you are rather gullible, Dr Caine. Let us summarise. You appoint a man to your staff who turns out to have a criminal record. You give him a trusted role in the preparation of the Cellini Exhibition, including some elements of museum security, and in face of almost watertight evidence of his criminality, you suggest the body we've found may not be his.

'At least, gullibility is one explanation of your behaviour. There is another – that you knew all along what was going to happen, and are being paid handsomely for your compliance, as Griffin was no doubt for his more active role.'

Robert turned away. 'You can of course think that.'

'But is it true?'

It had come out, and he felt calm. If he had given off any vibes of anxiety earlier, he was sure there were none now. 'No. Have you finished? I really must get up to the museum. I have appointments this morning.'

'I'm afraid I haven't quite finished.' Migliore looked around again. His eye alighted on Gabbi's furled red umbrella lying on a chair, and stayed there. 'You will pardon me, but I must refer now to a more intimate circumstance. This, I understand, is temporary accomodation of yours?'

'As I think you know, I've recently separated from my wife and have begun to live with Gabriella Bruneschi, one of the senior curators at the museum.'

Migliore grinned unpleasantly. 'If it isn't indelicate, may I congratulate you? Signora Bruneschi is a most attractive and delightful woman.' He left a grotesque pause. 'Previous to this – arrangement – I understand Signora Bruneschi lived with her husband at an address near to Termini station.'

'Yes, she did.'

'I gather also that her husband has no job, apart from certain political activities for which he receives no pay, and that hitherto at least, he has been kept by his wife.'

'I believe so.'

'How much does Signora Bruneschi earn at the museum?'

'About thirty million lire a year.'

'Thirty million. Not a princely sum, would you say, for a senior museum official?'

'None of our salaries is princely. We are a small private museum, having to earn our way without subsidy.'

'You would include your own salary in this parsimony?'

'Yes I would, by comparison with directors' salaries in state establishments.'

'Exactly so. You don't earn a salary with which it will be easy for you to start a new life with a new – er, consort – and no doubt with a continuing financial responsibility for your wife. Again you must pardon me for treading into such intimate areas, but it's necessary for us to think for a moment about your wife. Does Mrs Caine have an income of her own?'

'She has a modest one from her father's estate, and from the sale of her books.'

'Modest, you say. Quite so. And her books. They would be rather erudite publications, I imagine. Not exactly on the best-seller lists? Now I have seen your wife. We had a very full interview, of a frankness, I'm gratified to say, that surprised me. It did strike me – please inform me if your view on this is different – that your wife has expensive tastes. As a matter of fact she confessed to this herself. I formed the impression that if there is to be a question of alimony, she would press you to the limits?'

Robert had had enough. He stood up. 'I'm sorry, Inspector, but I really must go.'

Migliore was triumphant. He hardly stirred. 'I have a final question, Dr Caine. Your relations with Mr Ready. Would you describe these as amicable?'

'They are professional.'

'You wouldn't say there was any tension between you?'

'No. No more, that is, than you would expect between a private museum owner and a director, whose interests must diverge from time to time.'

'You've not had any major difference of opinion recently?'

'Not major, no.'

'He wouldn't have been critical of your directorship in any way?'

'How is this relevant?'

'It's for me to judge what's relevant. Can we proceed? Has he been critical of you?'

'He's had some criticisms. He always has done from time to time. But nothing of substance that has required change.'

'Criticisms of your treatment of staff for instance?'

'No. That is, yes. Some months ago there was a small matter. But it came to nothing. And it wasn't, I may say, concerning Griffin.'

'Not concerning Griffin. Are you sure of that?'

'Certain.'

'He approved of your appointment?'

'I have no reason to think he didn't.'

'He knew of the circumstances of your appointing Griffin?'

'Not precisely. There was no reason for him to.'

'Except that he *did* know, and considered it an odd appointment. Thank you, Dr Caine. I think that *is* all for the present.'

For a moment, Robert thought, Migliore looked what he was – no longer the powerful inquisitor, but a rather scruffy little man standing in a stranger's sitting-room, a cheap megalomaniac who enjoyed the temporary power which tragedy gave him over other people's lives. He must be careful, he told himself, to remember that. It would help him to remain dignified in their further dealings.

He had two intuitions. First, that for all his posturing and innuendo, Migliore had no leads. He was thrashing about helplessly. He would not catch the international gang of professional criminals who surely lay behind the theft of the Salt-Cellar. Reg's murderer or murderers would go free. After all the furore, the thing would end in bathos. His other intuition concerned Mortimer. He would bet any money Mortimer had told Migliore he distrusted Reg from the start. There was now no doubt in his mind Mortimer wanted him to go. His treachery had gone public.

If it was so, it further made up his mind. Of course he would go, eventually. How would he and Gabbi wish to stay on? But they would not go until all this was over and his name was cleared. The best thing would be for Mortimer to be forced to sack him. He would have no compunction about seeing there was a little compensation. He would put the money in trust, the interest to be spent on the museum.

24

They broke from low cloud and the tilted plate of well-nourished, well-ordered fields that was northern Switzerland came into view. The plane straightened, sauntered over a main road and houses. It touched down, and the retro-boosts roared. Suddenly the speed seemed too much. Robert endured those few seconds of anxiety which contact with the earth always brought him no matter how he lectured himself not to be such a coward.

The suppressed aggression of Swiss efficiency took over as, joining another incoming stream, they thronged into the spotless decor of Zürich airport. They queued silently in several lines at passport control to wait for the neat, grey-uniformed men to process them. He should not be here, he thought again as he inched forward, certainly not in these clandestine circumstances. But it had been too tempting, with the cast-iron alibi in Vienna.

The essential aftermath of the theft had been taken care of by letter. The national indemnity inspectors had returned to the Aemelia again, and as they had given their consent to the security arrangements for the exhibition before it began, they could be thought to bear some of the blame for the loss as well as financial responsibility. But Robert could not really feel this and adjudged a courtesy visit, particularly to the Director of the lending museum, was an expense that they should bear – in time as well as money. He would pay for it out of his own pocket if Mortimer proved difficult. He had also a personal reason for going. Migliore's version of how the theft had been effected had been leaked to the press and might well become canon. Some newspapers had even hinted at his possible implication in the crime. If it was possible to do so discreetly, he hoped to put his own view to the Austrians. He had after all to continue to live in the art world. He didn't want this hanging over him if it could be avoided.

Things had gone well in Vienna. Devastated as he was by the loss, the Director proved himself the civilised and decent man Robert had thought him before. The robbery, he said generously, was the kind of thing they all faced these days. Only obvious security aberrations were condemnable and, as he understood it, absolutely none had been demonstrated in this case. The Culture Minister was equally dignified and sympathetic, when he was also under attack from his own press and elsewhere. He had thanked Robert for his visit which, he realised, Robert had not been obliged to make.

Robert had decided in Rome to do nothing about Reg's will. The immediately obvious thing would have been to make no secret of it, tell the police, and express his surprise and embarrassment. But because of the turmoil of his thoughts about Gabbi, he had not done so in those first vital days. After that, every day that passed had made this line less advisable. After the conversation with Mortimer, then Migliore, it became even less politic. Gabbi agreed with him. At the back of his mind he had thought that if Gosser contacted him he would have to do something. But despite the press coverage, Gosser had remained silent. The whole business could perhaps just be forgotten.

The thought of going to Switzerland had not occurred to him until he woke in the Vienna hotel room that morning. The opportunity, and a sudden rush of curiosity, made him lift the telephone. What had Reg meant, among other things, by that cryptic message: 'it is not only assets I bequeath'? What especially intrigued him was that Reg must have foreseen the possibility of his death. Could there, even, be some important communication awaiting him, that would throw light on the theft and the murder?

He got Gosser's number from international enquiries and before he had fully considered what he was doing, was through to him. He made an appointment for the early afternoon, and managed to re-route his air-ticket. He could still go on to Rome this evening. Nobody need know, except Gabbi, that he had been here.

He took the airport bus into the city and found himself in a central square. A passer-by indicated the yellow tram he should take, which sped him smoothly out of the town. It climbed a hill, and the lake came into view, a great level stretch of placid grey, penetrating southwards to the distant shrouded Alps. Parallel with the lake's surface hung the low cloud base, severing the mountainside half-way up. In the tram a few well-dressed citizens sat silently, staring outwards.

Robert saw the name of the road they were travelling. It was the one Gosser lived in. He looked at the numbers on the American-style letter-boxes on the street. Apparently the road ran for miles. They were well short of Gosser's number. Passing Gosser's house, he got off at the next stop.

The houses were well-to-do, detached, mostly modern, but a few, made of stone, were not rendered with the ubiquitous Swiss grey stucco. Gosser's was one of these. There was an impenetrable iron gate on which was a bell. The gate was buzzed open by an unseen hand within. Robert wondered why Gosser had asked him to come to the house. Surely he would have an office in town? There was no advertisement of his name or his profession on the gate.

A maid opened the front door. She nodded when he said his name, and with no word led the way.

'Bitte,' she said, standing back to let him pass by her into the room with lowered eyes. She closed the door after him.

The room had a magnificent view over the lake. Robert watched the brisk progress of a lake steamer making for the town. The colourless scene was like a charcoal drawing.

Looking round the room, he realised that Gosser was a great deal more successful a lawyer than poor Storti. Reg would have paid dearly for the change. There was a baby grand, on which stood photographs of an attractive woman and three children sporting on a fair-sized yacht. There were several expensive-looking pictures of a Bond Street genre in gilded frames. Two were flower paintings. The shaggy, pale-blue pile of the carpet was half an inch high.

Herman Gosser entered quietly. He removed an eyeglass and let it drop on a black ribbon to a waistcoated stomach. Copious sleek brown hair was combed so immaculately it looked like a wig. He wore a spotted bow-tie. He approached, unsmiling, as if pursuing his outstretched hand. 'Dr Caine, good afternoon.' Amiable, good-looking features then creased with worry. 'But please, sit down, sit down. Did not Maria invite you to do so? And no coffee. She has offered you no coffee? Really, the girl is not efficient. She is new – Portuguese. My wife has not yet fully tutored her in our ways of hospitality, I fear.'

He moved determinedly to an electric bell beside the fireplace, then to the door which he wrenched open as if the girl might have been lurking behind it. 'Maria?' he shouted. 'You did not offer our guest coffee,' he said reprovingly, in Swiss German, as she appeared. He returned to the room, and switched again to his very competent English. 'You *would* like some coffee, Dr Caine?'

This was hardly now an option, Robert thought with private amusement. They settled in two of the chintzy chairs.

Robert received the life history of the luckless Maria, which was interrupted only momentarily when she reappeared with the tray. A further dissertation took place when she had left, on the whole topic of immigrant labour into Switzerland – 'a regrettable but necessary phenomenon', as Gosser saw it. Thinking of his flight to Rome, Robert had gently to remind Gosser of the object of his visit. He mentioned his encounter with Storti at Reg's funeral.

'Ah, Storti, poor Storti,' chanted Gosser. 'A good little man. Rather without style, I am afraid, but genuine, one has to say that. I think he was wise to hand on your little matter. It might have been rather outside his expertise.'

'Expertise?' Robert enquired.

'I use the term relatively,' Gosser continued with good humour. He waved his eyeglass in the air. 'Probate is always likely to contain complexities, and is best dealt with in the country concerned, especially when that country is Switzerland. But now, to business. To be proper I must first ask you for your passport for identification. A mere formality, you understand.'

Robert took the passport from his inner pocket and handed it. Gosser lifted his eyebrow to take the glass. He glanced quickly at the first page, then the photograph. 'Quite in order, naturally,' he said. He handed it back, and drawing a paper tied with green ribbon from his pocket began to open it.

'I say there are often complexities in wills, but this one is of the simplest,' he began. 'Probate could still prove difficult, but if things are as I suspect they are – in view of the steps I was able to persuade my client to take – I foresee no hitches except a certain passage of time. You are a fortunate man, Dr Caine. You are aware perhaps of the terms of the will?'

'No. I have no idea.'

'Something rather more than three-quarters of a million Swiss francs – that is a quarter of a million pounds – has been bequeathed to you, and the deeds of a property in South London.'

'But this is astounding, and most embarrassing.'

'I assure you it is true. The sum was in a large bank here. I persuaded Griffin that another, a much smaller one, would be more convenient for him, and assisted in the transfer of the funds. Unless withdrawals were made, they are still there.

'Now to return to probate. There could of course be parties who will challenge the will. However, I doubt it. I questioned Griffin closely on the matter when I learnt that the only beneficiary was to be someone not a member of his family. He was somewhat evasive, but I gained the pretty clear impression there was no immediate family. I have therefore every reason to hope that in a matter of months, given my relations with the bank concerned – which has some reason to feel indebted to me, not only for this introduction – the funds, and the deeds of the house, which are in their safekeeping, will be made over to you.'

Robert found himself blushing. 'This has come completely out of the blue. I must make it clear to you that I have absolutely no wish to act…'

'Illegally? Of course not, Dr Caine. A man in your position. A man in mine for that matter. There must be no question of either of us acting illegally.'

'But this man is almost certainly guilty of grand larceny. He has also been murdered, probably by the gang who hired him. It is quite possible the money is the result of his crime.'

Gosser closed his eyes. 'These are undoubtedly factors, Dr Caine. Undoubtedly they are factors. But I have always believed in keeping business in watertight compartments. I can see, from your point of view, there could be – complications. But, you will pardon me, these are not complications which should properly concern me. My duty is to my client, and to Swiss law.'

'Are you telling me that Swiss banks wink at crime?'

'I said no such thing. These days our banks co-operate widely with foreign police forces. They are also, of course, very wary of releasing money when there is a chance of litigation in Swiss courts. They have to be mindful of the possibility of losing their licences. On the other hand, it is not their purpose to act as bankers for world morality, of which there will always be more than one version anyway. Much the same kind of attitude inspires my own approach to this case. In short, my purpose is to execute this will as its sole trustee.'

Robert was on the brink of elaborating on his difficulty. He desisted. He knew what the outcome would be. Gosser would be willing to advise him, but on a professional basis, for a fee, and he was not sure he wanted Gosser's advice. He would have now, he thought, to tell the police. The source of the money in Reg's account might well be valuable evidence, if it could be established.

He remembered the other matter. 'It is not only assets I bequeath you'. *Was* it a joke of Reg's?

It was as if Gosser read his mind. He rose and handed Robert the copy of the will. 'There is something else I have to give you. Two packages Mr Griffin entrusted me with. I have them in my safe. If you will excuse me, I will get them.'

He returned with two used brown envelopes, the first of which simply bore Robert's name in Reg's handwriting. The second was addressed to Robert, 'care of' Gosser at Gosser's address and had been through the post. It had an Italian stamp and a Rome postmark. The ends of the envelopes had been sealed with red wax in several places. Across each seal Reg had written his signature.

'This is a little unorthodox. I agreed only to the first package because Mr Griffin pressed me when we met in Rome. The second one arrived by post, as you see from the postmark, somewhat mysteriously, only a day or so before the, er, events. If I had known what was going to happen I should not have accepted it. As it was, as far as the first package was concerned, I made the proviso that you came in person to my house to collect it. I have no idea what the packages contain. No signature of acceptance is required. It is off the record. I have not given them to you, if you please. If questioned at any time, I would be obliged if you would say that you obtained them by some other means.

'Now, with your permission, we shall go together to the bank. I have made an appointment with the director. It is important that he sees you and realises for himself that you are a man, if I may say so, of integrity and standing.'

Robert felt himself borne along. They travelled back to Zurich in Gosser's BMW. He was conscious of the large envelopes folded in his pocket.

Robert said goodbye to Gosser in the same square where he had taken the tram. It had certainly been one of the smaller of Switzerland's six hundred banks, in a side street several blocks away. The experience had not made him feel any better. It was clear that neither the manager nor Gosser took anything but a practical and self-interested view of the matter. This was the meaning of that word 'discretion', which had punctuated the speech of both men several times. Any reluctance was owing to their fear of falling foul of Swiss law, not from disgust at a notorious art theft. The final irony was Gosser's suggestion that he might like to open a numbered account with the bank himself 'pending the outcome of probate', which they would expedite as soon as was practicable. He had the impression there had been collusion between them. He politely refused.

It was a relief to emerge from the stuffy central heating of the bank to the chill of late afternoon outside. He sat on a public bench in the square to think what he would do. The money was of course dynamite, made the more explosive by his failure to tell anyone about the will except Gabbi. Sitting there, as the lights began to spring on in the buildings around, he wished Gabbi were here to discuss it with him. He looked at his watch. He had plenty of time to catch the plane. A raised arm, a taxi, and he could be at the airport in half an hour. In three hours he could be holding Gabbi in his arms.

All his impulses required him to leap into that taxi, to subordinate everything that had happened to the overwhelming desire to go back. But he had already realised that in implicating himself in this affair he was unwittingly involving Gabbi. No, he must not rush back. He must, this evening at least, read what was in that envelope, think, and decide calmly what was best.

He found a hotel just off the square, small but still very expensive. Installed in the room, he telephoned to alter the flight, took off his shoes and coat, and lay on the bed. He felt suddenly exhausted.

The next thing he knew it was dark. He put the light on. It was well past six. He had been asleep for two hours. Gabbi could be back in the flat by now. She would have been disappointed that he had not come back during the day, which he had said he probably would do. As he reached for the phone his pulses began a tattoo. Was she all right? Did she still love him? He heard the rings – three, four times – and their blessed severance as she lifted the phone.

'Gabbi, I'm not going to make it tonight, I'm afraid. I'm stuck here tonight.'

He heard the disappointment in her voice, and was absurdly glad. Did he think their love could evaporate in a couple of days? He began to talk about Vienna, deliberately making her think he was still there. He spoke of the dignified behaviour of the Director and the Minister, knowing, as they both knew, how secondary this was. 'Darling, how are you?' he said, before he had properly finished the story.

'OK.'

'I'm missing you terribly.'

'Me too.'

'Gabbi?'

'Yes?'

'Never mind.'

There was suddenly nothing they could say to each other, nothing a telephone wire could communicate.

'I'll be back tomorrow.'

'When? I'll meet you.'

He was for the first time ever with Gabbi, wary.

'No, don't do that.'

'Why not?'

'I haven't checked on my flight times yet.'

'You could do it and phone again?'

'Yes.'

'There's to be no dereliction of duty on my part, you mean?'

He laughed awkwardly.

'No dereliction of duty.' He had a desperate need to sever their communication. ''Night darling. I love you.'

'I love you.'

He hung up first.

The room, which had been so immaterial, reasserted itself, its silence, its emptiness. He had had the thought that the phone in their flat could be tapped. He thought back with an onset of concentrated energy to the opening of their conversation. When Gabbi had picked up the phone, there had been the usual click. Had there been another, secondary noise? Wasn't that what told you? Had he been subliminally aware of that other ear during their conversation? He could not be sure.

He decided he was getting paranoid. He could not honestly remember any clicks, nor had he sensed a third ear. Gabbi loved him. His life was transformed. There was nothing to worry about. He would have a bath, have food sent up, and read what Reg had for him. Then he would decide what he would do.

He called room service and included a half bottle of wine with the meal he ordered. Later, as the waiter withdrew, he slit the larger, unmailed envelope. There were about twenty closely typed pages, ordinary typing paper. He read the first words.

'The chances are you will never read this. I have a vested interest in hoping you won't.'

He poured the wine, and took a mouthful of soup.

25

'The chances are you will never read this. I have a vested interest
in hoping you won't. If you do, I try to imagine the circumstances.
Are you in the house of that Swiss creep, Gosser? Or perhaps
you're sitting in an aeroplane, conscious that your neighbour
might be looking over your shoulder. A hotel room? If the latter,
will Kate be with you? Would you want her to be a party to the
secret, or would you have to read this in the bog with the door
locked? Or will you now be with Gabriella Bruneschi?

Let me say, right away, Robby old sport, I hope La Bruneschi is
with you. If she isn't she should be. She deserves you. You deserve
her. Did you know I had to call off my own dogs from that
direction when I had the idea you two might be at it? Nice girl.
She might have reformed me if I'd got that far. But, now I think
about it, I probably wouldn't have got that far, with you in the
running. I'm also not sure she approved of me. I swung the cape at
her once. Got a pretty negative response. It's a nice point that we
shall never now be able to put to the test. More of all this later.

Of course you may have gone to the police already, if Storti did
his stuff. Dear old Storti. I like the fellow, don't you? As honest as
a lawyer can be. He could have stung me for the will. He needs
every lira he can get in the tin, I'd say. You should have seen his
fifth-floor, back-street office, which stank of rodents. Maybe you
have seen it?

The old boy didn't sting me. He passed me on to Gosser. I had
to agree that, from your point of view, it would be better if this
boring probate business was done in Switzerland. The money more
or less has to be in Switzerland, by the way. I didn't have a choice
in the matter. It was my patron's doing, not mine. I'm stuck with it.
Not that I criticise. The Gnomes are the world's shit collectors,
filthy lucre anyway. But I'm a shit merchant, too, so can't and
don't complain, not on that score. "Recognise your allies, even if
morally inconvenient." I've always had that burnt on a plaque on
my kitchen wall.

I am approaching the point circuitously. Did you go to the
police? I'll play a parlour-game and guess. Pause for reflection.

No, you didn't. Right? What happens? Storti tells you there's a will and that you're the lucky prize-winner. He doesn't tell you how much. I didn't tell him. But he delivers my message. I hope he did? Not just the assets, he says, modest as they will probably turn out to be (but not so modest, eh?), and the splendid old Caine curiosity stretches its neck. They are among your best characteristics, Robby, you know, those hairy nostrils of yours. They save you. I see your sensitive, patrician muzzle at this very moment raised skywards and quivering with the rich scents on the air. Truth? Self-revelation? Knowledge? An interest in life at last among all the banalities (how I agree with you there) which, without the greatest vigilance, so easily accumulate along one's path? How can you resist them? If you went to the police it might all be ruined.

Apart from this, how are you getting on with the police? One of my regrets is that I can't see how you are going to avoid being in trouble with them in the regrettable circumstances of my decease. You were a bit naughty in London, you know. Taking me off the street like that. Then giving me promotion. It was your curiosity again, wasn't it? You knew I was different, maybe even a bit dangerous? You wanted to see how I'd turn out. So they're bound to suspect you were in with me. Well, if it is like that, I want to try and help you. I think I can, up to a point.

I can't decide whether this is an Apologia Pro Vita Mia or a Humble Petition and Advice to you. The answer is probably that it's both. But you will be the judge of this. Mine is not at this point to reason why. I suppose I'm just drawing wildebeest on the walls, like Cro-Magnon man. It's for others to interpret. I'm going to begin, anyway, with something I've never told anyone. I can't even now use the right pronoun. I'll call him Jumbo. This is very definitely a wildebeest on the wall. Aren't they supposed to have depicted things they feared, those cavemen? I'm quite sure they were wise enough not to go in for shrinks, and drew on the wall instead.

Jumbo was bored that afternoon. Jumbo was often bored in those days, his dad being at sea so much in more senses than one, and his mum, well, his mum having her preoccupations. She loved him, mind. Oh, she loved him. Don't get that wrong. She loved him exclusively, Jumbo guesses, because on days when they went out together to do the shopping he felt the pressure of her hand tighten on his as people turned away or said things in low voices. Jumbo's mum used to sing to him too, usually when they, the visitors, had gone, and the house was still and full of peace and enchantment. There is an afternoon visitor on this day, and Jumbo is as usual on these occasions confined to his bedroom upstairs . He has his toys, plenty of them. Jumbo's mum lavished money on toys for him.

But something about the quality of the afternoon makes him bored. High grey cloud. Dim. Still. Winter. Not a leaf still attached in the park at the end of the road. Parties of wheeling gulls in from the Mersey, without much to do either, apparently. The very bottom of the year, when the party's elsewhere, on the other side of the globe. Jumbo's nose is against the window-pane, first one nostril then the other, savouring the cold like a penance, when who comes up the featureless street but his dad in his sailor-suit, a blue kitbag, long like a bolster, on his shoulder, and with his leading-seaman's gait (leading by dint of age not merit). The child is paralysed with fear, indefinably knowing. He waits transfixed on the bed, face down on the pillow.

He hears the noise, the shouts, the banging doors, something smashing, and converts them to the clangour of the ship he visited once with Dad and liked, the shiny brass bell sounding, the cheeky bosun's whistle, the exuberant whoops of departure, the scrubbed white wood, the grave but active officers with hands behind their backs, and Dad miraculously part of it all, part of the order and the purpose. Dad could be nice.

So powerfully does he conjure safety in this way, he does not take in that the house has continued to be quiet, quiet for a lot longer than it ought to have been. Now is the time when Mum ought to call from below, preceded by the smell of dripping toast for tea, perhaps a sugar bun. Maybe he has been waiting for her to call in spite of what he knows.

Gingerly he goes down, one step at a time, right foot leading, the banister rail just reachable for balance. The front door with its coloured glass pane is open, a coat, an alien coat, is on the floor. Had she gone out then, with Dad? A hand too small entirely to encompass the cold ceramic door handle nonetheless deftly twists it. The chaotic scene is before him, bedclothes everywhere. Mum is *there all right, with not much on, one leg bare, one with its slipper, lying over the bed, her head out of sight, hanging the other side. He calls. She does not answer. He knows she cannot answer.*

Instinct takes him through the front door. Outside he halts. The door of the garage that is squeezed between this house and the next is ajar. The garage door is never open. It is not a garage for a car. He goes in and there is the sailor man swinging, a chair tipped over at his feet. Jumbo remembers notably the black shoes. They were highly polished and shiny shoes, hanging in front of him about level with his stomach.

'Before we leave Jumbo there is another small matter to report. For a year or so it could be said Jumbo was not too pleased with life. The boarding school was what boarding schools usually are, whatever section of the community they serve, whether they are fee-paying or not, as two-faced as Janus. One side was for the teachers, the Inspectors, the Governors on Foundation Days (not for mums and dads, there weren't any), the other, the quotidian face, was for each other when the adults' backs were turned.

There was one boy, called Chunkie – his name was Chunkle, and he was fat – who bullied all of his group. He was larger than the rest, and led an infantile tyranny as harsh as anything Hitler thought up. A new hen thrown fluttering and squawking into the coop was fair game of course, especially as, given the circumstances, he arrived mid-term. Chunkie decided to hate Jumbo, principally, Jumbo considers from the vantage point of adulthood, because for some reason his shorts were held up with elastic when everyone else's were tethered by a belt. Surely as good a reason as any for despising someone?

There was a Sunday afternoon when he was stripped naked, tied to a tree and flogged in turn by his entire peer group with knotted dressing-gown cords (the Charity that ran the school was liberal with its bounty in supplying such details of clothing). It is unnecessary to say that Chunkie's blows were the keenest. Those of the others were tempered with the thought that there but for the grace of God and Chunkie... At Christmas they each had a box of chocolates from the Governors. Papally, in Jumbo's first term

Chunkie took Jumbo's for himself. A sort of First Fruit and Tenth.

This is to select at random two incidents from events that occurred daily. Jumbo would like *en passant* to record that it was not the acts which were particularly painful to him. On the whole Chunkie showed a singular lack of imagination in devising painful torments. Dressing-gown cords for instance do not really hurt. Probably he feared that visible stigmata on the victim's body would earn him retribution. The pain was the ill-intent, or, put differently, the pain was the attempt by Chunkie to distribute the load of his own internal suffering at being fat, at being an orphan.

It was not very long, this period of Jumbo's initiation into life. He looks back with a smile. The exit was so easy to arrange he thinks now it could have had an even shorter span. What does an impoverished schoolboy do when bored out of his mind by a divinity lesson in the head beak's study? He makes an inventory of the kind of precious objects in the room that he is never likely to possess. His eye alights upon a bottle of vintage port, the very stuff for which, only days before in a relaxed and imaginative mood, Chunkie had laconically confessed a sophisticated and insatiable appetite.

That night Jumbo makes a little detour, on his small hours' journey from the dorm to the lats, down the unheated corridors to the Head's study, where still stands the bottle on the sideboard. He makes a further journey to Lower Room, that aptly-named pit in which the smaller fry dwelt by day when not in class. Chunkie's locker is locked, but not so fast that it will not yield to the insertion of a pocket knife, as it had on countless other occasions in the past. No one will be able to isolate as evidence this the latest mark of prizing.

The beaks were out in full cry over the missing bottle. Twice a plenary assembly was held, when with pin-dropping silence, the Head in his black gown pontificated away up there on the platform like a reincarnation of the Grand Inquisitor, delineating the imperial-size boundaries of that public shame which must follow stealing, threatening collective retribution if the thief did not "overcome his cowardice" and come forward to confess.

Cowardice indeed. For a few hours, admittedly, Jumbo was affected by the word. He had thought his brothers would laugh to scorn this hypocritical, schoolmasterly rhetoric. He thought Chunkie would lead a chorus of laughter, and his own inability to join in would expose his act. But to his amazement there was no laughter. They all succumbed to the communal anaesthetic, grieved for the missing bottle and the missing decency its disappearance was said to represent, Chunkie among them. When it came to the crunch they were all on the same side, the beaks' side. Only he, Jumbo, stood against. "Decency." In an access of exuberance, he donned the power he had won from being able to recognise and stand aside from hypocrisy. Was the world really so manipulable?

Jumbo's final act in the small hours was to type a note on Matron's machine, placed obligingly on the table between the laundry basket and the medicine chest in the sick room. As soon as the hue and cry was raised, he addressed it "decently" to the prefects, not the beaks, and waited in the hope that Chunkie would not find and dispose of the bottle.

That evening after classes, it could be said Jumbo came of age. The prefects descended in a posse. Chunkie's amazement when ordered to open the locker was as convincing as that of his peers. It did him no good.

If Chunkie had accepted the plant and claimed the theft for himself, he could still have won redoubled prestige. As it was, Jumbo watched the disintegration of his authority in the space of seconds as he protested his innocence in the most abject way. He was reported, thrashed, publically named in Assembly, and ostracised for several months by the entire school.

Jumbo can claim that he was never vindictive. He did not need to be. Humbled as Chunkie now was, stripped of rank and returned like a Chinese feudal overlord to the peasantry, Jumbo was – not sorry for him, that would not be the word – he was "cognisant of his condition" is the better phrase. For he knew in his unique detachment, even at this age, that in real terms Chunkie had never been anything but a peasant. He had not fallen, he had just taken off fancy dress. Ironically, he and Jumbo became quite good friends. Jumbo never joined the witch-hunt against him and Chunkie was grateful.

'I wonder if you are thinking of the historical repetition, Robby boy? No, of course you won't be, for you were as hoodwinked as anyone by the till theft. I set up the slippery Pietro, yes, as Chunkie was set up. You never had any inkling of that, did you?

But I did you a service there, didn't I, as well as myself? You would never have got rid of the pig otherwise. And he deserved a spell in the cooler. Not for stealing – I could hardly claim that. But for a generally low attitude to life. Fancy crawling to a man like Mortimer Ready.

I'm sorry about Carmina, though. I would rather it hadn't been her, a worthy Gorgon to guard your till in that glass den of hers. As it turned out, no harm was done. She kept her job, thanks to your good sense. Instead of sacking her to appease the Mortimers of this world, you doubled her stake in the security of the place by giving her the keys. That was good thinking, generous thinking. Also Giulia, giving her the job, I was glad you did that. I would have been worried if she had been harmed.

Now to the crucial deed. Has anyone guessed the method of my departure? I'm tempted to remain as posthumously silent as I shall be if I survive the ordeal that awaits me. That I resist the temptation is partly vanity, partly a desire to defend you and Carmina, who might well be blamed again in some way. Wait for it. Here it is. This is no ordinary operation. My patron has style. I have the expertise. There is to be no crashing about. No business with keys and impressions of keys. I shall fly deftly upon the light airs of the night. At least, I hope they will be light airs. Not too much, not too little, horizontal, not vertical. There now, that should be clue enough. The other things, downstairs, you and the police will have to guess. It shouldn't be difficult. I shall have some nasty moments if I'm not mistaken. Theory is one thing...

Which brings me to Kate. Here, I realise, I'm on much thinner ice. I've known about you and Gabriella for some time. I suspected it, I guess, before you did, the way she talked about you, the way you spoke to her, and it was clear her relations with that red peacock, Giancarlo, were held together only by her exemplary loyalty.

It became obvious to me at the time you gave me the publicity job and I tried to get her to drive me round the town to look at the hoardings (a means to an end as you will readily appreciate). Secure in her unadmitted inner feelings about you, she was able to afford a very high tone. And when I saw her get out of the taxi at Termini, with you in the back seat after your day together in Tarquinia, the matter was clinched. You saw me standing there, *didn't you? I've always wondered if you guessed from that moment I knew your secret.*

Whatever the case, I really want you and Gabriella to get together. The socially-anxious Kate is not right for you, never has been, and you've been dragging the anchor for years, haven't you? This is your Uncle Reg speaking, and I would like to think I earn a little merit for this, though you may choose to hate me for my role as eminence grise.

Unknown to her, I saw Kate recently in the Forum. I was doing a bit of culture-vulturing on my day off, and there she was snapping one of the Vestals. I watched her from a discreet distance. That's what she should have been, incidentally – a Vestal. She would have done well wearing a pleated robe. She would have swung the incense with gusto, and no doubt been number one on interpreting the ravens' guts. Why is it the wrong people always get an overdose of willpower, or get pushed from behind, and get themselves by mistake into the ruling priesthood, and the natural leaders don't?

She didn't see me. I took good care about that. I've always kept a low profile in her direction. I sensed somehow she'd be the enemy if I did, and I've never been in the business of making enemies, which is a gross waste of effort for a start. But it was looking at her gave me my idea. I'd been thinking for some time how I'd get you both out of the building on the big night, whenever that proves to be. I know about your movements, though they seem stingily ungregarious during the exhibition. But her? Watching her fiddling with her camera, it became obvious. Her absorption in her task, the way she was completely unaware of the tourists gaping at her at a few feet's distance, the imprisoned look on her face. She's walled up in her lofty tower. She thinks she's secure. She doesn't realise, with her capacity for contempt and her will to hang on to a currency of rage that is no longer valid, how she depends on you. A couple of little whispers, I thought, and despite her haughty principles she'd be up and running with all the other jilted mates in the world.

I sent her a note the next day. She never showed it to you, did she? I'm sure now she didn't. I'd have seen the signs. I told her you were being unfaithful, and that she was to watch this space.

No doubt she's still watching. If all goes to plan, on the night she'll get her details. They won't be quite the right details of course, and it's only fifty-fifty she'll take the bait. But there's a chance she'll go rushing out. And really, you know, Robert, leaving out the small print, she'll be right to bite if she does, don't you think? I've always believed intention is much more important than action (the old law of literary obscenity used wisely to cite that). I bet you've dreamed of sleeping with that classy girl if you haven't done so. You are already, de jure, guilty of adultery. So, why not then cream the benefits, says I?

I'm pressing this a bit, I realise. I'm aware of my prose getting over-assertive, making too much of a case for myself. Do you know, I believe, for the first time I can remember, I've got a bit of a conscience going? It's true, goddam it. I do wonder at this moment if I haven't been rationalising a necessary act into a virtuous one to save my peace of mind. Or worse than that, I wonder if I haven't misjudged you and your emotions, and that you will hate me for this. I'm looking into the bowels of Christ and thinking I might be wrong. Am I wrong? I do hope not. I realise I wouldn't like to earn your dislike.'

The knock on the door startled Robert. It was the waiter, come for the tray. For some minutes he had been sitting back in the chair, absorbing what he had read. He felt as if he had been fired into space and was orbiting aimlessly, detached from everything that had been familiar.

He was grateful for the waiter's intrusion, but could think of nothing to say as the man stacked the crockery at a leisurely pace. His mind was filled with what Reg had written, and he could hardly discuss that. Finally the man said 'Goodnight, sir,' gave him a discreet look, and withdrew. The hotel was silent.

Robert picked up the second envelope, which had been through the post. He looked at the postmark. It had been posted, as Gosser had said, in Rome, the day before the robbery. He cut the envelope open with his finger. The first document had been typed. This was handwritten.

'I had no intention of adding to the agony, but the day after

tomorrow looks like being the day. You haven't been going out too much during the exhibition, have you? Also, there's a new development which frankly scares me. Hence this additional bison scribbled on the cave wall.

All along I've had to consider whether my patron is capable of violence. I thought first about Carlo Pelucci. (Have you?) The vacancy his disappearance created was convenient for my patron, wasn't it? Did he fall over a crag in the Abruzzi, or did my patron's men assist him? (And no doubt you heard, as I did later, Giulia's story from Pietro, about that week-end of his. Did he even go to the Abruzzi?) Well, pretty definitely, at the first of my two meetings with His Excellency, I was convinced he wasn't a murderer. It could have been wishful thinking on my part, but "He's a games-player, like me," I thought. Eccentric, yes, ruthless, yes. But ruthless in the field of deception, not surely with human life? You can see why I might be a bit interested in a thing like that, but I've trusted my intuition, as one should.

There were some disturbing moments after I got on the job. To start with, my flat was ransacked one day. I also realised I was being followed, intermittently. And one afternoon I caught one of your guardians in my office in suspicious circumstances. I'm not going to say who it was, but you ought to keep your eyes open. My success may give him ideas. At my second meeting with my patron, I was prepared to raise these matters, which seemed to indicate a lack of trust in me. I did raise one of them, the going-over of my flat. My patron is an inscrutable customer, but I was as sure as I could be that he knew nothing about it. I relaxed. I put it down to excessive zeal on the part of his minions, one or two of whom don't over-inspire me with confidence. As for Pelucci, I decided to believe the official assumption. I still do. Pietro's a lying bastard. He quite likely made up that story for some over-cunning motive.

But yesterday I made an unpleasant discovery. I've known right from the start of this game that my patron keeps an eye on me. Even during our tête-à-tête in that Baker Street restaurant, there were beady eyes at hand, beady ears as well. But yesterday I found there are two lots of people following me, independently of each other, it seems. One of the faces I know very well. It's my patron's man. I've got to the stage now when I almost feel naked without him. He is after all an ally, perhaps even a protector. But the other one is sinister. Is it the minion's? Could he be double-crossing his master? I wouldn't put it past him. I went into a building when I realised what was going on, nipped up a floor or two, and found a window with a view down the street. I convinced myself the two were not in tandem. My patron's man doesn't know of the other's existence.

'I just thought I'd put this on record. Don't know why, really, unless it's an attack of the jitters. Perhaps I should have become a don after all. No, cancel that. I don't mean it.

'At least I've put the jitters from me. I've got more important matters on my mind. Perhaps my patron's paranoid. He's certainly a strange bugger. Perhaps they think I'm in league with the first sleuth and am plotting to double-cross, which I am certainly not. Have you noticed a residual quality of loyalty in me too, Robert? If you haven't, you should have. I've never been a waverer. Let X equal something, and get on with it. That's always been my motto. The Greeks had something there. Have you ever thought of the philosophy involved in the mere fact of algebra?

'Now I've said it, I feel better. Exorcised the ghost. This is after all a kind of confessional, as I said. I wish you could say a couple of Hail Marys for me. If all goes well tomorrow, the police won't be able to lay a finger on me. I hope you won't suspect me, either. I'd like to stay with you a while at the museum. Truthfully. There'll be an element of necessity in staying on, I admit. Too rapid an exit would raise eyebrows higher than would be comfortable. But, you won't believe it, I really like the job, as jobs go. I'd like to see you shacked up with Gabbi. And we can get to know each other better perhaps. I'd like that. I'll say it, you're a "decent" guy, that word again. Yes, one of the few decent guys I've come across. A bientôt.'

26

Robert slept fitfully.

He had had recurrences enough lately, during the day as well, of that scene in the morgue, the pungent smell of spirit, the room brightly lit with a yellowish neon, the tiled floor, the massive lockers which pulled out like the drawers of a file, the naked, pathetically amputated body. Was it Reg's, he had so often asked himself? Could it, despite all the assumptions that had been made, have been the corpse of some other person? Was it possible that he had attended the funeral of this other person, and that Reg was still alive somewhere?

At least this anxiety was laid now. The will, the letters, Gosser's certainties, conspired with the other evidence to convince him the body had been Reg's. It was clear now from his letter that, if Reg had not been expecting death, he had envisaged its possibility. Robert's own thoughts had been the indulgence of wishful thinking, no more.

But he was racked now with new worries. He began to blame himself for what had happened. Reg was no ordinary felon. The letters proved it. He remembered in minute detail those moments they had spent together before the exhibition, when the Perseus arrived. He had been sure that evening that Reg had wanted to say something to him, that he had come within an ace of it. Could it not have been possible, by different behaviour, to have induced it from him? And could that somehow have prevented the theft, and the murder?

No, he argued with himself. All the evidence was that he could not have altered events. It was his liberal training speaking, the belief that there are common moral denominators in everyone, that however deeply buried these may become, they can be appealed to. Reg had been a villain. He would always have done what he had decided to do. Nothing he himself could have said or done would have changed that.

As usual, he did not entirely believe himself.

He was also left with his present feelings unexplained, unforgiven. The plain fact was he could not condemn Reg, not just like that, less now than ever. He had even found himself impressed by the incredible daring of his feat, which had fooled them all, fooled Migliore with his superficial logic, laughed in the face of the humourless power and the sanctimonious rectitude of authority. He regretted the loss of the Salt-Cellar, which might never be seen again. No one could 'forgive' that. But what did one do about oneself when, having sincerely said that, one still felt a sneaking affinity with the thief? Did that make him a kind of accomplice? He thought it might.

His alarm buzzed at five. He groped for the light switch. Instantly, as if banished, his mental torturers fled back into the shadows of night. Replacing them was a single thought of heavy practicality and banality. Whatever the consequences, he would have now to tell the police about the legacy. The money of course he could not keep, and to try to keep it dark, however he disposed of it, would be foolish in the extreme. Gabbi might be involved too, as she knew about the will. He would inform the police today.

He was thankful his plane was at an early hour and he did not have to hang about in this spiritless town. He paid the night porter of the hotel and went out into the icy darkness. An early tram whirred by. On the corner of the street a café was open. Standing at the bar drinking his coffee among the other silent people on their way to work, an elementary precaution prompted him. From his case, he drew out Reg's two envelopes, laid them on the bar, and readdressed them to himself at the museum. The barmen lent him paste to reseal them, and sold him stamps. He thought he would go to the police immediately on arrival in Rome, it could not be soon enough. It would be as well not to have Reg's letters with him. He had decided not to reveal their contents to anyone except Gabbi for the moment. There was no reason to, and they were private. He posted them at the air terminal.

At Fiumicino he emerged from customs. Though he knew she could not be there, he illogically searched the people waiting beyond the barrier for Gabbi. She wasn't there. As he turned to make for the exit, two armed city police stepped forward, one on either side of him. Behind them was Migliore.

'Good morning, Dr Caine. I must ask you to accompany me to my headquarters, if you please.'

Robert felt his stomach open like the trap of a gallows, but he managed to smile. 'That saves me an expensive taxi journey. As a matter of fact I was on my way to see you.'

Part Five
~ ~ ~ ~ ~ ~ ~ ~ ~ ~ ~

Part Five